THE
Truth
IN MY
LIES

A SECRETS OF SUBURBIA NOVEL

IVY SMOAK

ISBN: 9781942381174

2020 Hardcover Edition

For my husband.

CHAPTER 1

It was better when I had a routine. A routine kept my pulse even. Kept me sane. So I made sure every weekday morning was the same. At exactly 8 o'clock, I would go for a run. I glanced at the clock as I laced my sneakers. It was only 7:50, which was ten minutes too early. I finished tying my second sneaker and willed myself to stay still.

I was trying out this new thing. Long, slow, deep breaths. It was supposed to calm me. But my muscles wanted to move and I couldn't make my leg stop bouncing. The small movement radiated energy to all my limbs. Within seconds, I'd abandoned my slow, even breaths. I wanted to jump and run and scream. God, I wanted to scream. My fingers repeatedly tapped against the top of my thigh, one at a time, driving me slowly insane. I cringed when I looked back at the clock and only one minute had passed.

I clenched my hand into a fist so I wouldn't be tempted to grab something and throw it at the clock that wouldn’t speed up to my desired time. I looked back down at my bouncing leg. What would it feel like to scream at the top of my lungs? Would the neighbors hear? I shook the thought away. It didn't matter. I wasn't going to scream and wake the neighbors at 7:52 in the morning. 7:52? *Are you kidding me?* It was almost like time was standing still.

I stood up and started stretching to give my overactive limbs something to focus on. Sometimes change was okay. An adjustment to my schedule wasn't the worst thing in the world. But not today. Today was Thursday. My schedule couldn't change on a Thursday.

I smiled at the irony of it. Six months ago, my schedule changed on a Thursday. Not by choice. By destiny. It was like the universe knew what I'd needed at that exact moment. I used to run at 7 a.m. every day. Now I ran at 8. I was okay with being a few minutes early or late most days. But not Thursday. Never Thursday.

My route was timed out perfectly. That way I got to run past the same spot twice within a half hour. Once wasn't enough. It had to be twice. I wasn't sure I'd keep breathing for another week if it wasn't twice.

Some people might think my fixation was unhealthy. But it was the only thing I looked forward to all week. My world revolved around Thursdays at 8 a.m. Because the rest of my world was bleak. If my life was the only thing I thought about, I'd lose my mind.

Although it was possible I'd already lost it.

I walked into the pantry and reached into the far corner of the bottom shelf. My fingers wrapped around the container of pills. It used to feel like I was swallowing guilt when I took one. But now? I plopped one into my mouth and shoved the container back into the corner. Now it was part of my routine. And I felt no guilt. If anything, I felt relief.

I grabbed a bottle of water from the fridge and drank the pill down. *Nope, definitely no guilt.* My eyes lazily looked up at the clock and water dribbled down my chin as I started to smile mid-sip. It was time. I wiped my mouth with the back of my hand and placed the bottle down on the counter, not even bothering to put the cap back on. Who had time for bottle caps on a Thursday morning at 8 a.m.?

I put my earbuds in my ears and tucked the end of the cord into my shirt. It didn't lead to anything. But it was better that people thought I couldn't hear them. It was better that no one tried to talk to me. My whole world was for show. My run couldn't be any different.

I opened up the front door and breathed in the scent of autumn. The fall leaves were wet from the rain the night before. And there was an unmistakable crispness in the air. I loved autumn.

The thought made me pause. My fingers stayed glued to the door handle. Love? What a preposterous thought. I didn't love anything. I didn't believe in love. But addiction? I believed in that. I understood that better than most people. How could I not? I was almost positive I was addicted to him.

CHAPTER 2

I usually kept my eyes glued to the pavement in front of me, not daring to let my gaze wander. But today, I couldn't seem to stop looking at the houses. They were all the same. Beige siding. Brown front doors. Perfectly inviting cookie-cutter houses. Designed for cookie-cutter families. I used to crave that. When I was a little girl, I dreamt of everything I didn't have. I wanted it desperately. Much like how I craved him now.

I was naive back then. Now I knew that the things I craved should be kept at arm's length. Fool me once, shame on you. But fool me twice? Not going to happen.

My head snapped toward the sound of a lawnmower starting. The timing was pure perfection. My feet slowed to a light jog, unable to maintain my pace when I saw him. Somehow he always seemed to take my breath away. And all my senses became overloaded. Sight, touch, taste, smell, and sound. My lips parted slightly, an involuntary reaction. We were a whole lawn away. This was the closest I'd ever been to him, and the closest I'd ever be. So why was it so easy to imagine him kissing my lips? Tasting the saltiness of his skin? Feeling the whisper of his breath in my ear?

A daydream. A fantasy so oversaturated that it felt real. More real than anything in my actual life. I wasn't even sure what it was about him that consumed my mind. The way his hair fell slightly on his forehead? The tan that somehow highlighted the cut of his muscles? The kind smile that was much too kind for someone like me?

He looked up as I passed, that same smile I dreamt about crossing his lips. No, it wasn't the smile that had captured me. Although the kindness behind it was part of the intrigue. It was the dimple on his cheek. Not one on each cheek. Just the one. On his left cheek. It was an imperfection. An imperfection on an otherwise perfect physique. It was the imperfection that drew me in.

He waved as he continued to push the mower with his free hand. The first time he had waved to me, I'd immediately snapped my eyes back to the pavement. I had felt the heat cross my cheeks. He had caught me staring. My heart had slammed against my ribcage like I had been running for five miles instead of five minutes. And when I had looked back over my shoulder, he was still staring at me.

But that awkward moment had been 6 months ago. Now we had a routine. He waved and I would wave back. It was less awkward if I waved back. Less abnormal. Most people didn’t have to try so hard to be normal. To me, it was excruciating work. I didn't ever want someone to see through my exterior to the torment inside of me.

I lifted my hand and waved. He smiled and looked back down at the lawnmower. Our exchange was over. And I kept running, refusing to look back. It was better if I dreamt of him staring after me. It was better if I didn't know whether he was or not. I'd never looked back ever since that first day. But it was hard to shake that feeling that his gaze would be on me if I looked over my shoulder.

I picked up my pace as I turned the corner. My obsession with him was ridiculous. I knew nothing about him besides for his appearance. And I knew how meaningless appearances were. I knew I was attractive. My mother always used to say it was the only thing I had going for me. I hated when she'd say that. Maybe that was when my insides started to become twisted and unrecognizable. A compliment turned sour. Morphed into an insult. My insides definitely weren't attractive. I wasn't sure they ever were.

It was hard to not read into his flawless looks, though. When I jogged back in the opposite direction, his shirt would be gone and his appearance would be all I could think about. Perfect timing had its perks. I picked up my pace again. The feeling of my muscles resisting thrilled me. There was no better feeling than pushing myself to the limit. Knowing that my body wouldn't break. That nothing would ever break me no matter how hard everyone seemed to try.

I'd started running because it was the only thing that made me feel alive. I was addicted to the wind rushing through my hair. I'd stopped using hair ties because they lowered the thrill. I needed the wind through my hair, not through my ponytail. It made the cookie-cutter wives stare at me with disapproval. But I didn't care. They didn't know how badly I needed to feel alive. How badly I needed Thursdays.

Maybe that was something else I liked about him. The way he stared at me made me feel desired. Him staring lit something inside of me. Especially since I knew we'd never interact. Since I knew it would never be more than a wave. Or a smile.

I reached the dead end and placed my hands on my knees. The woods stretched out before me. I stared at the trees as I caught my breath. I used to want to run through them. I thought running so close to nature, tucked away from suburbia, would help ease my worries and fears. My footprints could easily make their own trail in the dirt. A trail just for me. But the one time I ran through the trees, I had been more terrified than ever. Because it was tucked away from suburbia. And there was definitely no one there to hear my screams. Not one soul. The thought irked me so fiercely that ever since then I'd never been able to look at the woods the same. Not to mention how the branches had cut my skin. I had come back to the house looking like I'd just escaped from the set of a horror movie.

I took a step back from the woods. They were why all the blinds in the back of my house were always drawn close. The trees gave me an unsettled feeling in the pit of my stomach. No, I didn't want to run through them ever again. I'd stick to the street. Worse for my knees, better for my mind.

Besides, my knees had never been fragile. But my mind was. That was basically what the doctor said when she'd prescribed me the pills. She ended up being right though. I felt better when I took them. They weren't helping anyone in the garbage disposal where I had originally put them.

Fragile yet stubborn at the same time. I ignored the inconsistencies and started running back the way I had come. I always ran faster on the way back to him, even though I was dreading my silent goodbye. Part of me always worried he'd be gone early. That he'd just disappear.

One day that might happen. He might stop cutting the lawn at that particular house. Or he might change his schedule. I couldn't exactly camp out on the street and wait for him. Whenever his disappearance ultimately happened, the one day I looked forward to would vanish. Every day would be exactly the same. And then what would happen to me? How had I existed without this one thing to look forward to? I couldn't even remember.

I turned the corner and saw him in the distance. He had stripped off his shirt. The sweat on his chest made his skin glisten in the sunlight. It made him look otherworldly. I laughed silently at the thought. *Otherworldly?* There was only one world. The current hell that I was living.

He lifted his hand and waved, that dimple appearing on his cheek. My world didn't feel like hell when I passed him. It felt airy like the breeze through my hair. Like anything was still possible, even though I knew in my gut that it wasn't. I lifted my hand to wave back.

I was completely distracted by his perfect imperfection on his cheek. It was all I could see. And I didn't want to look away yet. What if I couldn't wait till next Thursday? What if I was the one that disappeared?

The look on his face changed in a heartbeat.

I didn't understand the look.

I mistook it for anger. I always mistook expressions for anger.

Panic constricted in my throat.

What had I done? Had I stared too long at him? I had, hadn't I?

He called to me, but my mind blocked out his words. Something I was used to doing. A defense mechanism. The same doctor who had given me the pills had told me that's what it was. So all I saw was the supposed anger and his mouth moving fast. The words were drowned out by my own panic.

I crashed into something and my legs flew out from underneath of me.

CHAPTER 3

Leaves fluttered into the air as the bags deflated beneath me with a hiss. I reached my palms out to catch myself but my right wrist collapsed under my weight. I felt my hand skid across the pavement, ripping at my skin. *Ow!* I landed hard on my side as my wrist completely gave out. I tried to take a deep breath to access the damage. *I'm okay,* I tried to tell myself even though tears were biting at the corners of my eyes. *I'm fine.* I needed to run away. I needed to stop lying in this pile of leaves I had somehow managed to explode everywhere. There didn't appear to be any leaves left in the bags. *God.* This was worse than the time that I didn't wave back. *So much freaking worse.*

The pain that seared across my ankle as I tried to stand was significantly worse than the pain in my wrist. *No.* I rotated my foot in a circle and the pain only increased. *No, no, no, no, no!* I needed to run. I had to be able to run. My Thursdays depended on it. My sanity depended on it! I turned to push myself up but the pain was blinding. *Son of a bitch.* I couldn't do it. My body betrayed me and I collapsed back down on the bags. The air in them hissed again and a few more leaves fluttered into the air. I swallowed down the curses on the tip of my tongue.

I smelled him first. There was no doubt in my mind that he was standing above me. Because that smell could only belong to him. It was the only real sensation of him I had experienced except sight. And God, he smelled better than I had ever imagined. Sweet cologne mixed with salty sweat and something else that could only be described as all man. Dirt and grass and everything that exuded sexiness and...strength. How could he smell like strength? That wasn't an odor. I bit my lip as I tried and failed to stand again. *This can't be happening. He's not really standing above me. I'm just dreaming.*

"Ma'am, are you alright?" If he smelled like strength, he also sounded like strength. His voice was gravely and deep. Something about it made my own throat feel dry. Or maybe I was just parched from my run.

The sensory overload was jarring. *Wait. Did he just call me ma'am?* I pulled out my earbuds even though they weren't affecting my hearing. I had silently been pining for the man for months and the first time he talks to me he calls me ma'am? Did I look 80 years old? This was a mistake. I shouldn't have been here. I shouldn't have timed out my runs so perfectly. I never should have seen him, let alone been close enough for him to call me ma'am. My throat was definitely dry, because when I tried to speak nothing came out. I awkwardly cleared it. "I'm fine," I grunted. *Leave me alone in my misery.*

Then it was touch. His palms were rough from mowing lawns and they slightly scratched my skin. I already thought I was experiencing sensory overload. But his touch was what sent shivers down my spine and goose bumps up my arms. His touch is what made me finally look up at him.

"You don't look fine," he said.

My lips parted. There were words floating around in my head, but none of them seemed like an appropriate response. He had insulted me. So why were my eyes fixated on his lips? His perfectly kissable lips. I should have been giving him hell. Telling him to get his hands off my shoulder. Screaming at him to mind his own business. Instead, I stared dumbly. Apparently I became mute at the sight of perfection.

"Let's get you to your feet," he said. He didn't wait for me to respond. He effortlessly hoisted me off the destroyed bags of leaves. Like I weighed nothing. And my brain finally processed the fact that his touch excited me instead of frightened me. I looked down at his hands on my upper arms.

My sluggish brain quickly caught up to process the rest of the situation. Nosy neighbors could see this scene unfolding through their spotless windows. I needed to get home. People talked. And I did better when they were silent. I took a step away from him.

Ow. A pathetic whimper escaped my lips.

"Let's get you inside and clean up that cut." He stepped back toward me and wrapped his arm around my waist.

I should have stepped away again. Instead, I followed his gaze and looked down at my hand. There was blood on my palm that was already starting to cake. Just looking at it made me feel nauseous. I swallowed down the lump in my throat. Him offering to help me was something straight out of one of my fantasies. But going into a neighbor's house that I didn't know? Why did he even have a key? The members of my lawn service definitely didn't have a key to my house. There was absolutely no reason for that.

"No, I'm fine. I really need to get home." I cringed as I set my foot on the ground.

"You can barely walk. Come on." He started walking, forcing me to hop along with him.

"I'm not going in that house." God, who was watching us right now? Were rumors already spreading? As much as I loved his hands against my skin, they didn't belong there.

"*That* house? You're acting like something's wrong with it. It's a perfectly fine house, I assure you. And it contains Band-Aids and ice packs. Both of which you currently need."

"I'm not using their Band-Aids and ice packs." He was still pulling me toward the front door. It would have been a lot easier for my voice to sound demanding if I wasn't distracted by his skin pressed against mine.

He laughed. "Then you can at least borrow a pair of crutches so you can get home." He opened up the door like he freaking owned the place.

I pulled back. I wasn't going inside that house. It was like I could already hear the gossip. There was zero chance that this was happening.

"I promise I don't bite." The smile at the corner of his mouth made it seem like he was lying.

My words were gone again. He was standing there with his shirt off, practically begging me to come inside. How many times had I dreamt of this? But that's what dreams were for. This couldn't actually happen. I couldn't be alone with him. My eyes gravitated to his. For a moment, I was pretty sure I stopped breathing. I had never seen eyes the color of his. A bluish-green that put the ocean to shame. There was one other thing that made me feel alive besides running. Watching the waves crash against the sand. I loved the beach. But I hadn't been in years. I blinked as if I was trying to dismiss the memories.

His smile faltered when I didn't respond and his dimple disappeared. "At least come in so you can call someone to come get you."

Someone to come get me? Now I wanted to laugh. I had no one. Not one single person that cared about my wellbeing. So how exactly was I planning on getting back to my house? I couldn't walk. Was my grand plan to crawl home on all fours?

"Or you could tell me where you live," he said. "I can drive you home." He pulled his keys out of his pocket.

I didn't know which was worse. Going into that house or having him know where mine was. Which looked worse? My mind was spinning, but I couldn't come to a conclusion. They were both bad. Really bad. Why were those the only two options?

He raised both his eyebrows like he was growing impatient as he waited for my response.

I put my hands on my hips, somehow managing not to fall over. "Look, buddy..."

"Buddy? Really?" He laughed again.

At me. Somehow I hated and loved his laugh at the same time. "You called me *ma'am.*"

His smile was back. And that dimple that I couldn't ignore.

"That's why you refuse to come in? No Band-Aids or crutches from someone who calls you ma'am?"

"I'm not an old lady."

"No...I'm well aware of that."

Those ocean blue eyes scanned my body. They lit me on fire. *No.* The run had overheated me. That was all. And I was desperately in need of a glass of water.

"Stop it," I said. I kept my hands firmly planted on my hips. "I have neighbors. Gossipy, horrible neighbors that are probably staring at you staring at me right now. I have to go." *Somehow.*

He gave me a look that made me feel insane. "Stop what? I'm just trying to see how hurt you are. I'm trying to help you."

"Well, I...I don't know you." My rebuttal was pathetic. I wasn't a five year old outside a white van filled with candy.

"And I don't know you."

I had nothing left to say. He had to close this door that didn't belong to him. And we had to both go on our merry ways. Although, my way wouldn't be quite as merry. More like incredibly painful. "So, I'm just going to..." I pointed over my shoulder, like that meant anything. "Yup," I mumbled and started to turn around at the pace of a turtle.

"This is ridiculous," he said. He stepped forward and lifted me up in his arms. Like I was a freaking damsel in distress. *If only he knew.*

CHAPTER 4

Did he make a habit of whisking women off their feet and taking them into houses that didn't belong to him? I contemplated if this was something an axe murderer would do. *Probably.* So why wasn't I fighting him off? Why was I just enjoying being in his arms?

My bickering attitude had completely evaporated. I was already inside the house. The rumors were already spreading. For one moment, I wanted to just enjoy myself. I wanted to know more about him than just the way he looked and smelled. I wanted to be able to fill my fantasies with substance.

He deposited me on a pristine white couch. It didn't look like anyone had ever sat on it before. I was probably going to leave dirt and leaves on it. I pulled an offending leaf out of my hair as he wandered out of the room and down the hall.

I heard him rummaging through drawers, searching the owner's possessions. *We shouldn't be in here.* There was something thrilling about that. What we were doing was wrong. I was breaking the rules. I was tossing out my daily routine. My watch started beeping as if it had heard my thoughts. I quickly snoozed the alarm.

I heard his footsteps wandering back to me far too soon. It was almost like he had known where the items were. Maybe he was having an affair with the woman who lived here. Had I ever seen the couple in the yard? I internally shook my head. They had him to take care of their yard. I scanned the walls. They were completely bare. Not a single picture was hung. There was only a mirror above the fireplace. The reflection that stared back at me was horrifying. My hair was everywhere. There were more leaves than I even realized sticking out of it at odd angles. I thought he had been checking me out earlier. But his eyes probably were just scanning me to assess my condition. I looked like a maniac. My outside finally matched my inside.

I ran my fingers through my hair and tried to pull out the remaining leaves. All I really managed to do was smear blood on my cheek. I let my hands fall onto my lap as his steps drew even closer.

My eyes met his as he stepped into the room. The blue of his irises wasn't as bright inside. Maybe it was the sunshine that made them so intoxicating. The color almost looked stormy now, like when rain threatens the perfect beach day. But who was I kidding? His stormy eyes were just as addicting.

He pulled up a chair and gingerly lifted my ankle onto it. I didn't protest as he wrapped the ice pack around my ankle. He had even put a towel around it so that the coolness wouldn't sting. How many times had he done this before? Set traps for women and baited them into the homes of his lawn mowing clients?

"Here," he said and handed me a pill and a glass of water. "This'll help. It looks like a sprain. You should stay off of it for a few weeks."

I looked down at the pill. "What is it?"

"Advil. It's all I have."

It's all the owners of this house have. He was acting like he owned the place, which I knew he didn't. I ran by here every day during the week. His truck, touting his lawn care service, was only here on Thursday mornings between 8 and 8:30 a.m. Maybe this whole act worked on other women. But not me. I knew his schedule. I knew he was lying. The only question was why?

I was about to tell him off when he pulled his cell phone out of his pocket and handed it to me.

I just stared at him.

"Call someone to come get you. Unless you want me to drive you. I really don't mind."

Neither option would work for me. Eventually, he'd have to move on to his next client. He couldn't sit here with me all day. I'd pretend to make a call. And then whenever he left, I'd hobble home. Easy. Option C it was. I typed in my house number and pulled the phone to my ear. I listened to my voice on the answering machine and waited for the beep.

"Hi," I said into the receiver. "It's me."

Out of the corner of my eye, I saw him fumbling with something in his hands.

I turned away. "Everything's fine," I said, trying my best to make it seem like I was talking to someone who cared. Or anyone for that matter. "But you know how clumsy I can be." I laughed awkwardly at my own joke. "I tripped on my run and busted up my ankle. I'm sure it'll be fine in a few days but I can't exactly walk home." I paused for dramatic effect. "Mhm," I said into the receiver like I was listening to what someone else had to say.

I gasped when I felt his fingers on the back of my hand.

"I promised you a Band-Aid," he whispered. He wiped the disinfecting cloth against my palm like it was nothing. Like he didn't know his touch was making every inch of my body ache for the same attention.

I realized I hadn't said anything into the phone in a long time. "Mhm," I said again, forgetting the play I was putting on. My voice hitched on the word.

He looked up at me and smiled.

I was hoping he hadn't heard the quiver. But apparently he had. "Just come when you can, bye!" I ended the call.

He looked back down and smoothed the Band-Aid into place.

"All better," he said like I actually was a five year old kid. Which meant maybe he was a man in a white van offering free candy.

I bit the inside of my lip. He didn't look like he wanted to harm me. He looked like he wanted to make sure I wasn't in pain.

"Are they coming?" he asked.

"What?"

"Your friend. Are they coming to get you?"

"Oh. Yeah." I pulled my hand away from his. "She's at a dentist appointment. She's still in the waiting room but said that she'd be here as soon as she can."

"You didn't tell her where."

Crap. Had I really not? I guess I wasn't going to win best actress for that performance. I waved my hand dismissively. "I'll wait outside. She'll see me. She lives down the street from me. She has to drive by here either way, so..." I let my voice trail off. My excuse was pathetic. Also, I didn't want to sit outside. At least in here, the neighbors couldn't see what I was doing.

My watch started beeping again. I turned off the timer so it would stop.

"Somewhere to go?" he asked with a smile.

"Something like that." I needed to distract him. He was asking too many questions. "Do you think you could search for something stronger than Advil?" *Really?* My distraction was for him to pilfer their medicine cabinet for drugs? I wished I was speechless at the sight of him again. That was easier to manage.

He looked down at my ankle. "The Advil should kick in soon. I don't have anything stronger."

"You didn't even look."

He lowered his eyebrows slightly.

I needed a second away from him to clear my head. "Please, just..."

"There isn't anything stronger in the house. Do you want me to take you to the ER?"

"No." It came out faster and louder than I intended. I pushed my bangs off my forehead. Why was he so terrible at coming up with plans?

"Jesus." He sat down next to me and leaned in far too close.

Oh my God, he's going to kiss me. My mouth suddenly felt dry.

"I didn't realize you hit your head," he said. "Maybe we should go to the hospital."

"What?" It took me a second to realize that my fantasies were on hyperdrive. I touched my forehead. "I didn't hit my head." I leaned away from him. He was too close. His intoxicating smell was making me dizzy. "I don't need to go to the ER. My ankle is just killing me."

"You have a bruise..."

I caught my reflection in the mirror again. A small bruise was clearly visible above my left eyebrow. I pushed my bangs back in place. "Well, it doesn't hurt."

"You could have a concussion."

"I'm always this snippy. It has nothing to do with my head."

He laughed. This time I wasn't sure it was at me though. It seemed more like it was with me.

"Well, I'm glad you're always this snippy. I thought it was just your reaction to me."

No, it's definitely not you. Instead of speaking the words in my head I simply nodded.

"I'll go see if I can't find something stronger. Keep your eyes open for me, just in case." He lightly patted my knee.

Every time he touched me it felt like a spark coursed through my whole body. It made me want to rip off clothes and make buttons fly across the room. I swallowed hard as I watched him disappear down the hall again. I knew I shouldn't have come in here with him. Surely I was going to do something stupid. In a stranger's home. I looked around the room, searching for any hint at who it belonged to. The only thing I knew for sure was that they didn't have children. Everything was too white. Or maybe their kids just weren't allowed in this room.

CHAPTER 5

He came back carrying two glasses and a bottle filled with an amber colored liquid. *Bourbon maybe. Or whiskey.* I never drank. I wasn't supposed to mix alcohol with my pills.

"Will this work?" he asked and set the glasses down on the coffee table. He popped the cap off and started to pour some of the alcohol into the cups before I responded.

My ankle was killing me. I glanced to the left and looked out at the empty street. No one would know. The last time I drank was probably in college. I never liked the way it made me feel. Like I was completely out of control.

If I drank, I'd probably say something embarrassing. Most likely, I'd probably hit on him. I couldn't let my carnal needs take over. I turned back to him. I couldn't let anything about my life slip to the man who stared at me, patiently waiting for me to take the glass he offered me.

And it wasn't just my personal reasons. He had already used the owner's Band-Aids and Advil. What was he thinking?

"We shouldn't," I said. Saying the words made me want to accept the glass. I never did anything I wasn't supposed to. Well, rarely. I thought about the pills on the bottom shelf of the pantry. How was that any different?

"It's 5 o'clock somewhere," he said with a smirk.

That wasn't why I was protesting. Although, a drink before 9 a.m. wasn't exactly something most people did. I stared at him. He was a terrible lawn care employee. Really, I should have been making mental notes and been ready to report them back to the owners of this house. Instead, I grabbed the glass and took a big sip before I had time to change my mind.

It burned my throat. *Ugh.* It was disgusting. The last alcohol I had consumed in college was bad. It was some kind of cheap beer that only college students ever bought. This was worse if that was possible.

"Cheers," he laughed without clinking his glass against mine and took a sip from his.

The way I downed that, he probably thought I was an alcoholic. I had made assumptions about him. Maybe his assumptions about me were that I loved drinking before noon.

I took another sip. Not because of the pain in my ankle. But because, despite the burn of my throat, it calmed me. It made it feel like my heartbeat slowed. And I needed that around him. I needed my nerves to subside before I said something I regretted.

"Don't you have somewhere you need to be?" The words tumbled out of my mouth before I could stop them. "Another job, I mean." I immediately took another sip. I was unable to tell whether the alcohol made my social behavior better or worse. Maybe it made me worse. *Be normal.*

"No, not today."

Crap, what? How the hell was I supposed to go home if he wasn't leaving? I took a deep breath. There was no need to overreact. Just because this was his only mowing job today, didn't mean he could just stay here forever. He eventually had to go home.

"But you must have errands and other stuff to do. I don't want to keep you." I placed the empty glass down on the coffee table, trying not to cringe by the lack of coasters. If my lawn guy broke into my house, given that I would never willingly give him a key, and let someone put a glass down anywhere without a coaster, I would throw a total bitch fit. I'd sue. I'd call the police. I'd freaking lose it. I swallowed down the anger creeping up from my gut. Or maybe it was the alcohol threatening to come back up.

"Nope. My day is completely free."

Completely free. If this was happening in one of my dreams, I would have been thrilled. He'd already have me pressed against the wall. My clothes would have been shed immediately upon entering the house. I'd be relishing the taste of his tongue against mine. *Stop.*

"Do you run this early every day?" He refilled my glass but didn't add any to his. "Or is it just a Thursday thing?"

He was just making conversation. He clearly wasn't being accusatory. But for some reason, I took it that way. "I run every day of the week." My voice sounded too defensive, but I couldn't seem to alter my tone. "It has nothing to do with you." *Oh, shit.* God, the alcohol was definitely making me worse than usual.

"Well, I didn't think it did until now. Are you stalking me?"

I grabbed my glass and took another sip. I wanted to disappear into the burn.

"What is that old saying..." He tapped his lip in the most distracting way. "Silence is consent?"

I spit my sip back into my glass. "First of all, that is most definitely not the saying. It's silence is *not* consent. And second of all, I am not stalking you. I run every day of the week at the exact same time. Like I literally just told you. It has nothing to do with when you mow this lawn. Whenever that happens to be."

The smile on his lips grew with each word that tumbled out of mine. His silence was unnerving.

"I mean, of course I've noticed you. And the fact that you mow this lawn sometimes when I'm running. Is it always Thursday that you do that? Huh. I'm surprised I didn't notice the pattern. Usually, I'm pretty observant. I guess it was just that unimportant to me. I'm always completely focused on my pace while I'm running." I pulled on the sleeves of my shirt. It was suddenly stifling in the room and I wished I hadn't been so appropriately dressed for the brisk morning weather.

"So the fact that you were staring at me had nothing to do with you falling into a pile of leaf bags on the curb?"

My jaw had dropped. His forwardness was something that I was definitely not used to.

"It wouldn't be the first time I caught you staring," he said.

I snapped my mouth closed. "I wave at everyone. I was being a friendly neighborhood person. I wave to the trash man too when I see him. It doesn't mean I'm in love with him." It was a lie. I hid inside most of the time and had never once waved to a trash man. Not in my entire life.

"And I'm similar to a trash man because..."

"Well, you mow lawns. You make piles of trash for him to take. It's comparable."

He laughed. "I do more than mow lawns."

"Fine." He was exasperating. "What do they call you people these days? Lawn maintenance crew or something? I'm sorry I offended you." But I didn't sound sorry and I hadn't meant to.

"You people? Wow. Okay. You're awfully condescending."

"The company you work for has a truck that literally says lawn care. Grow a pair and stop being so sensitive about your line of work."

He smiled and set down his glass. "First of all, it's *my* company. And second of all, you didn't bother to read the rest of the sign. It's a landscaping company. We do more than just mow lawns. And I can assure you that I already have a pair."

I gulped. *Stop thinking about his balls.* I tried to focus on the rest of his words. *Landscaper? Huh.* How had I missed that? Probably because I was too busy staring at his abs.

"Well, I'm not the only one in this room with flaws," I countered lamely. "It's way too early to drink. Is this a habit of yours?"

He laughed. "No. I was just trying to keep you company until your friend came. No one should have to drink alone." He set down his glass that was still half full.

I glared at him. The word alone was bouncing around in my head. I was alone. My days were consumed by nothing but my own thoughts. Why was I snapping at him? All he had done was help me. He could have been a complete ass. He could have laughed at me when I crushed the bags and the leaves went everywhere. Instead, he had helped me to my feet. He had given me whatever was in that glass. Which made my head slightly fuzzy. No, it wasn't like all the times I had met him in my dreams. In my dreams he never called me ma'am. But at least he was a gentleman.

"Thanks for not leaving me out there." It came out as a whisper. I wasn't sure why.

He raised his eyebrows, probably as shocked by the change of gears as I was. "Of course I didn't leave you out there. What kind of person would do that?"

I bit the inside of my lip. *I know one.* I studied his features. "How old are you?" I said instead, hoping to change the subject. He looked younger close up. The whole model facade made him look older. Or maybe I was usually just not looking at his face. Plus I had never been fortunate enough to be close to him before.

"That's rather forward." He put his elbows on his knees and leaned closer to me. "You haven't even asked me my name."

"Okay, smartass, what's your name?"

He laughed. "Ben."

"Ben..." I needed to know his last name too. One syllable wasn't enough.

"Jones."

Ben Jones? His name was too average for his looks. I had imagined his name was Noah Hays. I had screamed that name in my dreams too many times to count. But as I stared at him, Ben Jones grew on me. Ben. Benny. Benny boo. *What am I doing?* "It's nice to meet you, Ben Jones." I liked the way his name felt on my tongue.

He put his hand out. "The pleasure is all mine..."

He was waiting for my name. I was tempted to lie. To tell him my name was something common like Jane. Jane sounded good with Jones. Jane Jones. I almost laughed at the thought. I knew him for a few minutes and I was already imagining us getting married.

I cleared my throat, trying to rid myself of the fake name that wanted to escape. "Adeline." It sounded harsh. It always sounded harsh when I told people my name. That was one of the many reasons I hated it.

He reached forward and took my good hand in his. "Adeline. Such a unique name. It's beautiful."

No, it was just plain odd. But I guess that suited me. "Not as beautiful as Ben." *What is wrong with me?* Had I really just said that out loud?

He laughed.

Yup, I had drunk too much. I was starting to be embarrassing. I could feel the alcohol as it spread to my limbs. My arms felt heavier. My mind felt...giddier. I laughed.

"What's so amusing?" he asked.

"It's been a long time since I've had anything to drink. And this bourbon already made my arms feel heavy." I laughed again.

"Made your arms feel heavy? I haven't heard that one before. Also," he said and leaned forward to snag my glass away, "it's scotch. And I think I should cut you off."

"Right." I dropped my voice and added, "We wouldn't want anyone to know we drank some."

He raised both his eyebrows. "Mhm. You've definitely had too much to drink."

Maybe. I leaned forward. I wanted to be closer to him. Just for a second. I wanted to smell him again. I wanted his hand to be back on my waist. He didn't realize how desperate I was. How much I truly needed this moment.

"You're right about me, Ben."

He didn't inch away from me as I leaned forward. If anything, he seemed to move closer too.

"That's why I'm cutting you off," he said.

"No, no." I waved my arm through the air. "The other thing." I shifted my butt on the couch, trying to get more comfortable. Or maybe I was just retreating. He was too close. He was supposed to be left in my imagination. The fact that he was right in front of me was too real. "God, my ankle really hurts."

"Here." His hands moved to my foot and he started unlacing my shoe.

He's undressing me.

"What other thing?" he asked.

"Hmm?"

"You said I was right about you. And then you said it was the other thing."

"Oh." I laughed. "I run every day at 8 a.m. because I know this lawn is on your schedule at 8 a.m. on Thursdays. And also it's better to run the same time each day because your body likes routine. It's scientifically proven."

"I understand the premise of the workout. But why do you time it so that you can see me?" He gently pulled off my sneaker.

I immediately felt relief. "Obviously because I'm madly in love with you." It came out as an exhale. I didn't even have any control over it.

His stormy blues danced with amusement. "Yeah, I figured that."

I laughed. "I was joking, buddy."

He sat back down in his seat. Even though I was begging him with my eyes to join me on the couch.

"We're back to buddy? I thought we were on a first name basis now."

I ignored him. "You never told me how old you were."

"Twenty three. And you?"

Only twenty three? He really was young. Of course he was. He mowed lawns for a living. *He's a landscaper*, I reminded myself. But wasn't that all the same? No wonder he had called me ma'am. "Older than you."

He smiled. "Well, I wouldn't have guessed that. What are you then, twenty five? Twenty six?"

I just turned thirty a few weeks ago. *Thirty*. I was officially a ma'am. I'd never speak to him again after this. What did it matter if he knew I was an old lady? "I just turned thirty actually."

He made this adorable whistling noise that put the smile back on my face.

"You don't look thirty. Not that it's bad that you are. I just would have assumed you were in your mid-twenties."

"Sure. You called me ma'am."

"I was being respectful."

"That's something you call old ladies."

He put his elbows back on his knees. "Trust me, that is not the way I intended it."

"Ben."

"Adeline."

"Oh, God, don't call me that."

"What would you prefer that I call you?"

"My friends call me Addy." A lie. I no longer had any friends. And when I was little, my mother forced me to go by Adeline. She said I'd never get ahead with a name like Addy and that she had given me the elegant name for a reason. And that reason wasn't to chop it in half.

"Addy, then, it was never my intention to make you feel old. Or demean you in any way."

“Then what was your intention? To get me drunk? And then what?”

I watched his Adam’s apple rise and then fall. That wasn’t in my head. It was an actual reaction to my words. He liked me too. Maybe we could still pop a few buttons.

“What do you think?” he asked.

He was saying all the right things. He was almost too kind. Too perfect. Especially for a twenty three year old male. He should have been out with his friends smoking reefer, not starting his own landscaping business. He looked young, but he acted mature. And I couldn't help but wonder how mature he'd be in the bedroom. Would he care about my needs? Or would he just get off as soon as possible? *What am I doing? He's twenty three. He's not going to seduce you, you old hag.*

I drank too much. And my libido was on too high of an alert. It was safer to go home, lock the door, and pretend this never happened. "I think that maybe it might be best if you could take me home?" Just because he knew where I lived, it didn't mean he'd stalk me. I was the stalker in this equation.

His smiled faded.

The expression made my chest ache. How could I already love his smiles so much?

"Yeah, of course. But what about your friend? I thought you wanted to wait for her?"

"She was still in the waiting room. She was going to be forever."

His smile faded even more.

He thinks you don't want to sit here with him. How wrong he was. This was the highlight of my month. My year. The past decade.

"Let me grab those crutches for you then."

"Oh, no need. I'll just stay off my feet until it's better."

He laughed as he stood up. "Don't be ridiculous." He wandered out into the hall and came back a few moments later carrying a pair of crutches. He was really helping himself to these people's possessions. I watched as he adjusted the height of them, lowering them to a position he thought would fit me.

Without asking permission, his hands were back on me, pulling me to my feet, arousing me.

Don't let me go. Don't send me back to my solitude. A horrible realization had just settled around me. I was hurt. I couldn't run next Thursday. And fall was ending soon. There wouldn't be any reason for him to mow this lawn in the coming weeks. When would

I see him next? The panic was rising in my chest. How was I supposed to breathe without Thursdays?

Once the realization hit, everything sped up. Before I even realized it, he was pulling his truck into my driveway. *No.* I couldn't imagine leaving his truck. It smelled like him with a hint of more grass in the air. I was obsessed with the smell. Just as obsessed as I was with him.

He cut the engine.

My breath hitched. He couldn't come in. Why did he stop the truck? What was he doing? My mind was at war with itself. *Come in.* I wanted to beg him. I wanted to get down on my hands and knees and beg him to stay. It felt like I was seconds away from bursting into tears. The war in my mind was too intense. Especially when the choice was so obvious.

"If you want, I can swing by tomorrow or something?" he said. "I'll bring you lunch. It'll be too hard for you to move around."

Please. "That's not necessary..."

"Really, I don't mind. I did put those bags on the curb. It's my fault that you're hurt."

It was your abs' fault. "I'll be okay, Ben." I pushed open the door and managed to somehow climb out of his truck without hurting myself even further. I pulled out the crutches behind me without making eye contact with him.

"Let me at least help you get inside..."

"I'm fine." The words were harsh. Much too harsh. And even more untrue. *I'm so sorry.* But I needed him to hate me. I needed to make sure he'd never come back. It was for his own safety.

"Addy?"

My whole life, I had so badly wanted someone to call me that. And from his lips? The sound was too sweet. I didn't deserve sweet.

"Can I at least..."

I slammed the door closed to muffle his words. I didn't look back as I limped up the sidewalk.

CHAPTER 6

The sobs I had been holding escaped my throat when I closed the front door behind me. They raked my whole body. I would have been stumbling even if I wasn't balancing on crutches. I needed my medicine. That was the reason I was feeling this way. I was late taking it, and it was the only thing that could calm me down.

I hobbled into the kitchen and threw open the drawer where I kept my pills. At least, the ones I wasn't hiding. My fingers wrapped around the container I needed and I fumbled with the lid. *Why do they make these so freaking hard to open?* I knocked the container to the floor and the pills spilled in every direction. They rolled across the spotless tiles, under the table, under the oven. *Damn it.*

I crouched down to grab one off the floor and winced at the pain in my ankle. Down on all fours on the cold tile, I had an epiphany. I was in pain. Not just physically, but mentally. Anguish. My mind was full of complete and utter anguish.

I wiped away the tears under my eyes. It had been the first time in months that I cried. That I felt anything but fear. I didn't want to be numb anymore. I didn't want to take the pills. Why were they forcing me to take them? Why didn't I have a choice? I deserved a say in my own damned life.

This time, I didn't worry about the neighbors overhearing me. I screamed at the top of my lungs. I screamed and tore the drawer from its hinges, dumping the contents to the floor.

I let myself feel. I let myself hurt. I let myself remember.

Until I couldn't bear it. Until I couldn't shed another tear. Until my body was as exhausted as my mind.

My fingers wandered across the floor until I found a sleeping pill. I was done with the others. But I couldn't take any more pain today. I placed it in my mouth and swallowed it down without any water. And then I curled up on the cold floor and willed sleep to come.

***

The light shining harshly through the window woke me up. The setting sun always seemed to weasel its way through the closed blinds. I blinked and sat up off the floor. I had slept through the whole day. I couldn't remember the last time I had slept so soundlessly.

But at what cost? My back ached and the pain in my ankle was throbbing. The combination of my swollen ankle and the pills scattered around the kitchen brought everything back to me.

I had been so close to him. Ben. I smiled to myself. Ben Jones. So close, and I pushed him away. *Why?* I wrapped my arms around myself. His touch had heated me. And now I'd never see him again. I couldn't walk. Soon the air would turn cold and crisp, and the grass would stop growing. I'd have to wait until the spring. A whole winter without him seemed impossibly daunting.

I eyed the pills on the floor. It was tempting to take one. I was supposed to take one. Instead, I crawled around the floor, pushing all the pills along with me. When I reached the sink I stood up on my good leg and dumped all the pills in the sink.

My fingers flipped the switch and the garbage disposal churned to life. I took a long, slow breath as I watched my pills being ground to dust. My mind was clearer than it had been in months. I knew exactly what I was doing. My memories made sense. I had slept for once. I felt great.

I looked down at my ankle. And for the first time, I realized I had left my shoe at my neighbor's house. Sitting in their pristine living room. A laugh escaped my throat. What on earth would they think about that? If Ben was having an affair with the woman that lived there, she'd be furious when she saw it. She'd think he was cheating on her. She'd break up with him.

A smile had formed on my lips. I laughed and shook away the thought. It didn't matter what Ben Jones' relationship status was. I was never going to see him again.

I hopped over to the fridge and pulled open the door to the freezer. The effort made me yawn. I could get used to this new exhaustion. Sleeping was better than being conscious. As long as my dreams didn't morph into nightmares. I pulled out an ice pack and slowly made my way toward the living room.

The room was as barren as my neighbors'. Like them, I also didn't have a family. There were no messy kids running around leaving sticky fingerprints everywhere. No one to bring laughter to my home. And there never would be. I swallowed down the lump in my throat.

Normally, I never stepped foot in the living room. But I was somehow still exhausted. The stairs weren't an option right now. I collapsed on the sofa. Before my eyelids shut, I couldn't help but realize that my walls were bare too. Not completely. Expensive artwork was displayed. But there wasn't a single picture of me. Which was odd, because I had so many pictures.

CHAPTER 7

My eyes flew open. It felt like my heart was beating faster than it ever had. *God.* The dream had been so real. I took a deep breath to calm my rapid heart rate. It was like Ben was right here. Holding me. Kissing me. I touched the side of my neck. His lips had felt so real. The coolness of my fingertips was jarring. Why was it so cold in here? I reached for a blanket but remembered I wasn't in my bed.

A knock on the door almost caused me to tumble off the couch. But I caught myself at the last second. Pain seared in my left hand. The one that Ben had bandaged. No wonder it was so easy to dream about his touch.

Another knock.

Go away. Was that what had startled me awake? A knock? No one ever knocked on my door besides for the mailman. And we had an understanding. He always left any packages on the doorstep because he knew I refused to answer. One time he had seen me staring through the curtain at him. He had waved. I had let the curtains fall back into place. Now we understood each other. Or so I thought.

I closed my eyes and readjusted myself on the couch. He'd go away. Unless it was a substitute. A sub would be more persistent if something needed signing. Had I even ordered anything recently?

Another knock made me groan. *Jesus. Just leave!* No mailman tried this hard. Actually, it was probably too late in the day for the mailman. It was…I swallowed hard when I looked at my watch. 11:45 a.m.? I sat back up with a start. How was that possible? I stared at the closed blinds. Light was streaming in through the slits. I had slept all day *and* all night? My stomach rumbled at the thought of all the missed meals.

I put my hand on my forehead. Sleeping pills had never worked well on me. I'd sleep for a few hours and then wake up restless. But I had slept for almost 24 hours straight.

The knocking had stopped. I was curious if he had decided to just leave the package. Or maybe there'd be a note for a redelivery date. I stood up on one leg and hopped to the front door.

All that sleep had given me more energy too. I felt like going for a run. If only I hadn't ruined that for myself. Just thinking about not seeing Ben again made me want to cry. It was like I was an addict and he was my drug. How could I see him again? Get a wheelchair and roll down the street to the lawn he mowed? I needed to think of a way. That one encounter would never be enough.

I opened up the door and it was as if I had conjured him to life. I blinked. No, he was really there. *Ben.* I placed my hand on the doorframe to steady myself.

"Addy, where are your crutches?"

Addy. I held back a sigh. How many times had he groaned my name in my dreams last night? How many times had he whispered in my ear? Or kissed my lips? God, he had just asked me a question. What had he said?

"Addy?"

The daydreams disintegrated as I saw a group of women walking in the distance. The gawkers I called them. Catty women who never took the time to get to know me. Gossiping witches. And they were coming this way.

"What are you doing here?" I hissed.

He lowered his eyebrows in the sexiest way possible. God, I didn't have time for him to look sexy right now. They were coming!

"I promised you lunch." He held up the takeout bag in his hand.

The aroma made me drool. It smelled like everything I never ate. Greasy, delicious fries were most likely in that bag. My stomach growled. "And I told you not to come!"

He smiled out of the corner of his mouth like I was amusing to him. "And I decided not to listen."

He wasn't supposed to come back. He wasn't supposed to be this sweet. He wasn't supposed to ever be more than a daydream. My eyes darted back to the women. They were drawing closer. They were probably already staring at us. Talking. *No.*

I grabbed the front of Ben's t-shirt and pulled him into the house. His chest collided with mine and he had to grab my back so that we both didn't topple to the floor.

The aroma of grass and all things manly filled my nose, making me pause in the middle of my plan to hide him. We stayed pressed together with the door hanging open for the whole neighborhood to see. A public display I couldn't bother to care about when I was in his arms.

"Well, hello to you too," he said and tilted his head down to look at me.

His ocean blue eyes were so gorgeous that it almost hurt to stare at them. If I stood on my tiptoes, our lips would only be a fraction of an inch apart. *What the hell am I doing right now?* I let go of his shirt and slammed the door shut.

"You shouldn't have come," I said as I hopped back into the living room and pushed the curtains to the side. The gawkers were walking past. One of the women turned toward the house and I quickly drew the curtains closed. *This isn't happening.* I could already hear the rumors. The damage was already done.

"Addy?"

I turned to stare at him. He had clearly asked me a question and I hadn't been paying attention again.

"If you don't tell me where your crutches are, I swear I'm going to carry you to the kitchen."

I laughed.

The foyer was dark, but his smile could light up any room. The realization that he was in my house made me bite the inside of my lip. What was I supposed to do with him?

I eyed the bag in his hand. *Right.* Eat. I held my head up high. "I don't need crutches or for you to carry me."

"Whatever you say."

I waited for him to move out of my way. I didn't need him, but that didn't mean I wanted him to stare at me hopping around on one foot.

"Well...the kitchen is that way." I pointed behind him.

"I want to make sure you don't fall," he said and waited for me to pass.

God he was infuriating. "We've already had this conversation. I'm not 80 years old." I hopped past him as fast as I could manage.

He grabbed me around the waist as I passed him, and lifted me up so that my back was flush with his chest.

"Put me down!" I squirmed underneath his grip as my feet hovered off the ground.

He laughed in my ear. The feeling of his warm breath and the sound of his amusement made me want to sigh. Instead, I said,

"I'm not a child either!" with much less force. Really, I didn't want him to stop holding me.

We reached the kitchen far too soon and he released me as soon as my good foot hit the tile.

His hand slid off my waist and he walked into the kitchen, completely ignoring my outburst. He set down the takeout bag on the kitchen table and started opening up drawers and cabinets.

"Excuse me," I said, putting my hands on my hips. What did he think he was doing?

"You're excused." He opened up another cabinet. "Aha." He pulled out two plates and set them down on the counter.

"Would you stop rummaging through my things?"

He glanced at me over his shoulder. "Would you sit down?"

I glared at him.

He gave me a similar look back before continuing to open up drawers.

I sighed and sat down.

"All set," he said and placed a plate and utensils down in front of me. "Want something to drink?"

"Are you trying to get me drunk again?"

He raised his left eyebrow. "It's barely noon, woman. What are you trying to do to me?"

Unspeakable things. I laughed. "The glasses are in the cabinet on the far left. And there's a Brita pitcher in the fridge."

"Two glasses of water coming right up. We can save the hard liquor for later."

Later? "How long are you planning on staying?"

He poured the water without answering me.

"Ben, I have a million things to do." Such a statement was always an exaggeration. But to me it was especially so. I had absolutely nothing to do.

"What things can you possibly achieve when you can't walk? Snort cocaine?" He sat down next to me in the only other seat and opened up the bag like what he had just said wasn't at all odd.

"Excuse me? I'm not going to do drugs with you. I don't know what kind of illegal things 23 year olds do, but I..."

"I saw the powder in your sink." He pulled out a wrapped sandwich and placed it on my plate without looking at me.

Powder? I looked over at the sink. *Oh, God.* "No, that's not..." my voice trailed off. Technically, I had tossed a bunch of drugs down the garbage disposal yesterday. Some of the grindings must have still been in the sink.

"It would explain why you're so fidgety."

"I don't do illegal drugs. And I'm not fidgety." I willed my knee to stop bouncing. He made me nervous, that was all.

"So...prescription drugs then?"

"No actually. Not anymore." I thought about the one prescription that I hid in the pantry. The one I'd never stop taking.

"What did you used to take then?"

"None of your business."

"Well, what were they for?"

"What, you want a list of my problems? How dare you barge in here and be...be... so demanding."

He put his elbows on the table and leaned forward slightly. "Doll, you literally pulled me inside your home. And I'm not being demanding, I'm just making conversation."

Doll. My mind seemed to focus on the most random parts of his sentences.

"But I wasn't trying to make you uncomfortable. Forget that I asked. He pulled out the other sandwich, unwrapped it, and then dumped some fries on my plate.

"How would you feel if I asked you what prescriptions you took?" I unwrapped my sandwich and tried to ignore him.

"I'd tell you that I don't take any."

"Just illegal ones then?"

He laughed. "No. My only vice is the occasional drink with a beautiful woman."

I stared down at the burger I had just unwrapped. It was topped with crunchy onion straws and there was a delicious looking sauce dripping down the sides. He had called me beautiful. Yet, I couldn't look up at him. I didn't want to know if he was being patronizing or serious. So instead of looking, I pushed the utensils to the side, lifted up the burger, and took a huge bite.

"Are you trying to make me fall in love with you?"

"What?" I said with my mouth still full.

He laughed. "The last date I went on, the girl ordered a salad and only ate half."

"If that's a challenge to see if I can eat this whole thing, you're on." I swallowed the bite still in my mouth. "I slept for 24 hours straight. I'm starving."

"Twenty four hours? Was meeting me really that exhausting?"

"Excruciatingly so." This burger was everything delicious in the world. I couldn't remember the last time I had eaten a burger. Or red meat. Or fries. I started to shovel those in my mouth as well without even realizing what I was doing.

Ben laughed.

I looked up at him mid-chew and realized I must look like a starving animal. I swallowed and cleared my throat. "Please don't stare at me while I eat, it makes me nervous."

"Please? Did you really just say please? I think that was the first nice thing that I've ever heard come out of your mouth."

"Don't be ridiculous," I said.

"Do you even know how to give a compliment?" He smiled as if he had me right where he wanted me.

"Of course I do."

"Then let me hear one." He leaned forward slightly as he waited.

"It's not a compliment if you have to beg for it."

"It doesn't have to be about me. I just brought you lunch. You could thank me for that."

"But I asked you not to bring it."

He shrugged his shoulders. "I think you just proved me right."

I didn't want him to think I hated him when it was so fiercely untrue. "You look very nice today. Cleaner than yesterday."

He laughed. "The first half of that was a compliment. The second half was an insult."

"There's nothing wrong with being dirty," I said and picked up a fry.

I thought maybe I imagined it yesterday. But I don't think I had. Because his Adam's apple had just risen and fallen again. The action made me press my thighs together.

"No, there's definitely nothing wrong with being dirty," he said.

I bit the inside of my lip. How long did he say he was staying? I had a feeling that as time ticked by I'd have a harder and harder time keeping my hands to myself.

CHAPTER 8

I squeezed the excess water out of my hair before wrapping a towel around myself. I was terribly out of practice with flirting. Somehow our conversation had taken a quick turn to the fact that I was actually dirty. The sexual innuendo evaporated completely when I had started talking about my greasy hair.

But the tension in the air hadn't gone away. It still swirled around me even though he was all the way downstairs. *Doing who knows what in my house.*

Just the thought made me hurry. I combed out the knots in my hair and applied a little too much makeup for a day at home. I pushed my bangs aside to see the bruise that Ben had pointed out yesterday. It was almost invisible under my foundation, but I added a little concealer just in case. In a few days, it would be gone completely and I wouldn't have to worry. But until then, Ben was asking invasive questions. And I was starting to wonder why. Was it really because he liked me? He was seven years younger than me. What could he possibly want from me that he couldn't get from someone his own age?

Was a seven year age gap enough for me to be considered a cougar? Just the thought made me feel nauseous. I wasn't one of *those* women. And it wasn't like I was going to act on my desire. I couldn't afford to act on my desires. I positioned my bangs back in place and hopped into my bedroom. Yoga pants and a tank top seemed like the easiest clothes to crawl around in. *And take off. Stop it!*

For some reason, I still pulled on a red lacy thong and matching bra. Just in case. Not that anything was going to happen. Geez, he was 23. He was too young. Too nice. Too naïve for...me. I caught my reflection in the mirror. So why did I put on so much mascara?

I turned away from the mirror. It was easy to picture this house being a home. Was that what I wanted? To feel loved again? To feel whole? I blinked quickly so that my mascara wouldn't start to run. None of that mattered. Ben could be my friend. Nothing more. I wasn't even sure why I let my mind wander.

I opened up the door and sat down on the stairs. My pride wouldn't let me call for him. Or maybe it was just that if I was in his arms again I'd lose all self-control. I scooted down the stairs a step at a time.

My legs were in good shape from running. But having to slowly hoist myself down each step made the muscles in my arms burn. I needed to add strength training to my workouts.

A deep chuckle made me look up. Ben was standing at the foot of the stairs with his arms folded across his chest. The amused look on his face made me press my lips together.

I wanted him. I wanted him desperately. That was why I threw insults his way. It was easier than admitting that I couldn't have what I wanted. I needed him to become something I didn't crave. "Would you stop staring at me? You don't need to be here." I swallowed down the groan in my throat as I moved down another stair.

"Why is it so hard for you to ask for help?"

Because asking comes with dire consequences. "I'm used to doing things on my own. I don't need anyone's help."

"So...you don't want me to carry you down the rest of the stairs?"

"No."

Ow. My butt hit one of the wooden steps hard when one of my hands slipped. I looked down at my hurt palm. I had forgotten to put a new Band-Aid on it. I tried to calculate how hard it would be to move back up the stairs.

"Addy, I'm offering to help you."

"And I'm telling you I don't need it."

"Here I thought that you'd be more chipper after a hot shower."

"You try balancing on one foot on slippery tile. This isn't exactly fun for me."

"How about you let me help you out until you're back on your feet?"

I stared down at my ankle. How long would that be? Why on earth was I even considering it? "Don't you have places to be? Things to landscape?"

He laughed. "If you haven't noticed, fall is here. Fall and winter are my down seasons. I can make it work."

Yesterday I was worried I'd never see him again. The thought had terrified me. Thursdays had always been the days I looked forward to. He was offering to be here...what...every day? For a few weeks? I needed to send him away. But it was hard. I wanted him here. I wanted to believe that this thing between us could actually be real.

"Let me help you." His voice was gentle.

And for some reason it brought tears to the corners of my eyes. I blinked to rid the pools that threatened to fall. "It's hard to get up and down the stairs." I sounded dejected. Small. But maybe just a tiny bit hopeful. What if he was the one that could actually save me from this hell?

The squeak of the bottom step let me know he was coming. But I didn't look up. I was scared to fall. Not down the stairs. I wasn't scared of bumps and bruises. That had never been my problem. I was scared of falling for him when I had no right to fall. Not again.

I squeezed my eyes shut tight as he lifted me into his arms. I thought that not seeing him would make it easier. But maybe that was worse. *Feeling.* One of his hands had slid slightly underneath my tank top. I could feel his callused hands against the softness of my skin. The contrast made me stifle a sigh in my throat.

I didn't open my eyes until he set me back down in one of the kitchen chairs. He had pulled out an ice pack for me. And next to that was a casserole of some sort. How long had I been in the shower?

Before I could ask him, he lifted up my foot and cradled it in his hand. He wrapped the ice pack around my ankle and let my foot rest on top of his thigh. Any thoughts I had about casseroles came careening to a halt. It felt like I could feel his heartbeat pulsing through my heel. Or maybe it was my own heart racing uncontrollably.

"Have you been icing this?" he asked as he gingerly rotated the ice pack. "It will heal faster if you ice it."

"I fell asleep right after I got home yesterday. But I iced it before I fell asleep the second time."

"Right." He shifted the ice pack again. "I forgot, you said you slept a whole day straight."

There was suddenly an awkwardness in the air. Did he feel it too? His face didn't show it. But he did look like he was thinking.

Where did his mind wander? I wished I could be in his thoughts. I wish I consumed them like he consumed mine.

He ran the pad of his thumb along the inside of my ankle. "How is the pain level? Did you want some Advil or anything? I could still take you to the doctor if…"

"No." Absolutely not. "But Advil might be nice. I have some on the top shelf of the medicine cabinet."

"Let me go grab it for you." He placed my foot on the chair he had been sitting in and disappeared down the hall.

I almost told him where the bathroom was, but then I heard the squeak of the hinge of the medicine cabinet. He must have already looked around while I was in the shower. The thought made my pulse increase even more than his touch. What else had he found? God, why had I let him in my house? I looked down at my ankle. I knew why I welcomed him in. It wasn't the women walking by on the street. It was because I liked his hands on me. I was playing with fire. I needed to send him home.

"Got it," he said. His footsteps sounded in the hall. "Took me a minute. I'm still not used to seeing the new extra strength bottle."

"I don't have extra strength…" my rebuttal died as he handed me the bottle. *Weird.* I didn't remember ever picking up extra strength. I liked the candy coating on the outside of the original. I must have bought them on one of my off days. My fingers wandered to the side of my head. *No.* Not off days. That's what the doctors would say. It was the medicine they gave me that made me forget. It made me have off days. And now I'd always be on. I felt my face flushing. I'd always be turned on if Ben was around.

"You must have grabbed these by accident then," he said. "I can pick you up some of the original if you'd like."

"No, no. That's okay." He had already done quite enough for me. I took the bottle from him and unscrewed the cap.

He watched me as I swallowed the pill and chased it with a sip of water. It was unnerving when he watched me. I cleared my throat as I lifted the aluminum foil to get a look at the casserole he had made beneath. I didn't remember buying this pan either. But then again, my memory was clearly fuzzy. I felt more alert without my prescriptions. Or maybe I just didn't realize I had that pan because I rarely cooked.

I leaned forward and inhaled a whiff of the casserole. *Mmm. Definitely lasagna.* Even though I had just devoured a hamburger and fries, my stomach growled again. Apparently one meal didn't make up for three missed ones. "Landscaper *and* chef? That's an impressive pairing. You're a man of many surprises."

He laughed and sat down beside me, pulling my foot back on his lap. "No, I wouldn't call myself a chef. Your friend just dropped it off."

"My friend?" My voice sounded strangled. What friend? I had no friends in this godforsaken neighborhood.

"Yeah. Must have been the one you called the other day. She seemed nice enough. Asked if you were feeling better."

"What was her name?"

"I think it started with a K." He scratched the back of his neck as he stared at me. He lowered his eyebrows slightly at the horrid expression on my face. "Or maybe not. It could have started with a C? No?" He shrugged his shoulders. "Regardless, she was nice. She had blonde hair..."

He was searching for something else to say. But all I could think about was the fact that he had answered my door. To a stranger. *No. This can't be happening.* "You talked to her?" I buried my face in my hand. It felt like my whole world had teetered and was about to tip.

"Yeah. I told her I was helping you out while your ankle healed."

Panic raked through my body. There was only one blonde nosy enough to stop by my house. *Freaking Charlotte Hallady.* I wanted to tell him to leave. To get the hell out of my house. I wanted to yell and scream and throw things. But the damage was already done. I swallowed down the lump in my throat. The action made a weird squeaking noise.

"Addy, what's wrong?" He moved one of his hands off my foot and placed it on the side of my knee.

"You can't answer my door to strangers while I'm showering upstairs. Do you have any idea how that looks?"

He smiled. "She's hardly a stranger. She said she was your friend..."

"That woman is *not* my friend. Don't you realize what you've done?" I lowered my voice slightly. "I was upstairs naked. She's probably going to tell everyone I'm sleeping with you."

"That doesn't sound like the worst thing in the world to me."

I was suddenly very aware of his hand lingering on my knee. *He wants to sleep with me?* I gulped. *He wants to sleep with me.* It was like every one of my dreams coming true. But I couldn't get rid of the strangled feeling in my throat.

"What was her name?" he asked. "Maybe I can pay her a visit and..."

"Please do not engage with Charlotte Hallady. She'll be the death of both of us." I meant what I said. My tone was completely serious.

But he laughed. He found the whole thing humorous.

"I'm serious, Ben."

"Addy." His hand slid up the outside of my thigh as he leaned toward me. "I told her I was helping you out while your ankle healed. She already seemed to know about your injury. Hence the lasagna. I don't think she's a big bad wolf out to get you. She truly seemed concerned."

"You don't understand how catty the women in this neighborhood are. Everyone on my street probably thinks we're having a scandalous affair."

"I hardly think it would classify as scandalous."

I knew he didn't know the truth. And I wasn't ready to tell him yet. "You're 23," I said instead.

"Age is just a number. The only thing that really matters is that we're both adults. Don't you agree?"

I snapped my fingers, ignoring him. "I'll go to their stupid bi-monthly civic association meeting next week and clear the air."

"There's a bi-monthly civic association meeting? I had no idea."

I waved my hand dismissively. "You're not part of the neighborhood. Of course you didn't know."

"Wow. Is there some sort of initiation I'm unaware of?"

"Ben, stop it, this is important. It's on Wednesday night. I'll just have to pray that she can keep her stupid mouth shut until then." There was a whole weekend before that. A huge stretch of time for gossip. It was likely the entire town would know the rumors by Wednesday. But it was the only plan I had. I couldn't exactly call her. I didn't have the woman's number. I didn't have any of the gawkers' numbers.

"Okay," he said and let his hand fall from my knee. "You'll go to the meeting and then what? Make an official decree that we're not banging?" Humor danced in his eyes. And his dimple was back. I didn't think I could ever hate his beautiful face, but I did for a second.

"Of course not. Mentioning that would just make it more incriminating. I'll tell everyone you…that you're my…gardener."

He rose his eyebrow. "Really? That's your grand plan? That just makes it seem like you're paying me to sleep with you."

Ugh. He was right.

"And trust me, Addy, you wouldn't have to pay me."

"Yeah right." I couldn't hide my gulp, though. He was looking at me in the most intense way. If I was standing my knees would be weak. Either way, he was definitely weakening my resolve. "You should probably go. Before you have a chance to answer more doors and make the hole I'm in any deeper."

He smiled. "If that's what you really want." An awkward silence stretched between us. He exhaled slowly.

I had the strangest urge to lean forward and inhale his exhales.

You're welcome by the way," he said. "For lunch."

"Yeah. Thanks." *Please leave.*

He laughed and stood up, gingerly resting my foot back down on the chair. "Keep ice on that. I'll see you tomorrow."

Saturday. "No. I mean, you can't…" my mind searched for anything to say. Any excuse that didn't sound insane.

"I thought you agreed that I could help you. Or be your gardener. Or whatever you'd like to call this." He was smiling, but it almost looked like he was begging to come back. Like he couldn't resist not seeing me for a day.

"I do want your help, but you can't come this weekend."

"Big plans?"

"You could say that. Monday. Please. Just…come back on Monday." My eyes darted to the clock on the wall and suddenly it felt like I was out of time. It was nearly 3 o'clock. I only had a few hours left.

"Okay."

"Promise me you won't come back until Monday."

"I promise," he said with a laugh. "Until Monday then." He started walking toward the front hall.

"No! I mean, could you leave out the back? I don't want anyone else to see you."

"You do realize how this looks?" he said as he backtracked and opened up the back door. "Me sneaking out the back of your house in shame?"

It made it look like we were having an affair. It just further validated the rumors that were certainly spreading at that very moment. "Fine. Go out the front door then."

"It's okay. I won't mind the rumors." He winked at me and went down the back stairs without another word.

I pushed the ice off my leg and hopped over to the back door. I couldn't resist pushing aside the curtains. Even the back of his head was handsome. I watched him as he disappeared into the woods. And I couldn't help but wonder if he had the same fears as me. I let the curtain fall back to place. Of course he didn't. Someone would be able to hear him scream. Someone would come to his rescue. I double locked the door. But it wouldn't be me.

CHAPTER 9

I emptied the dustpan into the trash and froze. There was nothing in the trash bin except for the dust. I tipped it closer toward me. It had been filled to the brim yesterday, hadn't it? I nodded to myself even though I was alone. *Definitely.* I always took the trash out on Friday afternoons when I got everything else ready.

Had Ben taken out my trash? Who came to someone's house without an invitation and took out their trash? What else had he done? I looked around the spotless kitchen.

I pushed the trash bin back into place. *God, I don't have time for this.* I could thank him later. I hopped back to the laundry room, hung the dustpan on its hook, and glanced at my watch. 5:37. I only had a few minutes left. But everything was set. Perfect timing.

I wiped my hands on the front of my pants. *Crap.* I looked down at my yoga pants. *Not quite perfect timing.* I had to change.

The stairs were even more difficult now that my arms were tired from scrubbing everything for the past two hours. And I wished that Ben was still here. I immediately dismissed the thought. I needed to stop dreaming of his arms around me. I needed to just...stop. Ben wasn't mine. He'd never be mine.

I rubbed my palm halfway up the stairs. Why did my body ache for his touch so desperately? I remembered the feeling of his fingers on the back of my hand. It wasn't in my imagination. There was a spark. And by the way he was acting, he felt it too. He wanted me back. How had I let this happen?

I looked back down at my watch. Only five more minutes. I held back the tears as I slowly climbed up the steps one at a time. It took every ounce of willpower not to collapse once I reached my bedroom. I was exhausted again. It felt like I could sleep another 24 hours straight.

5:43. There was no time left to change. I crawled into the room and opened the top drawer of my nightstand. I picked up the rings. They always felt so damn heavy. But today, they felt even heavier than usual. I slid them onto my finger and stared down at the diamond that was way too big. At the time, I didn't understand it's extravagance. I sighed and closed the drawer.

Maybe he wouldn't come home. All it took was one careless driver. One text. One drink. One. Single. Slip. It seemed so simple. If only I was so lucky.

The sound of the front door unlocking made me cringe. I pulled myself onto the bed. I was injured. I'd feign rest. I pushed down the covers to try to pretend I'd been in bed for awhile.

"Adeline! I'm home!"

His voice made all the hairs on the back of my neck rise. *Home? This was never a home.* He had made sure of that. All my energy was sapped by just the idea of him, let alone his presence. I heard his feet on the stairs and squeezed my eyes shut. *Leave me be.*

"Babe?"

Babe. An affectionate name that didn't belong anywhere in this house. Vomit rose in the back of my throat and I did my best to swallow it down.

His steps drew closer and the bed sagged beneath his weight. "Adeline." He gently touched the side of my face.

I groaned and turned away from him.

His fingers didn't move with me, and they dug into my jaw. Just a tiny bit. Just enough that they'd wake me if I had been asleep. Just enough to make it feel like my heart stopped beating. He didn't believe my act. That much was clear. This wasn't the way to start a whole weekend of him.

I slowly opened my eyes. Every time he came back from his business trips, I was always surprised to remember how handsome he was. His dark hair and eyes, his sharp jaw, and his perfectly kissable lips were all breathtaking. It was no wonder I fell for him so hard. I was naïve. I didn't realize love was a game. I trusted him. I trusted him with everything. And I lost the game. Because I knew better than anyone that it was what was on the inside that counted.

It should have been natural to miss him. He was my husband. I was supposed to be a loving wife, missing him, wanting him. I always counted the minutes until he returned home to me. But it wasn't because I missed him. It was because I was dreading his return.

I forced the corners of my mouth to turn up. "Oh. You're back. Welcome home, honey." *Vile.* The taste of vomit was back in my throat. I reached out my hand and ran it along his forearm. His dress shirt was stiff. It made me think of the soft fabric of Ben's t-shirt.

"What are you doing in bed, babe?" His fingers drifted to the side of my neck. I could feel his wedding band against my skin. A sham. It was all a sham. I had lost the game. But for some damn reason it wouldn't end. I couldn't make it stop.

I let my hand fall from his arm and gestured to my foot. "I twisted my ankle on my run."

The look of concern on his face made me want to laugh. "We should probably get you to the doctor."

"No." I kept my voice even. No more doctors. No more drugs. Even though I was exhausted, I finally felt like myself again. I didn't feel numb. His hand paused on the strap of my tank top and I kept the smile plastered to my face. I felt everything. For a moment I wanted to be numb again. I didn't want to feel his touch. I didn't want to be here. "I took some Advil. And I've been icing it. It'll be fine in a few days."

"Are you sure you don't want to go to the doctor? You look exhausted."

I laughed it off. "It's nothing serious." But it did hurt. It hurt and I missed the way Ben had taken care of me. For just one moment, I had felt almost loved. How quickly such a feeling could fade.

"Okay. I won't push it." His fingers toyed with the strap of my tank top. "I can whip us up something for dinner. Are you hungry?"

I saw no reason to delay the inevitable. I felt like an actress. Like I was performing a role I wasn't quite ready to play. But I had no choice. I had already been cast. I batted my eyelashes. "No, I'm not hungry. I missed you." I grabbed his hand and let him lower the strap he had been touching.

"I missed you too, Adeline. One day, I won't have to travel as much." He leaned down and kissed the side of my neck as he continued to pull the fabric down my arm. "One day soon."

One day soon? The words echoed in my head. It felt like my world was collapsing. What did he mean by one day soon?

I closed my eyes tight and tried to pretend Ben was the one climbing on top of me. Ben would be gentle. He'd be loving. And he'd never be mine. Because I'd never be able to escape my husband. Never.

CHAPTER 10

I pushed the kale around with my fork. It was bland and lifeless. It was almost like I was staring at the vegetable equivalent of myself. I wanted another burger and greasy goodness. I never minded the diet before. But now that I had met Ben, I felt different. I wanted to break the rules. I wanted a freaking brownie.

"Adeline."

My eyes snapped to his. The look on his face made it seem like he had been trying to get my attention. "Sorry, what did you say?"

He smiled. "How was your week?"

"It was fine."

"Just fine? Nothing out of the ordinary?"

My heart rate accelerated. *He knows.* He had only just arrived back to town. Had the gossip already spread so far? I set my fork down. I wasn't hungry for vegetables anyway. I needed to nip anything he had heard in the bud. "Actually, I hired a new gardener."

"What was wrong with the last one?"

He didn't seem suspicious. It's not like it would be the first time I had fired someone. "He didn't mow the lawn in straight lines. You know how that bothers me." My lie was stupid. Fortunately for me, I had grown to be quite the perfectionist. So at least it was believable. But with my mind less foggy, I doubt I'd notice whether a line was straight. Pieces of dust on the mantle didn't even seem to bother me anymore. I had done the worst cleaning of my life and it had nothing to do with my hurt ankle. I just suddenly realized I didn't care. My knee had stopped bouncing. I had stopped obsessing. The medicine was what had been causing me to be OCD. And the prescription they had given me to combat my OCD made me anxious. And the anxiety medication... I let my thoughts trail off. None of it mattered.

"You seem different today," he said.

"Do I?" It was a strange turn of conversation. I thought he'd question me about the new gardener. But he didn't seem suspicious at all. Well, maybe he was a little suspicious of me. He was staring at me peculiarly. Almost like he was studying me.

He smiled again. I hated when he smiled. "You seem...I don't know...lighter." He laughed. "Not in a weight way. Just in a mood way. Maybe that new depression medicine you started taking is finally kicking in. You're feeling good?"

"Mhm." I took a huge sip of my glass of water and my throat made a weird noise. I didn't want him to be analyzing me. For some reason, I wanted him to be questioning me. He should have been firing questions at me about the new help. Not...this. "You know Charlotte Hallady? Well, she was the one that recommended the new landscaping company."

"I'm glad you're finally making friends."

His behavior was infuriating. *Be suspicious of me!* Ben had been in our house. He had been so close that I could almost taste his skin. I wanted him. I wanted him desperately. But I stayed away. *I stayed away because of you.* I watched him cut up his steak. I should have just had the damned affair. Apparently he wouldn't have even cared. I pulled my hands onto my lap and twirled my wedding band around my finger. The most infuriating part was that he clearly didn't see how suffocated I felt. I was sitting in front of him drowning. *Let me leave.*

"How often have you been leaving the house?" He took a sip of wine as he stared at me.

I ran my tongue along my bottom lip. I wanted a glass. But I didn't ask. He'd want to know why I suddenly wanted a drink. And the answer was simple. *It will remind me of him.* "Just the running in the morning."

"And that's when you see Charlotte? On your runs?" Another sip.

I shouldn't have willed him to ask me questions. I wasn't ready with the answers. "Oh, and at the civic association meetings of course."

"When did you start attending those?" He topped off his glass.

Was that his second? Or his third? "It's important for me to go." I had only ever been to one since we moved to this neighborhood. But I had already started lying. I couldn't go back. Besides, I needed to attend the one next week. I needed to bury the rumors before they destroyed everything. "You wanted me to fit in. I'm just doing what you asked."

"What I asked? You know how I feel about you leaving the house. You need to tell Charlotte to come here from now on."

"I can't just stop going to the meetings. People will talk."

"I agreed on the runs. You didn't ask me about this. You're not going anymore."

"It's just a meeting twice a month. I don't see..."

He slammed his glass down. "We've have this conversation before, Adeline. It's not safe for you to be roaming about."

"It wasn't a conversation!" I shouldn't have yelled. God, I shouldn't have yelled. I couldn't even remember the last time I had raised my voice. Anger radiated off his body too, making me cower. "I'm sorry," I said before he could get a word in. "You *told* me what I could and couldn't do. I never agreed to anything, you…"

"Because I'm the only one capable of making decisions. For your own safety."

"I can make my own decisions. I'm fine. How many times do I have to tell you that I'm okay? I'm not a child."

He sighed. "One phone call. That's all it takes. Don't make me do it again." His tone scared me. This wasn't the first time he had threatened this. And I couldn't go back.

"I'm sorry." Tears bit at the corners of my eyes. "Please don't. I'm sorry."

"You're clearly still sick, Adeline. All I've done is try to help you."

"I'm so sorry. I'll be better."

He tilted his head to the side and the bones in his neck cracked.

I hated that noise. It was the only thing worse than hearing him say he was home. That handsome face that greeted me earlier was gone. The horrid one in front of me was what I was familiar with.

I needed to say something. Anything to stop this from escalating. "I promise. I'll stay in. I can't run anymore. I can't even walk. I'll stay here all day. I'll be good."

He reached across the table and took my hand in his.

My veins turned to ice.

"You'll be a good girl for me?"

The kale threatened to come back up. "I'll be so good."

"Promise me, Adeline."

I nodded. But I didn't say the words. I had no intention of actually being good. Because it felt like I was running out of time. He said one day soon he wouldn't be traveling as much. That meant one day soon I'd lose whatever scrap of freedom I had left.

"I just want what's best for you." His fingers slid up my wrist. "You know that, babe." His thumb traced the scars along my wrist.

I kept my hand completely still even though it ached to be away from him. I hated when he touched me there. He thought I was insane. But he drove me to insanity. It was him. I took a deep breath and tried to focus on his face instead of his fingers running along the scars. "I want what's best for you too." And what was best for him was to be dead in a ditch. Just the thought of covering his body with dirt made me smile.

He smiled back. "I'm sorry I got upset. I just...worry. Being away so much is hard. It's so hard."

I nodded.

He stood up and walked around the table toward me. "Look at me." He gently touched the bottom of my chin and tilted my face to his. "How about you show me what a good girl you're going to be."

"Okay." My voice sounded small. What else did he want? I had already given him all of me.

He grabbed my shoulder and pulled me to the floor in front of him. I landed hard on my knees and my injured ankle twisted awkwardly beneath me. I swallowed down the agony in my throat. He knew I was hurt. He knew I was in pain.

But I knew him too. I knew he got off on belittling me. Threatening me. Hurting me. And I prayed that this would be over soon. Not just this moment or this night. But us. Us and all the lies our relationship was built on. One of our hearts needed to stop beating. I just prayed it would be his.

CHAPTER 11

I pushed the curtains to the side and watched his sleek black sedan roll down the driveway. It already sounded like a clock was ticking in my head, counting down his return. If I was lucky, he and his pretentious car would be squashed by a semi.

I stumbled down the hall. My ankle hurt more than ever. I was exhausted. I needed sleep and a whole bottle of Advil. But there was only one thing I could think of.

I let my knees collapse when I reached the pantry. My hands pushed aside the rice and pasta until my fingers wrapped around the bottle. I popped off the top and put three pills in my mouth. One for Saturday. One for Sunday. And one for today.

The pills in my empty stomach made me want to puke. I swallowed down the lump in my throat and shoved the bottle back into its hiding spot. I didn't have the courage to read the label. Besides, I already knew the consequences.

I wanted to scream. I had always been able to slip away before. I had never missed a day. But my damn ankle had made it impossible to quietly sneak away from my husband. I let my head fall back on one of the shelves. I needed to go to the doctor as soon as possible. My stomach churned again, threatening to send the pills back up.

All I wanted all weekend was to hear Ben knocking on my door. I wanted him to rescue me. I wanted him to see the truth and save me from the hell I was living. But he hadn't come. I had told him to stay away and he had listened.

Ben was supposed to come today, though. I had already made up my mind to send him away. I didn't want him to see me like this. But how else was I supposed to get to the doctor's office? I had no car. And even if I did, I couldn't drive with my hurt ankle. I needed to get up and get ready. Why was I so exhausted?

When I reached my room, I was completely spent. I wanted to lie down in bed and milk my wounds. For years, I had learned to keep my mouth shut. For years, I had been numb. That's what the pills were for. I understood that now. They were supposed to turn me into the perfect wife. *Screw that.* This weekend had been different. I couldn't help my sassy replies. No matter how hard I tried to behave, I just...couldn't. I gingerly touched my shoulder. The pain was even worse than the pain in my ankle. No matter what my husband said, I didn't deserve that. Fighting with words was one thing. But I wasn't physically strong enough to defend myself from him.

A sweater would cover it up, though, and Ben would never see the bruises. I slipped on a pair of jeans too, being careful with my ankle. The leaves were changing outside and falling to the ground. Hopefully the air was crisp. Or else I'd be sweating all day, pretending to be cold. This time I didn't bother with fancy lingerie. There was no point. And I kept my makeup minimal. The bruise on my forehead had vanished and there was no reason for concealer. The person staring back at me was me in all my glory. That was the reason I had always had issues with men. They were attracted to my outside. But I had never made a point in tricking Ben into thinking I was good on the inside. We bickered constantly. We complained about each other. He saw what was behind my face. And I didn't want to trick him. I didn't want to put him in the crossfire.

But I craved Ben. I wasn't even sure why. Maybe because when we bickered, he didn't put his hands on me. He didn't laugh when I cried. Most of all, though, I craved him because he wasn't my husband. And I fucking hated my husband.

I pulled the rings off my finger, tossed them in my nightstand, and slammed the drawer shut. I was done being pushed around. Finished. It was time to find a way out. As soon as my ankle was healed. In the meantime, I needed a plan. And it had to be flawless or I'd be pulled back into hell.

A few Advil's and a blank sheet of ideas later, I drifted to sleep at the kitchen table.

***

A rapping on the back door made me lift my head. I couldn't help the smile that spread across my face. He had come to the back door. There was something thrilling about sneaking around with him, knowing that if I got caught… I let my thoughts trail off. That wasn't going to happen.

I limped to the door, the smile still glued to my face. "Top of the morning to you, Ben," I said when I opened it.

He laughed. "Well aren't you in a good mood this morning?" He leaned down and hugged me.

I wasn't expecting it. Not at all. Just the tiniest bit of physical contact. Like we were two old friends that hadn't seen each other in years. My smile vanished and my lip started to tremble. And I began to cry. Because I couldn't remember the last time someone had hugged me. Really hugged me.

"Addy?"

I couldn't talk about it. Instead, I gripped the back of his shirt, willing him to not let go. *Please never let go.*

"Addy." His voice was softer. Not a question. My name was simply a soothing sound. He was holding me like he understood. But how could he possibly understand my pain? His fingers gently touched my back, drawing me closer to him.

I was thankful he had come around back. Because I lost track of how long we stood there, our bodies intertwined. It wasn't inappropriate. His fingers didn't slip past my waist. He never once leaned down to place his lips upon mine. It really was like he was a friend. A friend I desperately needed.

He let me soak the front of his button-up flannel shirt. And all he did was gently rub my back.

Eventually I let my grip on his shirt loosen. I needed to say something before he started questioning me. So I gave him the only excuse I had. "It hurts." But I wasn't talking about my ankle. My heart hurt. It physically ached in each beat.

He slowly pulled back. "Let me take you to the doctor."

I was relieved he didn't press the issue. "Actually, there's a walk-in clinic on Wesserton Street. I tried to make an appointment with my usual doctor, but he couldn't fit me in until tomorrow. And I..."

"Let's get you to the car." He slid his arm behind my back.

"Could you grab my purse?" I gestured to the kitchen table. I had been ready to go for awhile.

He walked over and put it over his shoulder.

I was pretty sure that he did it so that I'd smile again. But he probably didn't expect me to start laughing.

"Don't you dare laugh at me," he said. The smile on his face said otherwise.

"I didn't say you had to wear it."

He ignored me and slipped his hand back around my waist. I leaned against his strong body all the way to the car.

CHAPTER 12

"Adeline Bell?" the nurse called.

I grimaced. I had awkwardly positioned the forms they had me fill out so that Ben wouldn't be able to see them. For some reason, I didn't want him to know my last name. If he really wanted to, he could look me up without it. He knew my address. He knew what I looked like. But my last name was the icing on the cake. The worst part was that he could find out that I was *Mrs.* Bell. I needed to tell him. I knew it. But I couldn't make myself say the words out loud. *I'm married.* It should have been easy. For me, though, the words were vile. And wrong. Just plain wrong. They summarized a story that desperately needed details.

I went to stand and Ben's arm immediately wrapped around me.

"You can stay here," I said.

"You can barely walk."

God, he has a point. But he couldn't come back there with me. I swatted his hand away. "And maybe you forgot, but I told you I didn't need your help." Today had been different between us. I hadn't lashed out at all. There was a calmness. And I had just broken it.

"This weekend, I thought maybe I just exaggerated your behavior. But alas," he dipped his mouth to my ear, "you are exactly as I remembered."

I ignored everything but the fact that he was thinking about me over the weekend. Instead of doing normal 23 year old things, he was daydreaming about *me*. I shook my head. He hadn't said daydreaming. Had he? "I was just trying to leave an impression."

"You, Addy, are unforgettable."

He was trying to make me swoon. But him escorting me back there wasn't an option. I wasn't even planning on talking to the doctor about my ankle. I had more pressing matters.

"Adeline Bell?" the nurse said again, irritation dripping from her voice.

"Right here," I said and pushed Ben away.

He forced his hand back around my waist. "We're coming," Ben said.

"Would you sit back down?"

But he was already guiding me toward the nurse.

"Stop it," I hissed.

He ignored me.

"Right this way," the nurse said and turned around without questioning who the man was next to me. She was supposed to make him sit back down. What happened to patient confidentiality? What kind of clinic was this?

I looked up at Ben and he was smirking. Not smiling. It was definitely a smirk. *Cocky bastard.* He was clearly used to getting what he wanted. My indignation evaporated when I started to wonder if he wanted me. If he did, I wasn't sure I was strong-willed enough to put up much of a fight. Because I desperately wanted him.

"You can take a seat right there," the nurse said and gestured to a few chairs in the corner of the exam room we had just entered.

We sat down and Ben put his hand on my knee.

"I'm Joanne," the nurse said. "Nice to meet you Mr. and Mrs. Bell."

Son of a bitch. I opened my mouth to correct her, knowing full well what might come out of it. I was a dependant on my husband's insurance. She'd wonder who Ben was and why he was here. If she hadn't already heard the damn rumors that I was sleeping with him.

"Nice to meet you," Ben said, completely unfazed. His hand momentarily left my knee to shake the nurse's hand. "My wife twisted her ankle on a jog last week. I tried to get her to come in sooner, but she's stubborn. Right, doll?" he said and winked at me as he placed his hand back on my knee.

What the hell is happening? I was about to open my mouth again but he cut me off once more.

"We're hoping to get it checked out. She's in a lot of pain. I'm not sure Advil is going to hold her until it improves."

"Oh, no," I said. "That's okay, I don't want any medicine."

He lowered his eyebrows slightly as he turned back to me. "Isn't that why we're here?"

No. I sighed. "Do you mind going back to the waiting room? I don't want to bore you with all this," I said.

Ben didn't stand up. "I don't mind."

Damn it. I leaned toward him. "Sweetie, please. Don't you have a call you need to make?"

"Nope. I have the whole day off. You know that."

"But that *important call.*" I smiled hoping that would be enough to persuade him to go make his fake call as my fake husband.

He smiled back. "Of course it can wait. For you. Anything for you, Addy." He reached up and pushed a strand of hair behind my ear.

This charade was ridiculous. He needed to leave. *Now.* But his fingertips trailing my cheekbone and behind my ear did feel nice. My body betrayed me and leaned into his touch.

"Let me get your vitals before the doctor comes in," the nurse said and shoved a thermometer in my mouth when I was about to protest again.

I felt like a petulant child. Ben smiled at me. I tried to frown at him without dropping the thermometer. How could I get him to leave?

The nurse pulled the thermometer out of my mouth. "Normal." She jotted something down in her notepad before grabbing my arm and attaching the blood pressure sleeve.

"Shouldn't she change into a gown or something?" Ben asked.

Was he trying to see me naked? I slapped his thigh. *God, he is trying to see me naked!* I wanted to see him naked. That much was for sure.

He caught me smiling.

"If the doctor is just looking at her ankle, there's no need to change," the nurse said. I hated the restrictive feeling of the blood pressure monitor as it whirred to life. Really, I hated doctors' offices in general. The only benefit of this one was that the doctor didn't know me.

"Normal." She un-Velcroed the sleeve. "Are you on any prescriptions?"

"Nope," I said.

Ben squeezed my knee.

I glared at him.

"She was on a few, though," Ben said. "She only just stopped taking them a couple days ago."

Stop talking. "But I'm not taking them anymore. So she doesn't need to know about that." I laughed awkwardly and bumped my shoulder into his. He was terrible at taking a hint.

"Actually, I probably should write them down," the nurse said. "They may still be in your system and we don't want to give you anything that will interact..."

"I won't be taking any new prescriptions either. I just need a word with the doctor."

She eyed me coolly.

"Addy," Ben said, pulling my hostility back to him.

"Ben."

He smiled.

I wanted to slap the grin off his face. Or kiss him. I didn't know anymore. "Please just wait in the waiting room." I begged him with my eyes.

A knock on the door sounded and the doctor walked in.

"How's everyone doing?" he asked as he took the clipboard from the nurse. She walked out of the room in a huff. He shrugged his shoulders and smiled at us.

"He was just leaving too. Weren't you shnookums?" I patted Ben's knee. *Shnookums?* I wished I could blame a prescription for making me loopy. What kind of term of endearment was that?

"Nah, I'll stick around, doll." He placed his hand on top of mine, effectively sandwiching my hand between his and his knee.

The doctor looked back and forth between us before tucking the clipboard under his arm. "Joanne forgot to get your pulse." He reached toward my wrist and I immediately pulled back, crossing my arm in front of me, and cringing because of my hurt shoulder. I'd take all the pain in the world to prevent him from seeing the scars on my wrists. I came here for the anonymity. I didn't want him to know about my medical history. There was no time for his judgment. And I certainly wasn't here for a lecture.

"My pulse is high," I said, trying to keep my voice even. "My pulse is always high, you don't have to take it."

"Due to…stress?" the doctor asked.

"No. Due to constant annoyances."

Both men stared at me. I thought at least Ben would laugh. But no one was laughing.

"I was joking," I said with a forced laugh. "Obviously I don't find either of you annoying. I don't even know you, doctor. I'm sure you're very competent in your profession. And I love my husband dearly." My throat felt like it dried up. Had I just confessed to loving Ben? I glanced at him out of the corner of my eye. At least his smile was back. But I was pretty sure he was laughing at me.

"She's a tad high maintenance," Ben said with a chuckle.

I didn't know what was true and what was part of the character he was playing. Is that really what he thought about me? I had basically just said I was in love with him. And that was his response?

"But I love her to pieces."

I definitely stopped breathing. It took me a second to remember this was all pretend. "I hurt my ankle," I said, turning my attention back to the doctor. I just want to make sure it's healing properly."

"Let's take a look then." He knelt down in front of me and pushed up the leg of my jeans. "Looks like a minor sprain. You should ice it and keep it elevated as much as possible. You'll be all healed up within two to three weeks."

"Great." I looked at Ben and then back at the doctor. "Could I have a word with you in private?"

"It's okay," Ben said. "Anything you say to him you can say in front of me."

"No." Again it sounded like I was whining. But I didn't know what else to do. "It's a private matter."

If they checked my blood pressure again, it would be through the roof. I had lost all patience. I had come here for one thing and one thing only. Ben was ruining everything. This issue was bigger than him liking me. I needed help. I desperately needed help.

"Addy, just spit it out," Ben said. "It's okay."

"Shnookums, that phone call..." Why did I keep calling him shnookums? What was wrong with me?

"It can wait. I'm here for you."

His words were more comforting than he knew. But that didn't make this any less mortifying. He wasn't supposed to follow me back here. I was never supposed to talk to him at all. I turned to face the doctor and tried to pretend Ben wasn't sitting next to me. But it was hard when his hand was so warm on top of mine. It was hard when every fiber of my being was so in tune with him. "I need..." The words got stuck in my throat. I wanted to scream in frustration. "I was hoping I could get a contraceptive implant." The silence killed me. "Today. If possible." To me, the silence was ear piercing. The words I spoke clearly made everyone in the room feel uncomfortable. "Please." I looked down at my hand that was stuck underneath Ben's. I thought he'd move his hand. But it stayed there. Locked in place.

"Alright," the doctor said. "An implant is good for three years." He looked at his clipboard. "You're thirty. You're sure you don't want to have kids within the next three years?"

"Positive." *So freaking positive.*

"Do you want to think about it for awhile? Of course, we can remove it early, but the pill is just as effective..."

"I don't remember to take them." *I'm not allowed to take them.* I couldn't look at him. My eyes were glued to Ben's hand. "And we decided to wait a bit. He's focusing on his career," I nodded to Ben. "And I'm just not...ready to have children anytime soon." At least the last part was true.

"There are other options. A shot perhaps. It's less invasive. We usually recommend visiting a gynecologist if you want the implant."

"How often do you get the shot?" I didn't have time to make a gynecologist appointment. I needed to get this done before my husband came back.

"Once every three months."

"Okay, just do that then." I lifted up my arm. I needed to get this over with and get as far away from this office as possible. And away from Ben. I could feel his eyes on me. Judging me. Maybe? I wasn't sure. I didn't know him well enough to even know when he was judging me.

"We need to do a pregnancy test first. And I need to know more about your medical history. Have you ever been pregnant before?"

I didn't want Ben here. I didn't want to be here. "I don't see why that matters." But I knew why he was asking it. My gynecologist would have asked the same thing. It was standard medical practice.

"I can't give you the shot without this information. Have you ever been pregnant before?"

I wanted the chair to swallow me whole. "Yes. But I lost the baby."

"Abortion?"

My eyes snapped to his. How dare he assume the worst in me? "No." I wanted to call him out on his rudeness, but all the fire in me was gone. I just wanted to go home and cry. "I lost the baby. I didn't willingly terminate the pregnancy. I would never do that. And I'm not pregnant now so just give me the cup to pee in so we can hurry this along." I sounded confident. But inside I was trembling. What if I was pregnant? The doctor had every right to assume the worst in me. Because if I was pregnant now I wouldn't hesitate to terminate the pregnancy. I wouldn't even blink.

He handed me a cup. "Bathroom is down the hall. Leave the cup on the counter for processing."

Ben stood up with me and I swatted his hand away. "I'm fine. Really." But I wasn't fine. I stumbled down the hall and into the bathroom. God, I wasn't fine.

Both men looked at me as I hopped back into the exam room.

"We really do need to get going," I said, without looking at either of them. Can you check on the results?" It felt like my knees were about the buckle. *Please don't let me be pregnant. Please.*

"I have a few more questions before we can administer the shot," the doctor said.

I sat down with a sigh. Maybe I was an ill-tempered child.

"We need a record of your sexual history," he said while staring down at his clipboard.

Was he being serious right now? Was it his mission to mortify me? "I don't know what you mean by that." But I did.

"How many partners have you been with?"

I'm sure my face was bright red. It felt like he was torturing me for no reason. "One."

"Great." He jotted it down. "And I just need to make sure you know that the shot does not protect you from STD's. You will still need to take precaution when..."

"I understand how sex works." I wanted this to be a dream. A terrible, awful dream. "If you have any other questions for me could you maybe just give me a form to fill out?"

"That was actually the last question. Everything else I needed to know was in the medical forms you filled out before coming in."

And why weren't the awkward, invasive questions a part of the questionnaire? It was as if he wanted to humiliate me.

Joanne stuck her head in. "She's good to go."

The doctor already had the shot ready. He was probably as excited to be rid of me as I was to be rid of him.

I turned away as he inserted it in my arm. And as soon as we were done I stood up and hopped toward the door.

"Thank you, doctor," Ben said from behind me.

"Of course, Mr. Bell. Mrs. Bell..."

But I was already through the door.

CHAPTER 13

"Addy?" Ben called from behind me.

I kept walking, biting down on my lip to divert my attention from the pain in my ankle.

"Addy! Wait!" He caught up to me when I reached the passenger's side of his truck.

I couldn't face him. Not even when he stepped right in front of me. Instead, I stared at his chest.

"Do you want to talk about what just happened?"

The tears bit at the inside of my eyes. I focused on the second button of his shirt. The top one was undone, giving him a casually inviting look. But there was nothing casual or inviting about this conversation. "What do you want me to say, Ben? You weren't supposed to know any of that. I didn't want you to look at me like you are right now."

"I'm not..."

"Like you pity me."

"I don't pity you. And how would you even know how I look? You haven't made eye contact with me for the past 20 minutes."

"I don't need to look at you to know how you're looking at me."

"You're ridiculous. You do realize that."

"I didn't want you to know." My voice sounded so small. It took me back to that moment I found out I had lost my baby. I put my hand on my stomach, instantly remembering how it felt to no longer have something to protect.

"We would have had to have that conversation eventually. Better to get everything out there."

What on earth was he talking about? I was never going to tell him about that. About any of it. "I asked you to leave a bajillion times."

"Only a bajillion? You should have made it two bajillion and I would have listened."

"Ben!" His stupid comment was what finally made me look up at him. He hadn't been lying. It didn't look like he pitied me at all. He just looked concerned. And slightly agitated. I sighed. "It's embarrassing for me to talk about stuff like that. Is that what you want to hear? I'm old. With old people problems. And I don't understand why you're being so nice to me. I haven't been that nice to you. Or nice at all really. You should be hanging out with some 23 year old girl that…"

"Now why would I do that when I could have you?"

Maybe it wasn't agitation in his eyes so much as it was affection. And concern. And…lust? Possibly? I didn't understand it. Why was he staring at me like that? He was supposed to pity my existence. I was a pathetic woman pining over someone seven years younger. "You can't…you can't have me, Ben." It was time to tell him the truth.

I didn't even have time to react. In a blink of an eye his fingers were tangled in my hair, arching my neck back.

"Ben…"

His lips crashed against mine, silencing me. How long had I been waiting for this moment? I parted my lips for him with the slightest nudge from his tongue. It was pure perfection. He tasted like heaven. And I had lost all control. My dreams had been only of him for so long. My thoughts only of him. No one would have had enough self-control to resist this temptation. Especially me.

I gripped the back of his neck, drawing him closer. His other hand slid down the curve of my hip to grip my ass as he pushed me back against his truck. A completely brazen display of affection. I should have felt shame. I know that I should have. But all I could feel was him. All I could focus on was him. And I wanted more. I wanted all of him.

He groaned into my mouth and I swallowed down the air he breathed. It was like he was breathing life into me.

Take me. That's what I wanted to say. I wanted to scream it from the rooftops. I wanted him to have me right against his car. I wanted to remember what it felt like to truly live. My body melted into his, fusing us together. I let his fingers wander down the side of my neck. His touch lit my skin on fire. The anticipation was too much. It felt like my heart was beating in my throat. I needed him.

His fingers dipped to my clavicle.

And then I was back in hell, the pain from my hurt shoulder searing through me. It was so much harder to fall back when I had tasted heaven.

I put my hand on his chest and turned my face away from him. I tried to catch my breath, but my words still came out airy. "We can't do this."

He let his hands fall from my body. "You have two seconds, Addy. Two seconds to stop me from proving that we most certainly can." He put his hands on either side of me, sandwiching me between him and the car.

I knew what he wanted to do. My libido wasn't dead even if it felt like the rest of me was. I had no desire to stop him. I wanted to say, "Then prove it." I so badly wanted the words to fall from my lips. There was a hotel a few blocks back. I could ask him to take me to it. I could make my fantasies a reality.

But fear had gripped my heart. And not just for my own safety, but for his. We were too exposed in the parking lot. "Please take me home." I found the door handle behind me and pulled it, but nothing happened.

"It's locked," Ben said.

"Then unlock it."

He didn't move.

"If you're not going to take me home, I'll call a cab."

He sighed and stepped back. I wasn't sure I had ever felt so cold. The car beeped as it unlocked. I scurried into the passenger's seat to get away from him. But the scent in the car just made him feel even closer.

I kept my eyes glued on the window the whole ride home.

"Thanks for the ride to the clinic," I said as he pulled into my driveway. I cringed when he cut the engine in my driveway. He grabbed my hand before I could reach for the door handle.

"You can't pretend you didn't enjoy that as much as I did." His voice sounded heavy like he was trying to hide his emotion.

"It was a mistake. We can't do this." *But God, it feels so nice to have my hand in his.*

"Give me one reason why."

I laughed. "You're 23, Ben."

He moved his hand to the side of my face. "Adeline Bell, I think you're beautiful and..."

"Stop."

His lips parted like he was about to say something else.

"Don't be fooled by what you see. It's the things you don't that really matter."

His lips closed. He was staring at me too intently. As if he was staring into my soul.

I took the opportunity to distance myself further and climbed out of his truck.

"Addy, I think we should talk about this." He sounded determined. Like he had just seen the worst and he didn't care. If only he knew what demons I was hiding.

"There's nothing to talk about. I thought we were friends. And clearly, we're not. And there's no undoing what happened. So just…don't come back here. Please stay away from me. Please." I slammed the door closed.

CHAPTER 14

I woke up drenched in sweat. I turned in bed and reached out to the other side. My fingers were met by empty sheets.

I had dismissed Ben Jones from my life. But I hadn't dismissed him from my dreams. It would have taken awhile, but I could have eventually forgotten what he looked like. I could have made the sight of him disappear from my memory. But I had experienced every sense of him. Smell, sight, taste, touch, and sound, and God I couldn't forget. And I'd be lying if I said I was even trying.

Stop. I rolled onto my back and stared at the ceiling. He hadn't come this morning. He had listened to my request. And now I wished I had never made it. A part of me thought he'd keep coming. He seemed persistent. So where was he? Was he lying in bed thinking about me too?

I closed my eyes tight. I was overloaded by all five senses of him when my eyes were shut. Maybe I'd just lay in bed forever.

***

There was a correct balance. But I didn't know what it was. If I wore too much makeup, the gawkers would talk. If I wore too little, they'd scoff behind my back. I tossed the eyeliner back down on the counter.

I was over-thinking it. All I had to do was march into their snotty meeting and make it clear that I wasn't having an affair.

Easy. I looked down at my ankle and sighed. Hobbling into the meeting didn't seem nearly as effective. But it would have to do.

Even though I had told my husband I had been going to the civic association meetings on a regular basis, I had only ever been to one. I had been to a couple hoity-toity book club meetings too, and that was enough to show me that these women weren't for me. I had feigned sick at first to avoid them and then they seemed to forget about me. I had tried to stay invisible for the past few years. And now I was willingly walking into the dragon's lair. I was doomed.

Not only did I need to make them not talk about me and Ben, I also had to make sure they didn't talk about me being *at* the meeting. Or else my husband would find out that I didn't obey his request. That wasn't an option.

I stuffed my swollen ankle into my boot and did my best not to cringe as I zipped it up. I would have worn yoga pants and sneakers, but I figured that wasn't the correct attire for these pretentious meetings. Besides, I hadn't bought new sneakers yet. I tried not to think of what my neighbor was doing with a random lone sneaker in his or her house.

Cheating. Lies. Scandal.

All of it was true. But it was on me. Not that poor, unknowing victim. Hopefully their marriage was strong enough to get through a women's sneaker appearing with no explanation.

Maybe it would come up in today's meeting. Item four on the agenda could be my sneaker. I tried to make an innocent face in the mirror and laughed. I was being ridiculous. Unless they had a neighborhood lost and found. Was that a thing?

I groaned and walked out of my bedroom. The boots kept my ankle straight, which made it a little easier to walk. But that didn't make it any less painful.

I downed several Advil before stepping outside into the crisp autumn evening. Limping into the meeting would cause talk. I needed to pretend everything was perfect. That's what the gawkers needed to think. That my life was perfect. That their lives were perfect. That everything in the world was freaking perfect.

What a lie. I crossed my arms in front of me. The air was chilly and I wished I had brought a jacket. But I wasn't going to expend the extra energy to walk back. Not when my ankle was already throbbing. A pillow would have been nice too. Why was I so tired all of the time?

The soles of my boots crunched on top of the leaves. I don't know what made me realize it, but the colors were breathtakingly vibrant and beautiful. Had I never truly seen autumn leaves before? Yellows, oranges, and reds of all shades. I smiled and I continued to crunch through them. I had been numb for so long. So long that I couldn't ever remember seeing such beauty.

The meetings took place in the elementary school in our neighborhood. I thought I'd see more people walking, but only cars passed by me. It was probably smart. The sun would be completely set by the time the meeting drew to a close. *I should probably try to catch a ride home with Charlotte.* I had pretty much claimed that she was my new BFF. There were consequences in lying. Horrible consequences.

I opened the door to the gymnasium. High pitched voices greeted my ears in the most unwelcoming way. But none of the voices were directed at me.

I stared at the other women, all clustered together at the front of the room. *Crap.* They were wearing dresses. *Of course they're wearing dresses.* I sat down in the back row before anyone could assess my jeans and sweater. My whole body seemed to expel awkwardness. *I should have walked to the front of the room to socialize.*

Instead, I pulled out my phone and scrolled through meaningless emails. At least no one would talk if I was invisible.

I almost jumped when someone put their hand on my shoulder.

"Adeline, hon, how good to see you," Charlotte said. "I hope you're feeling better."

"Oh, yeah." I waved my hand through the air and stuffed my phone back into my purse. "Just a minor sprain. I can barely feel it anymore."

"You're lucky Ben Jones was there to help. Such a sweet man, don't you think?"

"He's fine, I guess." I shrugged for added effect. The action made me wince. "I barely know him."

"Huh." She stared at me like she was waiting for me to say something.

Don't bet on it.

"Well, I had a long chat with him the other day. I guess you were in the shower when I dropped off the lasagna..."

"Thank you for that, by the way. It was so nice of you to think of me." It wasn't nice. She was being nosy. And I wasn't thankful. I was just trying to turn the conversation away from Ben. And the fact that I was in the shower when he was in my house. *Kill me.*

"Not a problem at all. But really, hon, you must spill. All the girls want to know what Ben is like. He's so secretive. We're trying to set him up with someone but it's hard when we don't know a thing about him"

Why are they all so interested in my gardener? I internally sighed. Mine? He wasn't mine. And he was so much more than just a gardener. He was smart and kind and had the lips of an angel.

"He's just my gardener. I barely even know him." It pained me to say the words.

"He was in your house."

I wanted to slap her. Instead, I clenched my hand into a fist and smiled. "Like you said, I was just lucky he was there to help me when I fell." This conversation was excruciating.

"Well, he likes gardens. That doesn't exactly add to our list. We all knew that already. Regardless, the girls and I have someone in mind." She waved a few women over from the front of the room. "Rosie, Phoenix, you remember Adeline."

"You haven't been to the book club meetings in forever," Rosie said. "Was the last book selection that bad?"

"No, no," I said with a laugh. "I haven't been feeling well for awhile." I really hadn't. Or rather, I hadn't been feeling anything at all.

"Well, we're glad you could make it," Phoenix said. "We all heard about you hanging out with Ben. We're hoping you could give us the dirt."

"I just hired him to handle my lawn care. Nothing more," I said with a laugh. It sounded so fake. But that didn't really matter. Everything about these women screamed fake.

"I'd hire him to handle my garden any day," Rosie said with a wink.

Phoenix laughed and elbowed her in the side.

I was going to rip their throats out. *Oh. My. God.* I looked down at my hand that was clenched in a fist. I *liked* him. I really, really liked him. Who acted this jealous if they weren't smitten? I knew I was attracted to him, but this reaction was intense. Ben and I weren't supposed to be a thing. We couldn't be. But if we were, in some crazy way, it would have needed to be purely physical. My emotions were completely out of control though. I unclenched my fist, placed my hands in my lap, and willed them to stop talking about Ben like he was a piece of meat.

"You should hire him. He does great work," I said.

"You really haven't learned anything else about him?" Charlotte asked.

"He drives a truck."

She laughed. "We've all seen his truck. He's so elusive, don't you think? It just makes him sexier. But you know Sally? Of course you know Sally."

I freaking knew Sally. Nosy Sally. The nosiest neighbor in the history of nosy neighbors. She was worse than Charlotte. For some reason since she was older, it was harder to hate her, though. "Yup. I've met Sally."

"Well Sally's daughter just moved back home after finishing med school. Her residency is at Kennett Hospital so it made sense for her to move back for the time being. We all think they'd be great together."

How could they think that? They knew nothing about Ben. "She's living with her mother?"

"Yeah, but weren't you listening? She's going to be a doctor. She's a catch. Ben and her would be adorable together. I'm going to try to convince them to grab a coffee together."

"I doubt he's into older women." It was a stupid thing to say. Because obviously he was. But they didn't know that.

"She's just a few years older than him. It's not like she's 30," Charlotte said with a laugh.

"Mhm." My hand had formed into a fist again. *Stop it.*

"What do you think?" Rosie asked. "Do you think they'd be a good match?"

"I don't know. Why are you so interested in his love life anyway?"

"Single people in the neighborhood is bad for resale value," Charlotte said.

That didn't seem like a true fact. "Really? How would you even check something like that before moving into a neighborhood?"

"Everyone talks. And if there's single people lurking around, it could lead to the neighborhood turning to a younger crowd…or affairs…or worse."

I swallowed hard. She knew. She obviously knew. Did she see me kiss him in that parking lot? They were all staring at me. *Say something. Say anything!* I laughed. "Worse?"

"Like porn factories," Phoenix said.

"What's a porn factory?" Rosie asked.

Charlotte shushed them with her hand. "You know what we mean, Adeline. Only bad things can come of it."

"Okay, but you could set Sally's daughter up with anyone. Maybe another doctor or someone with something in common with her?"

A bell jingled at the front of the room.

"Two birds with one stone, hon," she said and patted my shoulder. "We'll talk later. Wish me luck setting them up!"

"It was great seeing you," Rosie said and Phoenix added a wave before they followed Charlotte to the front of the room.

Crap, I forgot to ask Charlotte for a ride. I rotated my ankle slowly. The pain was on a whole new level. But I'd have to suck it up on the way home. I wasn't about to approach those women again. I was worried I'd knock one of them out.

CHAPTER 15

The president of the civic association was droning on and on about how important it was that no sheds were built in anyone's yard. Why did she care so much? No one would even be able to see them from the street.

I opened my eyes up wide to try to make myself stay awake. I should have tried to slip out before the meeting started. The conversation with Charlotte and the other women hadn't gone great. But I had held my ground. And if they were trying to set Ben up with Sally's daughter, then clearly they didn't think anything was going on between me and him. *Right?*

I started tapping my foot and immediately stopped. The pain was searing. This extra strength Advil was total bullshit. It was worse than normal Advil. All it did was make me sleepy.

Stay awake. I glanced down at my watch. How had it only been five minutes?

My mind wandered back to Ben. What was he doing right now? Eating dinner probably. My stomach growled. Nothing I ate was as good as that burger he had brought me. I wished I had asked him where it was from. Now I'd never know.

It was strange, but I had this overwhelming feeling of loss. Not because of the burger. Well, partially because of the burger. It was delicious. But mainly because of Ben. I barely even knew him. Why was I so fixated on him? All I knew was that I was happy when he had showed up on Monday morning. I had been looking forward to seeing him all weekend. For months he was all

I had looked forward to. And that was just when I would see him. Now that we had talked? Touched? Kissed? *God.*

He was perfect for me. Somehow I just knew. But I was technically committed to someone else. I twirled my wedding band with my thumb. I just needed to learn how to smile and hide the truth. It was something I was used to doing. I needed to bury my feelings in a pit and walk away.

But that kiss. How could I forget that kiss?

"Is this seat taken?"

I had been replaying Ben's voice in my mind on repeat. I knew before I even looked up that it was him. It felt like my heart started beating again when my eyes met his. His proximity made me feel cold and hot at the same time. He was the only one that could make me feel alive.

But what the hell was he doing *here*? I had just done damage control. He was going to ruin everything. "What are you doing here?" I shoved my left hand between my thighs to hide my wedding band and engagement ring. Had he seen it? *Why did I even care?*

He sat down as if my words were an invitation."It's for members of the community."

"Yeah, I know," I said.

He took off his jacket and settled into his seat.

"So...leave," I added.

"Does it really pain you that much to sit next to me for an hour?" He was smiling at me.

"That's not it." I was having a hard time keeping my voice down. "I just cleared the air with the gawkers. And now you're here sitting next to me. You're probably not even allowed in here. Are you stalking me?"

He laughed. "Gawkers?" When I didn't say anything he continued. "Addy, I'm here because I'm part of the neighborhood and I want to know what's going on. Honestly, it has nothing to do with you. But thanks for letting me know about the meetings." He turned to face the front of the room.

Nothing to do with me? What an ass. "You're hardly part of the neighborhood."

"You're really stuck up, do you know that?" He was still looking at the president instead of at me.

And it made me jealous. And sad that he wasn't here to see me. "I'm not..." I let my voice fade off. "You're not getting it. It's for people who live in the community. Not work in it."

He finally turned back to face me. "You've been to my house, Addy."

"No I haven't. You keep showing up at mine uninvited."

He put his arm on the back of my chair. He wasn't touching me, but it was like he was claiming my whole body as his. Any chill that I was feeling was replaced by warmth. "Were you so drunk the first day we met that you don't remember coming into my home?"

"I remember going into the house where you were mowing the lawn. Not *your* house. Some really organized couple who likes white."

"So you think that because I own a landscaping company that I can't afford a house in this neighborhood?"

"I didn't say that, but..."

"That was *my* house. I like things clean."

"I've run past that house every day for a year. You and your truck are only ever there on Thursday mornings."

"And I'm the stalker?"

I ignored his comment. "Fine. Whatever. I stalked you. But at least I'm not lying. You do lawn care at that house. There's no way you own it. I'd know."

"Owning a landscaping company means I need to go to other houses during the day. Thursday mornings I take off to make sure my property looks good. What kind of landscaper would I be if my own lawn was a mess?"

"I've been by at night a few times..."

"When I park my truck in the garage. Because I don't need my tools from it."

"If it's your house then...then...where is my shoe?"

"What shoe?"

"My sneaker. You took it off of me so I could ice my ankle. And I left it in that house. If you lived there you would have brought it back to me."

"I haven't seen your sneaker."

"Then you don't live there."

"I do live there."

"Then you stole my shoe!" *Oh my God.* How loudly did I say that? No one seemed to be staring at me besides for Ben.

"I haven't stolen your sneaker. You can even come look for it if you'd like."

"You're just trying to get me back to your place. Or someplace. Whatever that place is. Oh my god, do you run a porn factory there while the owners are away?"

"What? No. To both things."

I swallowed hard and turned to him. "No?" I had never hated that word so much.

"I heard you loud and clear the other day. You wanted a friend and I crossed the line. I'm sorry about that. Seeing you here was a coincidence. But I thought I'd take the opportunity to apologize. End of our story. Just like you want."

End of our story. I blinked at him. *Great. End of our fucking story then.* "Awesome. Well, it was great knowing you, Ben. I hope you have fun on your date with Sally's daughter. And just for the record, she lives with her mother."

I grabbed my purse and slid out of my seat. I was such an idiot. I had been so happy to see him. And he was probably pissed that I was here. I crossed my arms to hide my rings and practically ran out of gymnasium.

I didn't get far before my ankle gave out. *Damn it.* I sat down on a curb, pulled off my rings, and shoved them into my purse. I wanted to go back to last Wednesday. Before I had heard his voice. Before I had felt his touch. I wanted the memories to go away.

The leaves crunched beneath me as I leaned back into the grass. *What a lie.* I needed to savor those few good memories if I wanted to keep breathing. My eyes focused on the stars above me and I made a wish. A stupid wish that a stupid girl might make. *Let him chase after me.*

But I wasn't in a rom-com. If anything I was in a horror movie. And a knight in shining armor wasn't going save me. And a prince wasn't going to bring me my missing shoe. The stars started to blur above me.

"I don't want this to be the end of our story. I said that because I thought it was what you wanted..." Ben blocked out my view of the stars. The sight of him was more glorious than any starlit sky.

"I lied."

"Why?"

Because I'm so scared. I shrugged my shoulders. *Ow.*

He sighed. "I'm too old to play games…"

"You're only 23."

"Tell me what you want, Addy." His voice was demanding. He didn't sound 23. He sounded strong and competent and so sexy.

You. I wanted anything he'd give me. Everything he'd give me. But I couldn't say that. "A burger."

"That wasn't what I was expecting you to say."

"When do I ever say anything you expect me to say?"

"Fair point."

"I want one of the burgers like the one you brought me the other day. I'm starving…"

"Then let's go eat." He put his hand out for me.

I stared at it. I felt like I was imagining this moment. "Are you asking me out to dinner?"

He smiled. "Yes, Addy. I'm asking you out to dinner."

I glanced toward the school. No one else was walking or driving this way. He must have left the meeting early too.

I put my hand into his and I did my best not to cry. Because I wasn't sure my hand had ever felt so comforted by someone else's.

CHAPTER 16

"So you live in my neighborhood." I took a sip of my water. My stomach growled again. The burger joint smelled amazing. I was practically drooling. But it could have been because of the man across from me. I put my elbows on the table and leaned forward. It was very unladylike, and I didn't care. I just wanted to be closer to him.

"Or one could say that you live in mine."

I laughed. "I'm sorry. I just assumed..."

"And that's why I called you stuck up."

"I guess I deserved that." I leaned even closer to him. "And I'm sorry." I was. When had I become so pretentious? I was basically a gawker.

"Apology accepted."

I smiled. "Your house, though. It was so...white."

"I know you well enough now to know that your compliments are always backhanded."

"But really, Ben...it's hardly a bachelor pad."

"Why should it be? I don't want to be a bachelor forever. I'm looking for something lasting. Like I said earlier, I'm not into playing games."

We'd only been apart for a day. He looked good. Better if that was possible. The day apart had been agonizing for me. Like nails on a chalkboard bad. I had even rummaged around in the medicine cabinet to see if there was anything to numb the pain. It was a low moment. And luckily, there hadn't been any old prescriptions.

It seemed like he was waiting for me to say something. He had given me the perfect opportunity to tell him I was married. I took the silence that stretched between us to take a sip of my chocolate milkshake. "This is so good." I immediately took another sip.

He laughed. "You're doing that thing again."

"What thing?"

"Using food to make me fall in love with you."

His gaze was unnerving me even more than his words. I pushed the milkshake to the side and ran my thumb along the condensation outside the glass. "Are you going to go on that date with Sally's daughter?"

"Who?"

"I don't know her name. The doctor. Charlotte was saying she was going to set you up with whatever her name is. She might be good for you."

"Charlotte never mentioned it to me. I don't even know who Sally is."

"Really?"

He put his elbows on the table and leaned forward too. "Really. Why? Are you jealous?"

I laughed. "No."

"Then why'd you ask?"

"I was just wondering if you were dating anyone else."

"Dating anyone else?" He smirked. "Are we dating?"

I felt my cheeks flushing. "You knew what I meant."

"No, not really."

"I'm thirty."

"We've already had this conversation, Addy."

"And I'm not really any clearer on what we're doing." I gestured back and forth between us. I wanted it to involve a heated session in the bathroom of this restaurant.

He pressed his lips together and leaned back in his booth.

The action made me want to climb over the table and kiss every inch of his perfect face.

"I asked you what you wanted earlier and you said you wanted a burger. Clearly I'll give you whatever you ask for." He licked his bottom lip. It was possible it was absentminded. But it made me cross my legs under the table regardless.

"I don't know what you want me to say." I couldn't tell him that I wanted him. Not until I told him the truth. And I wasn't ready for him to walk out that door. A part of me wanted to say nothing at all. The nurse thought he was my husband at the clinic. She did that because she knew I was on my husband's insurance. And he easily could have seen my rings earlier tonight. There were plenty of signs. Maybe he knew and didn't care.

"How about we just get to know each other?" he asked.

I sighed in relief. "I'd like that."

"What's your favorite kind of meat to have in your mouth?"

"Ha. Ha."

"I was asking a serious question. If I was to cook for you, I'd need to know what to make."

"The burgers from here would be hard to beat. But I don't believe you for a second that your question wasn't a sexual innuendo."

"It's not my fault if you have a dirty mind."

I glared at him. "What kind of meat do you prefer in your mouth?"

He laughed. "I can assure you that I'm not gay."

"Caught you red-handed." I pointed to him. His smile was contagious. I wasn't sure I remembered the last time I smiled quite this hard. It was my turn to ask a question. I wanted to know more about him, but I needed to make sure the question wasn't invasive. Or else he'd ask me questions I didn't feel comfortable answering. "What's your favorite color?"

"Blue."

"Because it matches your eyes?"

He laughed. "No. Because it reminds me of the sea."

Did he not realize that he carried the brightest ocean around in his irises? "I love the beach too."

He put his elbows on the table, mimicking how I was sitting again. "What's your favorite season?"

"Summer," I said. The hue of his eyes seemed to brighten. "Don't look at me like that. It has nothing to do with you being around more. If that was the case, I would have said autumn. This autumn, specifically."

"Mhm. So why is summer your favorite season?"

Because of you. Because it's my husband's busiest time of year. I shrugged my shoulders and tried not to grimace from the pain. "Because it's warm. Even on the days it rains you can still go outside and dance in it."

"Why can't I picture you dancing in the rain?"

"I dance in the rain." When was the last time I had? Maybe in college? It felt like a lifetime ago. "I used to dance in the rain."

"So why did you stop?"

"Because I'm not happy." I was lying about my husband. I didn't have to lie about this too.

He reached out and grabbed my hand.

My body tensed. My eyes darted around the small restaurant. I didn't know a soul. I looked back at him and let myself enjoy the warmth of his skin against mine. Every time we touched I had this overwhelming sensation of comfort. Like my hand belonged in his.

"How long ago did you lose your baby?"

He wasn't supposed to ask questions like this. I closed my eyes. "Six years ago." Had it really been that long? It felt like yesterday but at the same time it felt like a lifetime ago.

"I'm sorry."

It hurt to think about. But I knew it was a blessing in disguise. I knew it, but I still had to hold back my tears. "Do you want children?" *Why? Why on earth did I ask him that?* I opened my eyes to see the disaster unfold.

But he didn't flinch. Or laugh. "Yes. At least two. I was an only child growing up and I so badly wanted a brother or sister."

"Me too."

He squeezed my hand.

"I can have children. I lost that baby, but it...I wouldn't lose another one necessarily." I wanted to say it was an accident. But I knew that those words weren't true. There was no reason to say them. He wasn't judging me. He was just trying to understand.

"Are you trying to proposition me to put a baby in you?"

"What? *No.* This conversation took a strange turn, I just..."

"I'm messing with you, Addy."

"Well, stop doing that."

"One of my new favorite activities is pushing your buttons."

I laughed. "I've noticed that."

He was silent as he stared into my eyes. And I just knew he was about to do it again. He was about to ask me something I didn't want to answer.

"You flinched when my hand slid down your neck. I knew you were as caught up in that moment as I was. And then you pushed me away. What happened?"

Why was he doing this? We had been having such a nice time. "You're asking too many questions."

"Addy, I'm not trying to be nosy. I'm worried about you."

"Why? Why do you care?" I pulled my hand from his. "I'm not your problem."

He exhaled slowly and pulled his hands onto his lap.

For just a moment I thought he was going to drop it. But then he stood up and joined me on my side of the booth. He slid in until his thigh was pressed against mine.

"You winced in the doctor's office when you crossed your arms."

"Please don't press this."

"And whenever you shrug your shoulders, you favor your right one."

Wasn't he Mr. Observant.

He lightly touched my shoulder.

I turned away from him. He already knew. What would seeing it matter?

He pulled the fabric down my shoulder and I heard his sharp inhale. The black and blue splotches on my skin would alarm anyone. Red flags raised on high alert. The jig was up.

"Addy?" His voice was soft. Not upset, just...gentle. Kind. The sweetest noise in the world.

I couldn't look at him. If he saw my face he'd know the truth. He'd see my whole story in my eyes. I was so good at hiding. But I knew that if anyone ever truly looked at me, they'd see below the surface. At least, I prayed that one day someone would.

He lightly touched the bottom of my chin to turn my face toward his. And he waited. He waited for me to confess everything. I was so sick of hiding. But I wasn't ready to tell him the truth. I wanted him to like me. Not pity me.

"If you hurt your shoulder when you fell the other day, why didn't you just tell me?"

He didn't even realize it, but he had just given me the perfect out from the truth. A flawless lie. He saved me. "You already felt so bad about my ankle..."

"This looks worse than your ankle. You should have told me."

Thank you for the out, you sweet, wonderful, perfect man.

He let the fabric of my sweater fall back into place. "I'll be right back." He slid from the booth without another word.

Maybe he didn't believe me. Or maybe he had seen all the red flags and decided to leave. I turned around to look out the window. His truck was still in the parking lot.

I didn't want tonight to be over. The pain in my shoulder was minimal. I had experienced much worse. My husband was hundreds of miles away and he was still finding a way to ruin my life. I needed to just tell Ben the truth. Rip the Band-Aid off.

He came back carrying takeout bags and a smile on his face. "Your house or mine?"

"We're not going to eat here?"

"We need to get ice on your shoulder. So, which would you prefer?"

He didn't want to run away. Not even a little bit. He was inviting me into his home again. And I hated my house. It reeked of sadness and hostility and death. "Take me back to your place."

CHAPTER 17

For the first time in my life, it felt like the universe was on my side. I walked into his dark house. His masculine smell was everywhere. Now that I knew that it was his house, I wanted to see everything. I heard the click of the lock behind me.

The foyer was bathed in darkness. And I realized that I didn't really want to explore anything but his body. I turned around and bumped into his hard chest.

It took less than a second for my mouth to find his. I heard the bags of food drop to the floor. And in less than a minute my legs were wrapped around his waist, his hands squeezing my ass. We were a tangle of knotted limbs. I was back in heaven.

No one should have had such a talented mouth in addition to such a perfect physique. It wasn't fair. He should have had some flaw. But I hadn't found a single one. Besides the dimple in his cheek. And that wasn't a flaw at all. It was gorgeous. There wasn't one thing wrong about this beautiful man. And being with him felt so damn right.

He slammed my back against the wall. "Ow." And in that one second, I ruined everything. *Don't stop.* The words were on the tip of my tongue, but I didn't have time to say them before he released my thighs. I slid down his chest. God, why did I have to spoil that perfect moment?

"I'm sorry." His voice was strained. "Ice. As much as I want more, ice is the reason why we're here." He reached around me and switched on the lights.

His lips were slightly swollen from our kiss. It just made them look more kissable.

He took a step back from me. "You shouldn't even be walking, Addy. What happened to the crutches I gave you?"

"I didn't want to make a scene at the meeting tonight." *So much for that.* "Did anyone say anything when I left?"

"They were in a deep debate about leaf raking etiquette. I don't think anyone noticed that we left. Make yourself comfortable. I'm going to get you some ice."

We. That's the word that went round and round in my head as he left me in his foyer. How badly I wanted to be a we again. I looked right toward the living room I had already been in. I wanted to see his world. Besides, the pain was minimal. My want for him outweighed it twofold.

I limped into the dining room. It was as barren as his living room. White walls. A solid oak table that looked like it had never been used. I walked through the room and into a hallway. The kitchen was to the right. I could hear the fridge door close. I turned left and wandered into his family room.

I smiled when I saw the blue throw blanket on his couch. It was the first touch of color in the place. And I had just learned that it was his favorite. The couch was black leather, which in itself screamed bachelor pad more than the white one in the other room. There were still no pictures on the wall, but there was a shelf full of movies. I limped over to it.

The titles were all comedies, action, dramas, and classics. Not a single romance in the mix. I ran my fingers along their spines. For someone who said they wanted more than a game, he didn't seem that interested in the more. Although, what real man curled up alone and watched The Notebook? Besides, love like that wasn't real. It was fiction for a reason.

My elbow knocked into something and I grabbed it before it had a chance to topple over. *Huh.* I stared down at the binoculars. I had never even held a pair before. I lifted them up to my eyes and turned to the window. It was too dark to see anything.

"Searching for something in particular?"

I jumped at his voice. "No." I set the binoculars down a little too hard and they banged against the wooden shelf. "Not at all." I tucked a loose strand of hair behind my ear. He had caught me snooping. But he didn't look upset. His smile was easy. If anything he looked like he was expecting me to snoop around.

"You can see deer sometimes in the woods." He reached around me and lifted the binoculars up. He hit a switch on the side and handed them back to me. "But you have to use the night vision." He turned the light off in the room and we were once again in darkness.

"Really?" I put them back up to my eyes. The woods were suddenly alive in a neon green glow. They didn't seem so scary in the glow. Maybe I needed to get myself a pair of these. It would put me at ease to be able to see through the trees at night. "That's so cool."

He laughed. "See any deer?"

I looked to the left and then to the right. I could see my backyard, just barely in the distance. If I played around with the settings I might be able to see it really well. Which meant I'd be able to see his yard from my house. I shook away the thought and handed the binoculars back to him. I didn't want to spy on Ben. I wanted to spend time with him. "Nope, no deer."

He switched the lights back on. "Maybe next time." He placed the binoculars back where I had found them.

I liked the idea of there being a next time. "You have quite the movie collection." I wasn't sure why, but I was suddenly nervous. I turned away from him and scanned the titles again.

"We can watch one while we eat if you'd like."

"Dinner and a movie? That's quite the first date, Mr. Jones." My words hung awkwardly in the air. "Unless this isn't…I didn't mean…"

He placed his hand on my waist as he stepped beside me. "I wasn't answering because I was trying to think of what would make the perfect date movie." His fingers slid slightly down my hip as he leaned forward to look at the movies.

"Oh." It came out as a sigh. I had no control over myself around him.

"Are there any you haven't seen?"

I couldn't stop staring at him. My eyes were fixated on the 5 o'clock shadow along his jaw. I wanted to rub my palms along it. I had been too busy pulling him closer in the foyer to take the time to touch his jaw. To keep my hands busy, I reached out and pulled a movie off the shelf without looking. "How about this one?"

He looked down at the movie and then back at me. "You haven't seen Rocky? Are you kidding me right now?"

I looked down at the movie in my hand. Actually, I had never seen Rocky. "Nope. Never."

"Well, you have to see it. It's a classic." He walked over to the TV.

"It's hardly a classic. Anything in color isn't a classic."

He shook his head as he hit play. "Maybe this is where our age difference plays a bigger role."

"I didn't grow up watching black and white movies. I'm not *that* old. It's just the principle of the thing."

"That a movie has to be black and white to be considered a classic?"

"I don't know why we're even arguing about this. You have black and white movies in your collection."

"Would you please just sit your perfect little ass down and experience the greatness that is Rocky."

"You think I have a perfect butt?" I sat down on his couch and stared up at him.

"Delectable." He sat down next to me. "Scrumptious." He grabbed my foot and unzipped my boot. "Mouth-watering."

My mouth was the one watering. I was practically panting as he tugged off my boot. He placed my foot gently on his coffee table. The same table we were eating off of. And I didn't even flinch. I was transfixed on the words coming out of his mouth.

"And completely off limits for tonight."

"What? Why?" I hated how it sounded like I was pleading.

He positioned an ice pack on my ankle and then one on my shoulder. "You were walking around all night on a sprained ankle. And I just found out your shoulder was hurt too."

"I'm not as fragile as you think."

He adjusted the ice pack on my shoulder. "I never said you were fragile. If my shoulder looked like that, I'd probably be whining nonstop." He pushed my hair away from the ice pack, his fingers hesitating on my neck. "I bought a few bottles of wine since you were here last. Wasn't sure if you preferred red or white. Unless you want scotch again. I know how much you liked that."

"You thought I'd be back here again?"

"I hoped you would be." But his eyes screamed, "Doll, I knew you would be." He let his fingers drop from my neck.

I swallowed hard. "Red would be great."

"I'll be right back." He paused the previews and disappeared out of the room.

God, my stupid shoulder. I had to admit, though, the ice did feel good. I leaned forward and grabbed one of the takeout bags from the coffee table. He hadn't bothered with plates. Probably since last time we had eaten burgers at my house, I had eaten mine so quickly it barely touched the plate.

I pulled out my burger and fries and positioned the bag on my lap. The burger was even juicier than I remembered.

Ben dimmed the lights when he came back into the room. He looked good every time I saw him, but there was something special about the way the light of the TV hit his face. No one had a right to look that good in casual lighting. How was I supposed to concentrate on a movie when all I wanted to do was look at him?

He handed me one of the glasses. "Here's to you discovering what a classic truly entails."

I laughed. "Really? That's your toast? Not, here's to a lovely date? Or here's to a romantic evening in?"

"I thought all those things were implied. Obviously the best date of your life involves ice packs."

I smiled. "Ice packs aside, I have no doubt that this will be the most memorable date of my life."

Something flashed across his eyes. *Shock maybe?* I wasn't sure. It was gone too quickly to tell.

"Okay, scratch what I said before. Here's to the best first date of your life."

I smiled and clinked my glass against his. My eyes stayed on his as I took a sip. Red wine was definitely better than whiskey.

"I'd tell you to start eating," he said and grabbed his bag off the coffee table, "but you've already started without me."

I looked down at my half-eaten burger. "I tend to be an incredibly rude houseguest. Feet on your table kind of houseguest."

"Trust me, I don't mind. It's nice to have someone to spend the night with."

And with those tantalizing words, he restarted the movie.

I tried to pay attention, but I had a million questions running through my head. Was I spending the night here? Would I spend it in his bed? With his arms wrapped around me? And when was the last time he had someone to spend the night with?

CHAPTER 18

"Addy you have to watch it to fully experience all its glory." He pointed to the TV.

"Thank you for coming after me." The wine had given me courage to say what I had been meaning to all night. No one had ever come after me before. He made me feel like I was in a fairytale. "When I stormed out," I added when he didn't say anything.

"You're worth chasing."

The way he said it made my whole body feel warm. It had been a long time since I had felt anything but worthless.

He lifted his feet onto the coffee table beside mine. "I'll keep on chasing you if you make me. But I'm hoping you'll like tonight so much that you stop running." He winked at me before turning his attention back to the screen.

I'm sure the acting was good in Rocky. And it probably was a great movie. How could I not stare at Ben instead, though? I ran his words through my head on repeat. He wanted me to stay still. To stop resisting him. He wanted...*me.*

He pointed to the TV again.

I reluctantly turned back to the screen and took another sip of the wine. It truly felt like we were having a classic first date of dinner and a movie. Except for all the ice packs. But tonight, I was actually grateful for them. My body would have been overheated if not for the ice packs on my ankle and shoulder.

Whenever I was near him, my heart always raced. The mix of alcohol and ice packs somehow managed to calm me down.

Maybe it made me bold too. When I set down my wine glass, I repositioned myself so that I could rest my head on Ben's shoulder. I held my breath as I waited to see what he'd do. But I didn't have to hold it long.

His arm looped lazily around my back, his hand resting on my hip.

For this one second in time, life was good.

It got better when he started tracing circles around my hip-bone with his thumb.

I closed my eyes, completely forgetting about the movie. I never wanted to leave Ben's side. I never wanted tonight to end.

The last thing I remembered was Rocky yelling for Adrian. And how similar it sounded to Adeline.

***

Apparently the combination of wine and ice packs was so relaxing that it put me right to sleep. I woke up alone on the leather couch, a blanket draped over my body.

I immediately pulled the blanket up to my chin. Without Ben beside me, the room was cold. *Ben.* My eyes flew open. Had I spent the night at his house? The birds were chirping outside. There was light flooding into the room through the blinds. It was definitely daytime.

Jesus. I must have been out cold. I cringed at the thought. Had he heard me snore? Had I mumbled something embarrassing in my sleep?

None of that mattered. What mattered was that I had spent the night on the couch, not in his bed. How had I managed to squander away that opportunity? I reached for my purse to check my phone, but it wasn't where I had left it. My eyes wandered to my watch.

11:25. I blinked. The watch still read the same time. I pushed myself up into a seated position. 11:25! How had I slept so long? I pinched the bridge of my nose, trying to erase my headache. I barely had two sips of wine. How did I have such a bad hangover?

I looked around for my purse again and cringed. My whole body felt sore, like I had just run a half marathon. I swallowed down the groan in my throat. I was too old to sleep on couches.

"Did you enjoy watching Sly last night?"

I ran my fingers through my hair and wiped the side of my face as Ben came into view. "Did I enjoy what?"

"Sly?"

I gave him a blank stare.

"Sylvester Stallone?"

"Oh. Yeah. He was good."

"Good? Not great?" He handed me a cup of coffee.

"I actually had a hard time paying attention." I looked down at the cup in my hands. I didn't drink coffee. The caffeine in it made me anxious. Or was I told that the caffeine made me anxious? I didn't remember ever having a cup and freaking out. I took a sip and sighed, the memories flooded back as soon as it touched my tongue. I used to drink it in college. And it had definitely never made me anxious. If anything, it helped me focus. And I loved the heat of it in my hands. It was so soothing. How had I forgotten about that?

"I thought for sure you'd admit it was a classic."

"That was never going to happen anyway. It's in color."

He shook his head. "What is this obsession with black and white? It's a little dull."

Maybe he was too young to know. Maybe he hadn't experienced anything like what I had. "Everything is black or white. Good or evil. There is no in-between."

"That's the most pessimistic thing I've ever heard."

"It doesn't make it untrue."

He sat down on the edge of the coffee table, his knees bumping against mine. "What if someone committed a crime with good intention?"

"One good deed doesn't cover up the evil."

"So what are you, Addy? Good or evil?"

Evil. I didn't have to think about it. But I didn't need to offer him the truth. He'd discover it soon enough. "You'll have to figure that out for yourself."

"Well, can I trust you alone in here while I go do a few jobs?"

Absolutely not. "Of course." There was a zero percent chance I wouldn't snoop. I was pretty sure he had done the same thing at my house.

"I didn't know what you liked for breakfast. I pulled out some different cereals for you. And there's milk on the counter."

"That's because you didn't ask what my favorite food was. You asked what kind of meat I liked in my mouth."

He smiled and stood up. "Is there anything else you need? The ice packs are back in the freezer. You should probably use them again this afternoon."

"I'm sorry I slept so long."

"I would have woken you up, but you looked so peaceful. And non-argumentative."

"Fair enough."

"I'll see you in a bit." He leaned down and I thought he was going to kiss me. Instead, he placed his lips against my forehead. It felt more intimate somehow. The action almost brought tears to my eyes.

"Okay," I whispered as he walked out of the room. I heard the front door close and his truck roar to life.

I was all alone in Ben Jones' house. A smile curled over my lips. *I'm all alone in Ben Jones' freaking house!* I stood up and ignored the pain in my ankle. Screw the pain. And screw the cereal. I had some exploring to do.

CHAPTER 19

Nothing. I sat down on a stool at the kitchen counter. Ben had absolutely nothing incriminating in his house. *How was that possible?*

His underwear drawer wasn't hiding any weird sex toys or a gun. His medicine cabinet didn't have any odd prescriptions or foot fungus cream. There were no journals or dirty magazines under his mattress. But God did his sheets smell good.

I told myself that it was okay to snoop around his house. Because he had stolen my sneaker and I wanted it back. But I couldn't even find that. Maybe it was in his truck. Or maybe it was in my house somewhere. I had been so sleepy recently, maybe I had just put it someplace random that I didn't remember.

Ben had even left his laptop on. Signed in and everything. He was practically begging me to look at his internet history. And again...nothing. Not even any porn. There weren't any files in the recycle bin or in the folder marked "Important." What kind of weirdo labeled a folder "Important" and didn't put anything in it?

He was so much on the good side of the spectrum that it was almost disappointing.

The lack of anything juicy had made me come back downstairs. That with the combination of my growling stomach. I had given up on finding Ben's flaw. Or maybe I had already found it. He was too perfect.

The only thing slightly odd was that his basement door was locked. At least, I thought it was the basement door. His house was a similar model to mine. And the only room I hadn't found yet was the basement. The door was in a different spot than my basement door, but what else could be behind it? I was pretty sure every house in the neighborhood had a basement.

But even the fact that his basement door was locked wasn't very suspicious. I kept mine locked. It was just annoying because his was locked with a key and mine was locked with a bolt. It just meant I couldn't go down there and explore. But it was probably empty. Or filled with gym equipment. He clearly worked out and I hadn't found any of that anywhere. That's most likely what it was.

Although, I kept my basement door locked because I was terrified of intruders. Ben didn't really seem terrified of anything. He had left a relative stranger alone in his house for God's sake. I could have been a Russian spy. I could have been putting cameras up all over his house. I smiled to myself. Now that would have been a good idea. Then I could finally see him naked.

I sighed. I was definitely the evil one. And he was a goody-two-shoes. I poured myself a bowl of some healthy cereal I had never heard of and wandered back to his family room. My feet stopped at the basement door in the hall. I pressed my ear against the wood and then laughed at myself. *What am I doing?* I kept walking and sat down on the couch.

Searching through all his stuff had been a complete waste of time. Not only had I not found anything interesting, but I hadn't found my sneaker either. And now that I thought about it, I still couldn't find my purse. Where the hell was my stuff?

I looked over my shoulder into the hallway. At the locked door. It was going to drive me crazy. I could have searched how to pick locks on my phone, but my phone was missing. And I didn't want to add anything suspicious to his perfect internet browsing history. I knew how to delete recently browsed things, but I knew that meant nothing to a computer nerd. Those guys could search through years of deleted data. What were the odds of Ben being a computer nerd? I hardly knew anything about him. But he did have those fancy binoculars. And he'd look damn good in a pair of glasses. It was probably better not to risk it.

I left my cereal to get soggy and walked back over to the locked door. Maybe I could climb in or see something through the basement windows outside. But then the neighbors would probably see me. And how would that look? I was hoping they believed my story from last night. I was also hoping they hadn't noticed Ben run after me. Or me stepping out of his truck and into his house last night.

If Sally saw, maybe she'd keep her big mouth shut. Especially if she wanted her daughter to date Ben one day. Smearing his name wasn't the best start to a relationship. Just the thought of Sally's stupid daughter upset me. And it was even more upsetting that she wasn't actually stupid. She'd probably be able to figure out how to pick a lock.

Bobby pins. I snapped my fingers. I had seen that on TV once. I pulled one out of my hair and stuffed it into the lock. *Nothing.* I wiggled it back and forth. *Nothing.* Was it supposed to click or something? I put my ear to the lock and wiggled the bobby pin again. *Nothing.*

I sighed. Maybe Ben had a movie that involved lock-picking. All I knew was that I had to get into that basement or it would drive me crazy.

I felt vindicated. The coffee definitely hadn't made me anxious. It made my hyper-focused, just like I remembered. Hyper-focused to the point of destruction.

CHAPTER 20

I turned off Ocean's Eleven and sighed. I had been fast-forwarding through a handful of movies for over half an hour. Why did no movies about robberies have a helpful lock-picking scene?

Probably because they didn't want to aid lunatics like me. I'd just need to keep trying my bobby pin. I put the movie back on the shelf and walked over to the basement door.

Again, I pressed my ear against the wood. I wasn't sure what I was expecting to hear. Someone crying for help? An animal begging to be let up? But it was completely silent. I couldn't even hear the whirl of a sump pump. Not that it had been raining.

It's just a basement. A normal, regular, everyday basement. My thoughts didn't stop me from dropping to my knees and stuffing my bobby pin back in the door. *Come on.* Opening that door had completely taken over my thoughts. I needed to get in. I needed to know what secrets he was hiding. Because I couldn't be the only one with skeletons in my closet. There had to be something wrong with him too. I couldn't be with someone so perfect.

That wasn't really the issue. The question was, why the hell would he want to be with someone as messed up as me? He should have seen me fall and ran in the opposite direction. I was trouble. And Ben was out of his mind if he wanted me.

But he did want me. Every glance, every touch, I wasn't insane. I wasn't making our connection up in my head. He liked me. So he was the crazy one. Maybe that was his flaw. Wanting me. Desiring something so clearly broken. Wanting to save someone who couldn't possibly be saved.

Come on. I wiggled the bobby pin to the left. My psychologist said I needed to think more positively. So for once in my life, I was attempting that technique. The lock would make a click or something soon. Any second now the door would open for me. *Any second now.* The bobby pin snapped in my fingers, half of it jammed into the lock. *Shit. No!* I put my eye right up next to the doorknob. *Oh God, oh God, oh God.* The end of it was lodged into the lock.

I grabbed the small piece that was jutting out and tried to pull it, but I couldn't make purchase on it. It just slipped from my fingertips before I could even try to get it out.

How long had Ben been gone? An hour and a half? Tops. He said he had a few jobs. It took him a little less than half an hour to mow his lawn. That meant he could be home any minute. He couldn't see this.

I had looked all over his house and I hadn't seen a toolkit. Where did men keep their toolkits? I slammed my palm against the basement door. *The basement.* They kept them in the basement. *What have I done?*

My fingers slipped from the end of the bobby pin again. I couldn't give up. There had to be something I could use. I ran into the kitchen and started throwing open drawers.

I lifted up the wine opener. With all the metal things sticking out of it, I thought one might be useful. But of course none of them were. I threw it back down and opened up another drawer. I almost screamed in delight. *Tongs! I could use tongs!*

I pulled them to my chest and thanked a God I didn't believe in, before running back to the door. I knelt down and pinched the bobby pin with the tongs. The tongs immediately slid off the piece of metal. *No.* This was going to freaking work. It had to. I moved my fingers to the end of the tongs and tried to keep my hand steady as I performed what could have been classified as the hardest medical procedure ever known.

The end of the bobby pin was just starting to come out when I heard the front door open.

"Addy, I'm back!"

It felt like my heart was beating in my throat. *Come on you stupid piece of…* The bobby pin flung out of the doorknob, pinging against the wall behind me.

"Addy?"

I did the first thing I could think of and kicked the mutilated bobby pin under the gap underneath the basement door. *No! Why?* I reached my fingers underneath the door but couldn't find it.

"Addy?"

His voice was closer. There were scratch marks all over the front of the doorknob. A perfectionist would notice. I would have noticed. But Ben was a guy. He wouldn't notice. *Please don't notice.* I stood up and stuffed the tongs into the back of my jeans. "I'm here." I sounded out of breath. I'd be suspicious of me. I ran into the kitchen and started shutting the drawers and cabinets I had opened.

"What are you doing?"

My hand froze on a drawer handle. "Oh. Um…" I closed the drawer and looked up at him. Half of the cabinets were still hanging open. *Jesus.* "I…" My voice trailed off. "Looking through all of your things of course." He had caught me. There was no use lying. Besides, I couldn't come up with a lie even if I had wanted to. The sight of him was too distracting. His shirt was damp with sweat below his neck and he had a smear of mud across his cheek. And all I wanted to do was jump him.

He laughed and leaned forward, resting his elbows on the island. "I was able to avoid temptation." He set my purse down on the granite countertop. "You must have left this in my car last night."

I had been so suspicious of him, yet he hadn't done anything wrong. We were the personification of good versus evil. I grabbed my purse off the counter and put it over my shoulder. "Okay, well…I guess I'll just go."

He laughed again. "I don't want you to leave."

"I was going through your things. I'd want me out. I get it. Really, I'm just going to go before I make things even worse." I tried to brush past him but he caught my arm.

"You're adorable."

Adorable? Ha. Not even a little bit.

He ran the pad of his thumb over my bottom lip. I hadn't even realized I was pouting. "Stay. I need to go shower. You can finish snooping around before I get back down."

I sighed. "Honestly, I'm already done."

He raised both his eyebrows. "You've looked everywhere?"

"Pretty much."

His smile never faded. "Find anything good?"

I was very aware of the pair of tongs shoved down my pants. The metal was digging into my back. "No. You're officially perfect."

He leaned forward, until his lips almost brushed against my ear. "I'm far from perfect. You're just not looking hard enough."

I gulped.

"I'll be back down in a minute. Have fun looking around." He walked away without another word.

Maybe he wanted me to get into the basement. My fingers itched to try to break into it again, but I didn't want another disaster. Looking through drawers was one thing. Picking a locked door was another.

I couldn't even believe he wanted me to stay. Although, he had been in my house while I showered. He had probably looked around. He had at least looked around enough to know that my trash needed to be taken out. He wasn't as good at avoiding temptation as he claimed.

As soon as the water started upstairs I pulled the tongs out of my pants. I was just about to wash them when I heard my phone buzz.

I lifted it out of my purse. Ten missed calls. *What the hell?* Twenty text messages. A knot had formed in my stomach before I even clicked on the most recent text. It could only be from one of two people. And both would be bad. It was from my husband.

"Don't make me come find you."

The blood in my veins turned to ice. I scrolled back to the first text.

"I have a layover. I'm stopping by for a few hours so we can get lunch."

Shit! I shoved my phone back into my purse. He was home and I wasn't there. He was going to kill me. But I couldn't let him find me here. I wouldn't let him hurt Ben too.

But I couldn't just leave. Ben would come down from his shower and wonder what was wrong. He'd come to my house. I grabbed a slip of paper and a pen from my purse and jotted him a quick note.

Ben,

Something came up. I'll be back later. Thank you so much for the best first date ever.
-Addy

I ran to the door and cringed. His tongs were still on the kitchen counter. I didn't want him to put butt tongs back in his drawer. And I didn't have time to wash them. I went back to the kitchen and stuffed them in my purse. He stole my sneaker, I stole his tongs. We were even.

I grabbed the note I had left him and added my number to the bottom. Just in case he needed to reach me. Hopefully he'd call me instead of showing up unannounced. I was already in enough trouble.

CHAPTER 21

I paused before opening the back door of my house. My only play here was to pretend I hadn't seen any of his calls or messages. I turned off my phone and shoved it back into my purse. The back of my hand brushed against my engagement ring. I pulled out my two rings and slid them on. The diamond glinted in the sun, teasing me into thinking it was beautiful. But it wasn't. It was hideous and so was everything it represented. I unlocked the door and prayed he was in a good mood.

He was pacing the floor. His cell phone was pressed to his ear and he was yelling into the receiver. His other hand was waving in the air frantically. When we locked eyes, we both froze.

Me in fear.

Him? I had no idea what was wrong with him. But something was definitely wrong. And I had a feeling that it actually had nothing to do with me.

The silence was unnerving. I wanted to turn around and run. I wanted to disappear into the woods and never be found. But I couldn't move. "You're home." I plastered a smile on my face. "What a wonderful surprise."

"Never mind. She's home," he said into the phone and tossed it onto the table.

In two steps he was right in front of me.

I closed my eyes, expecting the worst.

He wrapped his arms around me, leaving a trail of kisses from my jaw to my neck. "I thought something happened to you, babe." He took a deep breath, like he was breathing in my scent in order to remember it for eternity. The thought was haunting.

I tried to step back, but he wouldn't release me. "Why? Have you been home long?" The scent of him made me gag.

"Hours." His arms wrapped tighter around me, suffocating me.

"I'm so sorry. I went for a walk. Why didn't you call?"

He took a step back and ran his fingers through his hair. "I did call. I left dozens of voicemails and texts. I was so worried."

"What? I would have heard it." I pulled my phone out of my purse. "Oh, no." I put my hand on my forehead. "It's off. Something in my purse must have bumped the power button."

His sigh was heavy. I was terrified he wouldn't believe my lie.

He went to the fridge and opened up the freezer. "You have a twisted ankle. What on earth were you doing walking around for hours? Sit down, Adeline."

"It's a mild sprain. And I was growing restless. I needed exercise. It's hard to be cooped up in here all day when I'm used to running in the mornings. I must have lost track of time."

He pulled an ice pack out of the freezer. "Sit. Down."

I sat down in one of the kitchen stairs and took my boots off. He watched me the whole time. Assessing me. Analyzing me.

"I drove around looking for you. I didn't see you out walking."

"I was walking in the woods." It wasn't a terrible lie. It's not like he knew I was scared of the rustling of leaves in the wind. Or the shadows that lurked in the darkness.

"The woods."

I watched his face as he let the thought settle. He believed me. I took a deep breath.

He placed the ice pack down on my ankle. "You missed your last appointment with Dr. Nash." He didn't look up at me. He kept his gaze on my ankle. Like he cared.

"You called my psychologist?" That was unacceptable. "We had a deal."

"You were missing, Adeline."

"I was hardly missing. I went for a walk. I needed fresh air."

"Regardless, we had a deal too. You promised you'd go to your appointments. Fortunately, she has an opening in an hour."

"I'm not going."

"Why? Because you're done taking your pills? You think you don't have any problems? News flash, Adeline, you're a mess. Who goes walking in the woods for hours on a sprained ankle? You've lost control."

"I haven't lost control. I needed fresh air. You can't keep me in this house!" I was panting. He had pushed all my buttons. On purpose. I could tell because he looked happy by my outburst. Like I had just proven to him just how out of control I was. But I was completely in control. And all I could think about was the fact that he said I was done taking my pills. Had he looked for them? Did he really know that?

"It's for your own safety. Look what happens when you leave." He gestured to my ankle.

"It was an accident."

"And I'm supposed to trust your word on that?"

"Yes. Trust me. I haven't done anything wrong. Please." I reached out to him, but he took a step back.

"Okay, I'll trust you. In the spirit of mutual trust, how long have you been off your pills, Adeline?"

"I'm not. I've been taking them every day." I didn't know how to tell the truth anymore.

"Bullshit. You haven't been going to your psychologist and there are no pill bottles in your drawer."

"You're not allowed to talk to my doctors."

"I'm the one paying for them!" He stepped back up to me and put his hand on my shoulder. Right where he knew I was hurt. Right where he had hurt me. "How long have you been off your medicine?" His fingers dug into my bruises.

"I haven't..."

His fingers dug in deeper.

"Seven days! I haven't taken them for a week."

He released his grip.

"I'm sorry. They were making me sick." I was already blubbering. "I couldn't think straight. I..." my voice trailed off as I watched him pull something out of his back pocket and set it on the table.

"And what's your story about these?" He removed his hand.

My bottle of birth control tablets was sitting there, staring at me, mocking me. Why hadn't I thrown them away? I didn't need them anymore. It was a careless oversight. As was throwing out my other prescriptions. I should have kept the bottles. Of course he'd look. He had no respect for my privacy.

"They're old," I said.

"I called the pharmacy. It's new enough for you to still have refills available."

"No..." I let my voice trail off. What was the point in lying anymore? He had caught me. "You said you wanted kids. I can't..." I was losing it. I was becoming the crazy person he thought I was. "I will not have your children."

"Get dressed."

"I am dressed."

"You know what I mean. Something more appropriate." He waved his hand dismissively.

He meant a dress. Like the gawkers wore. I would never be one of them. He couldn't mold me into something I wasn't meant to be.

"We're leaving in ten minutes," he added when I didn't move. "And if you say one more word, I'll make that phone call and we can put this conversation on hold for a few months." He dumped my birth control pills in the trashcan.

He was trying to fire me up. He wanted to send me away again. But the joke was on him. I didn't need those pills anymore. The shot I had gotten would prevent anything with his genes from growing inside of me.

I stood up, letting the ice fall from my ankle. He could go to hell. I'd tell my psychologist everything. He'd be in jail before dinner. He was fucking done. I was done holding onto his secrets. I was done protecting my past. Done. I didn't care what happened to me. It was time to end him.

CHAPTER 22

My hands were fidgety. This woman brought out the worst in me. Our sessions usually ending in one of two ways. The first was with me screaming and getting kicked out. She pried and pried. The second was I just refused to talk to her about anything and she poked and prodded until our time was up. My life wasn't her business. The only reason I came here was to appease my husband. I didn't need a shrink to tell me about my problems when they were so abundantly clear. And I definitely didn't need to rehash the past. It belonged buried.

"Please take a seat," Dr. Nash said.

I sat down, eager to be able to hide my hands. I placed them between my thighs. She'd pounce on the movement and try to force more medicine down my throat. This whole session would be focused on a nervous tick when I needed it to be focused on my confession. It was time. I had the evidence I needed. This had to work. "I need to tell you something."

"What made you miss your appointment earlier this week, Adeline?"

She never listened to me. She had so many questions, but never cared about my answers. Today she needed to care. "I didn't think I needed to come anymore. I was feeling better. I've been great actually. Really great."

"Better? Describe what that means to you." She held her pen in her hand, ready to analyze me.

I didn't have time for this. "I need to tell you something. I'm in danger. My husband..."

"Your husband told me that you went walking today and lost track of the time. You were wandering around in the woods for hours. How were you feeling then? Great? I feel like you must have been scared. Your hands are still shaking."

I shook my head, pressing my thighs together to further hide my hands. *Stop shaking.* "That was a lie. I wasn't walking. And that isn't what I need to talk about. My husband..."

"He's very concerned about you. I understand that you haven't been taking your medicine. And I have to be honest with you Adeline, I'm concerned too."

"Dr. Nash, please listen to me. I'm in terrible danger."

"Your psychosis flares up when you abruptly stop your prescriptions. We've talked about this numerous times. And if you ever were to go off your meds, we'd need to wean you off slowly. Stopping like this wasn't the right way. And in my opinion, you shouldn't be stopping at all. This medicine makes you better. It's been working so well. You've been happy."

Happy? Was she high? And we had never talked about this before. Stopping my prescriptions had never been an option. Or I would have stopped ages ago. Every time I came here I seemed to get more and more pills, never less. "They've been numbing me. I've been having trouble remembering."

She leaned forward in her seat. "Remembering what?"

I hated that I was giving her what she wanted. "Remembering that I have evidence." I shook my head, trying to push aside the doubt on her face. "A whole box of it. It's under my bed."

"I know," she said with a sigh. "It's what you always say. But the pills don't numb you. They help control your outbursts. And your rage."

I don't fucking have rage! I bit the inside of my lip. I didn't. And why was she focused on that one thing? Didn't she hear me? "The evidence is…"

She held up her hand to stop me. "I know. It's under your bed. I'm doing my best to help you move on. But you don't want to talk about that night. How do you want me to help you if you won't talk about it."

"It doesn't matter!" It felt like I was choking on the air around me. Slowly suffocating in Dr. Nash's stupid office.

"It does matter, Adeline. Talk to me."

"It doesn't! What's done is done." Why? Why couldn't she move on? I had. "I need your help now. I don't need to talk about the past. He's hurting me *now*."

She jotted something down in her notebook. "Who's hurting you?"

"My husband. He's been abusing me. Mentally and physically."

She sighed. "Adeline." She said my name like I was a child. "We've talked about this too. You know that…"

"We haven't talked about this!"

"I have records. You've brought this up numerous times to distract yourself from your past."

"That's not…" I pinched my fingers on the bridge of my nose. It wasn't true. I had never opened up to anyone about this before. "You're lying."

She leaned forward. "Do you need me to show you the records?" She flipped to another page. "April 17th, you said that your husband had caused bruising on your left thigh. You claimed to have all of the evidence in a box under your bed." She flipped to another page.

No. I shook my head.

"January 23rd, you said your husband had broken your elbow. And that you had all the evidence in a box under your bed."

No, no, no! "I never told you that!"

She flipped some more pages. "You first started mentioning this box right after you lost your baby. The first time you mentioned it, I went to your house, Adeline. We looked under your bed together…"

"Stop lying! You've never been to my house. I'd remember if you'd been to my house."

"I have been to your house. I've looked for the box under your bed, just where you said it would be. It wasn't there. The box doesn't exist. You just mentioned that you've been having trouble with your memory. You admitted it yourself."

"Not about this, Dr. Nash. I have the evidence. There's photos…"

"I know." Her voice was falsely soothing. Everything about her was fake. "And you always mention the box when you're hiding from your past or something *real* is currently bothering you. Something completely unrelated to your husband. Is something bothering you Adeline? Have you done something wrong?"

I've been seeing Ben behind my husband's back. "No."

"Nothing at all? Nothing that would cause you extra stress?"

I hated her face and her stupid soothing voice. She was judging me. It was like she knew I had kissed another man. Wanted someone that wasn't my husband. "I sit at home all day doing nothing. What stress?"

"This is important. We need to know what's causing your outbursts. Please talk to me. Stress can make your medicine not as effective. Can't you think of anything that may have altered your stress levels?"

"I'm not crazy. You're saying that I'm crazy. I haven't done anything wrong."

"I never said you were crazy. But I know you're making up the box. I know it has nothing to do with your husband. You're hiding something."

"The only thing I've been hiding is the fact that my husband hurts me."

"Your husband loves you. I've never seen a more devoted spouse."

I pulled my cardigan off my shoulder to show her the bruising.

She pushed the box of tissues toward me. "Your husband told me about your accident. You fell on your run, yes?"

"And hurt my ankle. But *he* did this to me." I pointed to my shoulder. "He pushed me into a wall. He's been hurting me for so long. And I couldn't tell anyone. There was too much at stake. But I'm tired." I'm so *tired.* "I need someone to help me. He needs to be behind bars. It's the only way to keep everyone safe."

She jotted something into her notebook. "Usually when we talk about this, something else is bothering you. You create this issue in your head to hide from the truth. What's really bothering you, Adeline?"

Usually when we talk about this? Screw her notes. We had never talked about this. Not once. I'd remember. I know I'd remember. The room was stifling. I was finding it hard to breathe. "I'm not...this is the truth. Aren't you going to call the police? Or something?"

"Does this have to do with you starting to take birth control? I thought you two were trying to have a baby. You've so badly wanted a child. What made you start taking those pills?"

"My husband is a monster."

"You've had fertility issues in the past. Neither one of you is to blame for that. He's not a monster. And neither are you. You're human. Humans aren't perfect. I know that's what you strive for..."

"I'm not blaming him for our lack of fertility. That's not what this is about!"

"You lost your baby, Adeline. But that was six years ago. You can try again now. It's safe to try again now."

I couldn't breathe. What kind of sick game was she playing with me? "I will never have his children. He'll hurt them too. Just like he hurts me."

She closed her notebook. "It's clear that we're not going to be having a serious conversation today."

"Dr. Nash, please, you have to help me!"

"You want me to believe that your husband is abusing you? The same man that's sitting in the waiting room worried sick about you? The one that deals with your moods like a saint? Come back next time with a better story. Or tell me the truth. For once in your life, stop lying to yourself and stop lying to me. All I want is to help you."

I stood up. "Go to hell!"

She sighed. "I'm afraid we've run out of time. I'm going to double your dosage of anxiety and depression medicine. And next time, please call in advance if you're going to miss an appointment. But I expect you to be here. And I expect you to tell me the truth so that I can help you."

"You'll be sorry. If I die, someone will find out the truth. And you'll be so, so sorry that you didn't listen."

"That's enough!" She shook her head like she was trying to clear it. Her eyes were like stones when she looked back at me. She slowly stood up and smoothed down her skirt. "Now if you would please sit in the waiting room, I need to have a word with your husband."

"He's lying to you."

"We both know that isn't true."

"You can't talk about this with him. You can't tell him what I said. He'll punish me."

"He's your custodian, Adeline. He needs to be aware of your progress."

She said progress. But her tone screamed "lack of progress."

"I don't need a custodian. I can make my own decisions."

"The state of Delaware thinks otherwise. Now, if you would, please go to the waiting room and send your husband in."

I wasn't crazy. He had hurt me. He'd been hurting me for years. And I didn't need drugs. I didn't need someone else to make decisions for me. I was going to go home and find my box and go to the police. They'd help me. And if not, I'd kill my husband. I'd hit him over the head with a shovel and use the same shovel to dig his grave in the backyard. I couldn't wait for his lifeless eyes to stare back at me. He had made mine lifeless for so long.

I walked out into the waiting room and plastered a smile on my face. "She wants to talk to you."

He folded up the magazine he had been reading and walked over to me. "Feeling better?" he asked with a smile that was probably as fake as mine.

"Oh, I'm smashing." Right after I killed my husband I was going to kill Dr. Nash.

CHAPTER 23

I looked down at the bland piece of chicken on my plate. All I wanted to do was find that box. But he was breathing down my neck.

"Eat, Adeline."

I glanced up at his face. It was odd. At one point, I thought I loved his smile. His eyes. His nose even. Now each feature made me feel nauseous. "Are you going to send me away?" I hated how pathetic I sounded. But he'd barely said a word since we left Dr. Nash's. What had they talked about?

He finished chewing and set down his fork. "You're acting like I want to. I never want to."

"Then why do you threaten me with it?"

"Why do you continue to defy me?"

Because you don't own me. I was done fighting with him. All I had to do was wait until he needed to leave to catch his flight. Whenever that was. He'd originally said he'd be stopping by for lunch. It was almost 3 o'clock. And I couldn't force this food down my throat. "I'm sorry."

He sighed and leaned back in his chair. "I can take some vacation time. I can…"

"No. That's not necessary. You have to work. And I told you I'd take the pills."

He stared at me, as if he was trying to gauge my honesty. "Then take them."

The bag from the pharmacy sat on the table between us. A divide we'd never cross.

But if I wanted him to leave, I had to put those pills in my mouth. At least I didn't have to swallow them. I pulled the bag toward me and took out bottle after bottle. It was an endless supply of ways to cloud my thoughts. Exactly what he wanted. Exactly what Dr. Nash wanted. But it wasn't what I wanted. Why didn't my opinion count? Why didn't I get a say? I wasn't insane. I didn't need a custodian.

I'd had one moment of weakness. One instance where I had lost control. That didn't earn a lifetime of damnation. It didn't. That's what hell was for. I deserved to live my life the way I wanted. They were robbing me of that.

I unscrewed the cap to the first bottle and popped two of them in my mouth. Two for depression. I unscrewed the second bottle. Two for anxiety. I drank some water, being careful to keep the pills tucked under my tongue. Bottle after bottle. Paranoia. Nausea medicine to counteract the side effects of all the other pills. Claustrophobia. One to relieve symptoms of OCD. A thyroid problem they couldn't prove. Way too many pills to hide underneath my tongue. But my husband didn't take his eyes off me.

I screwed the last cap back on and tossed the bottle into the bag. "Happy?" My words sounded gargled. *Damn it.*

"Swallow them, Adeline."

"I have." Even I could hear the slurred tone of my voice.

He stood up and walked over to me.

I tried to force my throat to make a gulping noise, but failed. My mouth was too full.

He grabbed my jaw and yanked my face up to his. "Now, Adeline."

I tried to shake my head, but his fingers dug into my jaw.

"Swallow."

"I...need...water."

"Now!"

I swallowed a few of the pills dry. They scratched my throat the whole way down. He kept my chin in his grasp.

"All of them."

Tears bit at the corners of my eyes. One by one, the pills went down. I felt sick to my stomach.

"Stick your tongue out."

I clenched my jaw shut. Screw him. I'd done what he had asked. And it felt like I had just swallowed poison. My mind was already muddled. The moment stretched on and on.

He pinched my nose closed. "Open your mouth!"

I grabbed his wrist with both my hands to push him off. He responded by putting his free hand around my neck.

I couldn't breathe.

He tightened his fingers.

"Stop!" I tried to yell, but no sound came out.

He took my opportunity of weakness to pry open my jaw. He shoved me backward when he was satisfied.

My butt slid off the chair and I landed on the ground.

"I wanted a nice afternoon, Adeline."

"I'm sorry." It felt like I was still choking. I gasped for air.

"Why do you always have to test my patience?"

"I'm sorry."

He crouched down beside me. "If I come home this weekend and find you in the same condition I did today, then I'm going to have no choice."

"I'll take the pills. I promise."

"Good girl." He leaned forward and brushed a strand of hair out of my face, completely ignoring my tears. "Now that wasn't so hard, was it?"

There was no question in his sentence. But I shook my head anyway.

"Dr. Nash suggested someone coming and checking in on you once a day. Until my schedule eases up."

He was talking about being home more again. Just the thought made it feel like my heart stopped beating. "I don't need someone to check on me. I had a bad day is all. I missed you. This house feels small without you here." Claustrophobia was apparently one of my issues. I could play that up.

He nodded. "Only one more day apart until this weekend, babe." His fingers wandered over my neck, landing on my injured shoulder. "Try not to hurt yourself while I'm gone."

You're the one that hurt me. He was so obviously the crazy one in our relationship. I just wished I didn't feed off of his insanity. Instead of fighting, I nodded my head.

He leaned forward and pressed his lips to mine. It took every ounce of restraint I possessed not to bite him. I imagined it was Ben. I imagined the smell of grass and the taste of lust. And when he pulled away and his face came back into focus, I had this horrible fear. What if I had made up the box? What if I had made up my hurt shoulder? What if I had made up Ben?

My heart rate accelerated. *Paranoia.* I did have it. But it was because of the medicine. *Right?* The thought of Ben not being real made me want to cry.

My husband cupped my face in his hand. "I wish I could stay. I wish I could be here to take care of you. And help you get better."

I nodded, despite the fact that I loathed the idea and didn't need a lick of his help. My eyelid twitched. I needed to find that box. I needed to go to Ben. I needed to throw up. My mind was consumed and the man in front of me blurred away.

The sound of the front door closing pulled me out of my trance. He was gone. I stood up on wobbly legs and started running for the stairs.

My sprained ankle. My shoulder. The pain still emanating from my neck. Nothing could stop me from getting to that box. I had been taking pictures of the injuries he had given me. We had no pictures of us hanging in the house. No lies in images. But I had the truth in a whole shoebox of images.

I threw myself onto my hands and knees at the base of my bed. *No.* There wasn't a single thing under our bed. Not a loose sock or a dust bunny, let alone a box. *No.* I pushed myself away from the bed. *No!*

I buried my face in my hands. I had lost all control of my body. It heaved up and down as I cried harder than I ever had. I touched my neck where it still felt like his hands were. I knew I had lost my freedom. I had no choice but to give it up to him. But when had this happened? When had I lost my mind too?

CHAPTER 24

I had scoured my house just like I had Ben's. Every single drawer. Every single inch of closet space. Twice. Because the first time my vision was blurred with tears. The second look further proved what I had feared. There was no box. There was no evidence of his abuse. Just my own memories. And who would believe the words of a lunatic?

I was terrified to turn my phone back on. As soon as I did, I'd know if Ben was real. He would have texted me. We had such a lovely evening together. And then I left so suddenly. He'd be worried. *Right?*

Every minute that passed made me feel like I was slipping away. And maybe I was. I had been staring at the basement door for over half an hour. My body was paralyzed. My eyes stuck on the bolted lock.

I wasn't scared to go into Ben's basement. If anything, I had been so eager that I had almost ruined my relationship with him. Hell, maybe I had. Maybe he had seen the scratch marks on the knob. Or my broken bobby pin on the stairs. Or maybe none of that had even happened. That thought was the most horrifying.

But my basement? I wanted nothing to do with it. Basements were for intruders and items of the past. I was scared of both. Despite what I had said to Dr. Nash, I wasn't over my past. I wasn't over that night. How could I be? Every mistake I had made in my life had led me to this moment. And this moment was hell.

Unlock the door. I lifted my hand up to the lock. I cringed when my fingers touched the metal. I pulled my hand down. Today had been bad enough. Why did I want to make it worse? The box wouldn't be down there. Because the box didn't exist. I folded my arms across my chest and stepped back.

I needed sleep. I needed...I didn't know what I needed. No, that wasn't true. What I needed was Ben. The thought made me want to cry again. I cared way more about Ben than I did about the box. And that was terrifying too. I barely knew him. Why did I care so much? He couldn't help me out of this mess. Continuing our relationship would only make it worse.

But that didn't stop me from walking back to the kitchen and picking up my phone. It was as difficult as unlocking the basement door. I forced my thumb down on the power button.

Please be real. God, please. It felt like my whole body was pulsing. My heartbeat was everywhere. In my ears. In my throat.

The screen turned on. And...nothing. I blinked. Dr. Nash was right about everything. Every. Single. Thing. I would have started crying again, but I didn't think it was possible. The medicine had taken full effect. It was hard to cry when I was numb.

So instead, I screamed at the top of my lungs. I screamed until my throat ached.

And I threw my phone against the stupid white wall. It made a cracking noise and fell to the floor. I screamed again and choked on the noise. My next scream sounded like a wounded animal. That's what my husband had turned me into. An animal. He had stolen everything from me. I opened my mouth to scream again but only made the tiniest peep.

Because my phone buzzed and danced across the tiled floor. And then it buzzed again. And again.

I flew to the ground and looked down at the cracked screen. The tears that didn't come with agony somehow came with joy. Maybe my medicine couldn't dull every emotion. It was just rare for me to experience joy when I was doped up. I wiped underneath my eyes and clicked on the text from the unknown number. It had come in four hours ago. Probably several minutes after I had left Ben's house. My phone just hadn't loaded the messages yet.

"It was definitely memorable. Although, our second date could be mind-blowing. I never did find out your favorite food. Maybe I'll just prepare an assortment of meats for you for dinner tonight."

I smiled. He didn't ask if I wanted to come to dinner. He basically just told me it's what was happening. I wiped away the remaining tears and clicked on the next message. It was from an hour after the first.

"It's Ben by the way. In case you didn't get that. You said something came up. Is everything okay?"

He was worried. For some reason that comforted me. I never had anyone in my life to worry before. At least, anyone I believed. Because my husband claimed he worried. But he only truly cared about himself. I clicked on Ben's last message.

"Addy, you can't exactly ghost me. I know where you live."

I laughed and typed out a response. "I wouldn't dare. I'm sorry, I had an appointment I forgot about." I pressed the backspace until what I had typed disappeared. I didn't want him to ask about my appointment. Honestly, I didn't want to talk at all. I wanted to feel his strong arms around me. I wanted to feel whole for just one moment.

"You already have the only meat I want. Do you want to come over?" I pressed send before I chickened out.

I only had to wait one agonizing minute before my phone buzzed back to life.

"Do you want me to come in your back door?"

I laughed. The sexual innuendo wasn't lost on me. But I actually wanted him to use the literal back door. "Absolutely." I pressed send. I needed to get out of this ugly dress and into something a little more…me.

CHAPTER 25

I didn't want Ben to fall for my pretty face. I wanted him to fall for me. Every broken piece, every untapped corner, every fiber of me. It wasn't fair to ask him to do that.

But life was always unfair. It wasn't fair that I was stuck in a relationship with no love. And it wasn't fair to pull him into that mess. It wasn't fair to trick him into falling for me. So I wiped off my lipstick and exchanged my jeans for the sweatpants that I usually reserved for cleaning. I pulled my hair into a knot on the top of my head and turned back to the mirror.

This was me. Sweatpants and all. Or was it? It was so rare that I got to be myself that I wasn't even sure I remembered how. I was happy scrubbing every inch of the house on Fridays. Which meant sweatpants made me happy. *I think*. That made sense. I tucked a loose strand of hair behind my ear.

Life truly was unfair. My pretty face hid the darkness inside. Even in this outfit and without makeup, I knew that I was attractive. But everyone knew that looks could be deceiving. Sometimes I wished that I'd have huge pores and warts. Maybe my husband would divorce me if I was hideous. I sighed and turned away from the mirror. That was wishful thinking. My face wasn't what made him say "I do." I had just found that out a few days too late.

Tonight wasn't about my mistakes. It was about my sanity. Ben would be here any minute. And I somehow needed to determine if he was real. I wasn't sure how that was possible. I could picture the box in my hands. I remembered putting pictures into it. I remembered taking them. Years of documentation. And that wasn't real.

I pinched the bridge of my nose with my fingers. Unless my husband had found the box. He could have thrown it away. Burned it. Buried it in the backyard. A smile curled over my lips. How fitting would it be if I buried his body beside the box filled with the reasons why.

I pinched the bridge of my nose harder. God, I was insane. Who dreamed of murdering their husband? What kind of person smiled at the thought of death?

It was the pills. They were changing me. I shook my head. *No.* I had thought about killing him when I wasn't on them too. I thought about what it would sound like when the bones in his neck snapped. Or how much blood would splatter on the walls if I hit him in the face with a frying pan.

I lowered my hand to cover my mouth. Was I crazy? Was the medicine actually helping me? I felt sick to my stomach. I looked toward the bathroom. The pills had been in my system for a while now. I wasn't sure if making myself throw up would even help. Besides, I didn't even know how to do it.

And what if Dr. Nash was right? It's possible they were helping me not act upon my thoughts. It was even possible that she had been here and looked under my bed. There wouldn't have been anything there. But I'd remember. I would have. Something like that would have stuck with me. And my husband would have responded when she left. He would have punished me.

Or maybe she did come. And she did find a box. And they were both plotting against me. *That stupid whore.* I'd love to hear her try to scream when my hands were around her neck.

I wrapped my arms around myself. How long had I been having those thoughts? Did insanity happen suddenly? Or was it a slow progression? I wasn't sure I could remember being normal.

What if I had imagined looking for the box, but hadn't actually done it? I knelt down on the ground again and looked under the bed. And I tried not to cry. My world had turned upside down. It felt like my mind was rewinding and fast forwarding at the same time.

I needed the pills out of my system. They were messing with my head.

A knock on the door downstairs made everything slow down for a moment. *Ben.* He'd know what to do. I struggled down the stairs. I had been on my feet all day, and my ankle was starting to protest.

Part of me wanted to be sexy when I opened the door. I wanted Ben to rip my clothes off and take me on the kitchen floor. But none of that prevented my lip from trembling when I saw him standing on the top step with a bottle of wine and a bouquet of roses. He was real. His ocean blue eyes. The dimple in his cheek as he smiled at me. And he was as perfect as I remembered.

Above all else, he had become my friend. And at that moment, I just needed to know that I wasn't alone. I threw my arms around the back of his neck instead of inviting him in. I wanted him to hug me back so hard that it hurt to breathe. But his hands were full.

Instead he kissed the side of my forehead. I felt the velvety rose petals touch the back of my neck as he hugged me the best he could.

"I missed you," I mumbled into his shoulder.

His laugh was hot against my neck. "And here I was all day thinking you were never going to speak to me again. I was wondering if you found something in my house you didn't like after all."

"No." I squeezed him even tighter. "I didn't find anything weird at all. Although, that in itself was a little unnerving."

He laughed again. "Aren't you going to invite me in, doll?"

God, I wanted his breath on my skin all the time. And I wanted to hear him call me doll over and over again. "Of course." I made myself unwind my arms from his neck.

"These are for you." He handed me the flowers.

They weren't ordinary roses. They were a soft orange with a little red on the tips. I had never seen anything more beautiful. "Thank you. Come in," I stepped to the side. *Before the neighbors see you.*

I started looking for a vase and then froze. Seeing his gorgeous face had made me completely forget about my dilemma. "Ben, I almost forgot." I turned back around and almost bumped into him. "I ate something that I shouldn't have. Something rotten. How do you make yourself throw up?"

"Whoa. Let's back up for a sec. What did you eat?"

"Something gross."

"Then why did you eat it in the first place?" He smiled.

"Ben, this is important. How do you...you know." I pretended to put my finger in my mouth.

He grabbed my hand. "Usually your body will force you to respond the way it needs to. If it was bad, you'd throw it back up."

"I'm not going to sit around until I have food poisoning."

"If you had food poisoning, you'd be sick already," he said. "Maybe it wasn't rotten."

This wasn't working. "I…" I didn't know how to say the words. "It wasn't food. I took these pills…"

His whole demeanor changed in flash. The smile on his face vanished and his body became rigid. "How many did you take?"

"It wasn't like that."

"Addy, how many did you take?" He pulled out his phone.

"Stop." I grabbed his arm. "I didn't overdose."

He suddenly looked older. Wiser than a 23 year old should be. "Would you please just tell me what happened?"

"I didn't want them. They forced me to take them. I don't feel right. They're messing with my head. I have to get them out of my system."

"Who made you take them?"

"My doctor." *My husband.* I wanted to tell him the truth. It felt like there was a weight on my shoulders that was too heavy to bear. "She's forcing me to take them."

He ran his palm along the scruff on his jawline. "Your doctor forced you to take pills? Most doctors suggest medicine…"

I walked over to the kitchen table and lifted up the bag from the pharmacy. "It was never a suggestion for me. She makes me take pills I don't need, for issues I don't have."

"What issues?"

"Ben, you're missing the point. They're in me and I need them out right now."

"Then drink some water and flush them out of your system. You don't have to make yourself throw up."

"I thought you'd want to help me." I suddenly felt alone again. It didn't help that he was looking at me like I was crazy. "I'll figure it out myself." I grabbed my phone and clicked on the internet icon.

"I do want to help you."

I opened up the top article. The best way to make yourself throw up was to watch someone else throw up? That wasn't going to work. Ben wasn't going to be willing to assist me with that. I clicked on the next article. Your index finger easily triggers your gag reflex. I stuck my finger into my mouth.

"Addy, stop it. They'll be out of your system by the morning."

I shook my head back and forth. Why wasn't this working?

He pulled my hand out of my mouth.

"Ben!"

"Stop it." He looked pissed. "Please, just stop for one second."

"I have to do this. They're making me crazy." I stepped back from him. "They're trying to make me think I'm insane."

"Your doctor? I'm pretty sure it's her job to help you. Not convince you that you're crazy."

I shook my head. "You don't understand. It's not just her."

"Then who else is it?"

"Everyone!" *Everyone was out to get me.*

"I'm trying to help you. If your doctor is giving you prescriptions you don't want, then go to a different doctor. I'll drive you myself. We'll figure it out."

"It doesn't matter who I go to. They'll just do whatever he wants. He controls everything."

"Who?"

"My husband!" That wasn't the way I wanted to tell him. Whatever we had was over just as quickly as it started. I finally told him the truth and he just stood there silently. I watched him shove his hands into his pockets and I quickly turned my head away.

It was fine. I was used to being alone.

But that was a lie. It wasn't fine. It hurt. He was supposed to say something. Anything. I pushed my finger back in my throat, harder than before, and instantly gagged.

I ran to the bathroom and threw open the lid on the toilet just as the contents of my stomach came back up to haunt me. And I enjoyed the burn. I enjoyed the hurt. Because pain was the only emotion I had felt in ages before Ben. It was the only thing that reminded me that I was alive.

I felt his presence in the bathroom. I didn't understand why he was still here. He was supposed to run away. I was married. I was a monster.

He sat down next to me on the bathroom floor and gently rubbed my back. He wasn't supposed to be doing this. He wasn't allowed to be kind in the face of my cruelty.

I wiped my mouth with the back of my hand. "What are you still doing here?" The fingers of my other hand gripped the edge of the toilet bowl. "You don't have to stay."

He was quiet for a long moment, his hand running up and down my back. "They thought I was your husband at the clinic. You were wearing a wedding band and engagement ring at the civic association meeting."

I didn't have anything to say. I thought I had been so smooth.

"There were tons of signs, but I convinced myself that you were going through a divorce or something. You're always here alone. You never mentioned him."

Because I'm an awful person. But how I wished those things were true.

"But none of that really matters. I knew. It was easy to put together. I knew and I kept pursuing you."

I sat back on my heels. It didn't seem like anything else was going to come up from my stomach. I just had to suffer through this goodbye instead. "I get that. The chase is fun. And I was unobtainable. You can go now. I'll be fine." I couldn't look at him. I just couldn't.

"That wasn't what I was saying."

"Really, Ben. You're a good guy. You didn't even make a mistake. I lied to you. No one has to know about this. We never even did anything but kiss. It's not a big deal." I flushed the toilet and rinsed my mouth out in the sink. He waited for me to turn off the water before he spoke again.

"You're not getting it." He lightly banged the back of his head against the wall. "I can't seem to stay away from you, Addy."

I finally got the courage to look at him. He was in pain. I was causing him that pain. But I didn't know how to fix it. And honestly, I didn't want to. He couldn't stay away from me. Wasn't that what I wanted?

"Why did you ask me to come tonight?" he asked.

"Because I don't love him."

He sighed and slowly stood up. "So you're using me to get back on him…"

I shook my head. "That's not it. I don't care what he thinks at all. I tried so hard to stay away from you. I have. But I feel it too. I can't stop. I'm pretty sure I'm addicted to you."

He smiled, but it was sad. "So what is this?" He gestured back and forth between us. "Just fun for a while?"

I shook my head.

"I've told you what I'm looking for. But you never told me what you want. Are you planning on leaving him?"

"It's not that simple."

"It seems pretty simple to me."

I didn't know what he wanted me to say.

"I know I should leave." He sighed. "I know it, but I can't make myself walk out that door." He ran his fingers through his hair. "You're still gorgeous even when you just forced yourself to puke. How is that possible?"

I laughed.

"This isn't funny." But he was smiling too.

We stared at each other in the small bathroom. Him being here didn't make sense. Me asking him to come made even less. But here we were.

"You're right, it is simple," I said. Getting a divorce wasn't. That wasn't the only way to part ways with my dear husband, though. There'd been another way this whole time. It had been calling to me. For years it had been calling.

"I shouldn't have said that. I know it's more complicated than just one question. And despite how much I like you, I don't want to break up your marriage."

"It's already broken." I couldn't divorce my husband. I couldn't leave. But I could kill him. "I'm going to end things with him. But I need some time." My plan would need to be flawless. Good enough to kill him and good enough to get away with murder.

CHAPTER 26

He didn't ask me how much time I'd need. He didn't say anything at all. All he did was help me out of the bathroom.

I silently watched him go through my pantry. It wasn't like he could find anything in there that would reveal anything else about me. *He knew.* He knew I was married and he was calmly going through my things.

He handed me a ginger ale. I didn't ask for a cup or ice. I was just grateful to get the vile taste out of my mouth. I downed the soda as he watched me.

Say something. I certainly didn't know what to say to him. I was asking him to have an affair, for Christ's sake. The silence stretched between us.

I excused myself to brush my teeth. Not one word in the past 15 minutes besides for my exit from the kitchen. We were at an impasse. I spit out the toothpaste and brushed my tongue for the tenth time. I needed to fix this. The only way was to tell him the truth. He needed to know just how bad my marriage was. Because my marriage wasn't based on love. It was simple, really. My husband owned me.

But how much could I tell Ben if I wanted him to stay? I needed him. It was wrong, but I didn't see any other way. I'd tell him enough. Just enough so he'd be on my side. Just enough so he wouldn't leave me.

I splashed my face with cold water. Ben already knew I was married and he wasn't running. Maybe he wouldn't leave if he knew everything.

No. I grabbed a towel and wiped off my face. No one could know the truth. That's what got me into this mess in the first place. I'd kill my husband and my skeletons would die with him. I'd live the rest of my life in peace at last. As tempting as it was to confide in someone, the stakes were too high.

I walked down the stairs, cursing under my breath each time my hurt ankle held my weight. If I kept running around it would never heal. For once in my life I needed to stay still.

Ben looked up when I walked into the room. His cell was pressed to his ear.

And for a moment I thought he found something. I stopped, terror running through me. I had been so desperate to get into his basement. Had he been equally eager to get into mine? Unlike his basement door, there was no key required. Just a simple sliding lock.

He said my address into the phone.

I grabbed the doorframe to steady myself. They were going to take me away. "Ben, please…"

He hung up the phone and looked up at me.

God, it was too late. I didn't want to go to jail. I was only just learning what it was like to be free.

"What?" he asked. There was humor in his eyes. "It looks like you've seen a ghost."

"Who were you calling?"

"I ordered us some food." He set his phone down on the kitchen table.

My hand released the doorframe and I sighed in relief.

"You should be sitting down and icing your ankle. And your shoulder. Do they make full-body ice packs?" He walked over to the freezer to examine the options.

"I think what we should be doing is talking about this." I gestured back and forth between us.

He grabbed two ice packs and turned back to me. "What do you want me to say, Addy? Do you want me to ask where you two met? When you had your first kiss? How he proposed?" His voice was strained. "I don't want to know any of that."

I couldn't make myself move. "That's not what I meant."

"Then what did you mean? All I care about knowing is if he's going to come in that door and try to beat the shit out of me. Otherwise, I don't need any specifics."

That was exactly the problem. Ben's words made it hard to breathe. Every time my husband came home, he beat the shit out of me. But for Ben? It would be so much worse. What was I doing? I'd told Ben as much of the truth as I needed to. He was supposed to run away. He was supposed to save himself. But he hadn't left. And now I held the power to save him. I couldn't afford to repeat my past mistakes. I had lost sight of that in the face of his beauty and warmth. "I think you should go." The words made me want to vomit again.

He lowered both his eyebrows. "I'm sorry, Addy, I didn't…"

"Really, it's better if we put a pin on this until my marriage is over."

"No."

No? I repressed my smile. He was fighting for me. How was I supposed to turn him away when I had no one else on my side?

"And I do have questions." He walked toward me. "Why does he force you to take pills? How long have you been married? What caused your miscarriage? Why did you say yes to his proposal in the first place? And why, Addy, why does talking about him make your hands shake?" He grabbed my hands in his to steady them. "I want to know none of it, but all of it at the same time. Tell me whatever you want. I'm not going anywhere."

He's been hurting me. I'm terrified of him. And I'm so scared for you. Instead of saying anything, I buried my face into his chest. He didn't know it, but he was putting his life on the line for me. I breathed in his grassy scent. Combined with his embrace and the softness of his flannel shirt, I felt a wave of calmness surround me. "We should probably sit down."

"That's what I've been trying to get you to do."

I laughed and grabbed his hand, pulling him toward my family room. It was the one room in the house that didn't feel so cold. It was also the only room that didn't have tan walls. One week when my husband was gone, I had painted the walls a seafoam green. A very light seafoam green. So pale that it was really almost white. My husband had never noticed. It was a silent act of rebellion. It seemed fitting to talk to Ben in here.

We sat down on the couch, him on the opposite end. His distance was unsettling, but it was better like this. If his arm was slung over my shoulder while I talked, it would have been harder. He probably needed the distance as much as I did. I turned to face him, putting my legs up on the couch between us. I didn't know where to start, so I adjusted the ice pack on my ankle.

I awkwardly cleared my throat. "My husband and I have been married for ten years. I thought I loved him for maybe…two…" I quickly met Ben's eyes. "Two months. Not years." My throat was dry and scratchy. "And even that? Looking back on it, it felt forced." It didn't feel forced at the time. But it was easy to look back now and know. Easy to see the signs. Because I knew it was all a lie.

"So why did you marry him?"

I shifted in my seat. "My mother raised me with the idea that I needed to marry up. That all I had going for me was my looks. That I was worthless unless I was some stupid trophy wife." Resentment bubbled up in my chest. "She was furious at me for going to college. But I wanted more. And I loved school." I smiled. I could still remember the classrooms. The smell of chalk and the wooden desks.

"What did you study?"

"Psychology." I swallowed down my laugh. I knew it was ironic that I was the patient and not the doctor. My life had taken a horrible turn. But it was all my fault. There was no one to blame but myself.

I cleared my throat, shoving the bitterness aside. "My mother got sick during my sophomore year. We didn't have much. I was paying for college through student loans and a waitressing gig that barely paid for books. Her medical bills were astronomical and it got to the point where she couldn't even afford the medicine to help with side effects of treatment, let alone the treatment. I was drowning in debt.

"Growing up, I hated my mother. She never understood me. And she certainly never wanted me."

"I'm sure that's not true."

I laughed. "No. It's true. She said it to me on numerous occasions. She blamed me for my father leaving. Everything that went wrong with her life, she put that on me. And she wasn't afraid to voice that. But when she got sick, none of that mattered. Blood is blood. It was my responsibility to take care of her.

"I had this brilliant idea that if I found my dad, maybe he'd help me. Maybe he felt guilty for leaving. Maybe he'd suddenly care. I know how ridiculous…"

"It's not. It's not ridiculous to think someone would care about you."

I swallowed hard. Ben believed in me so strongly. But I was weak. And pathetic. And so freaking stupid. "He left my mother as soon as I was born. Trust me, he didn't care. But I didn't really have any other options.

"I looked everywhere. But I couldn't find him. It was like he disappeared after my birth. No records, no anything. And I was growing desperate. My studies were slipping. I was working night shifts and it wasn't even close to enough.

"And then I met my husband." I rubbed the spot on my finger where my engagement ring and wedding band were supposed to be. It felt good to not be weighed down by the precious metals. "He kind of just appeared when I needed him most. He was graduating in the spring and already had this amazing job lined up. He had a hefty inheritance after his parents died in a car accident a few years prior. And he was charming and such a smooth talker. He was everything my mom wanted for me." *Even if it was all a lie.* "He promised me the world. He'd pay my debts. He'd pay for my mom's treatment. He even hired a PI to help me find my dad." God, there were so many signs.

"Sounds too good to be true."

If only he knew. "Something like that. We got married right after he graduated. Only a month and a half after we met. I dropped out of college because he thought it was best. And I wanted to give him what he wanted so that he'd deliver on his promises."

"Did he?"

"Yes. Every single one. My debts vanished. He started paying for my mom's treatment and he kept looking for my dad." I didn't want to tell him anymore. But all of this made my husband look like a saint. I had to keep going. I bit the inside of my lip, trying to keep the demons inside.

"How is your mom now?" Ben asked, breaking the silence.

"She's dead." That was the simplest way to put it.

"I'm sorry, Addy."

"It's okay." It wasn't. Nothing about her death was okay. But he was skipping too far ahead in my story. This wasn't coming out right.

"And did you find your father?"

I looked down at my hands. "Yes."

"Did you get to have a relationship with him?"

"I talked to him. Once." I could still remember his eyes. I had never seen so much fear in someone's eyes before. Except maybe my own. Sometimes when I looked in the mirror, my eyes looked just like his. "He's since passed." Wording it that way made me cringe.

"Addy, I'm so sorry."

I shook my head. I didn't want to talk about my lack of family or their untimely demise. Ben would recognize my husband as a monster because of what he did to me. Not my family. Besides, if I was to believe my husband, it was my fault that they died. And deep down I knew that was true. I had led my husband right to them.

"None of that's really important," I said.

"Do you have any other family?"

I forced my hands to stay still. Because it was tempting to touch my stomach. It was tempting to remember the pain of almost having a family again. "No. It was always just my mother and me. And now that she's gone…" *I'm all alone, Ben. Please don't leave me too.*

"I'm sorry."

I wish he'd stop saying that. I hated when people said they were sorry when they hadn't done anything wrong. Probably because I was all too quick to say it to my husband when he was the one that needed to apologize.

"I didn't even really mean to talk about losing my parents. What I'm trying to say…God, you're going to think I'm crazy."

"I promise I'm not going to think you're crazy."

He would if he knew how I lost the capability of making decisions for my wellbeing. If I told him the story about how I landed myself in a psych ward. But I couldn't tell him about that day. Because I wasn't exactly sure when I lost my mind. How could I tell a story I didn't understand?

I pulled my knees to my chest, letting the ice pack fall from my ankle. "I wanted to get to know him better. I had gotten enchanted by the idea of a knight in shining armor. But I kind of dismissed how important it was to see what was beneath the metal. I had been so swept up in this whirlwind that I realized I didn't really know the man who saved me."

I laughed. It sounded sad and weak. Just as vulnerable as I felt. "I started asking him questions. I was curious about the roots of his last name and his ancestry. I wanted to know if he had any other family. I just wanted to know him. I didn't even mean to pry. And I was changing my last name to his. I wanted to know what I was becoming, if that makes any sense."

I was rambling. I didn't want to tell Ben any more than necessary. It would just give him more reason to judge me. "But he wouldn't talk to me about anything but work. Which was fine. I let it go. But a few weeks later, I got a certified copy of our marriage certificate in the mail. I needed it for my name change. I hadn't looked at his parts before. I had just signed mine, eager to get on with it. So it was kind of exciting to look through it.

"There were so many inconsistencies in that document. It terrified me. A different date of birth. Even his parents didn't have the same last name as him. I didn't think it was odd that his family didn't protest our elopement. Because his parents were dead and he was an only child. I didn't have any cousins or anything either. And my mother wasn't upset that she couldn't attend. She was just thrilled that I was getting married. But there was something unsettling about the fact that his parents' last names weren't Bell.

"So I asked him about it. And he said he was adopted and that no one really knew his birth date and that it was hard for him to talk about. He immediately changed the subject.

"But I couldn't let it go. I had this nagging feeling that something was wrong. I should have been sympathizing with him. If what he said was true then his whole childhood had vanished, you know? But I never, not even once, believed his story. Nothing was adding up. So I looked up the names of his parents and I found a phone number. I couldn't not call it. And when I did...a woman answered. I asked to speak to her son and she said he wasn't home. She said his name, Ben. And I know what you're thinking...it could be a coincidence. But what are the odds that all three of them would have the same names as my husband and his parents?"

"I don't know, Addy." He shifted in his chair. He looked uncomfortable, but he wasn't staring at me like I was crazy.

"I think pretty slim. So I figured he'd lied to me. About everything. Who he was, the fact that his parents died in a car crash, all of it. So I confronted him and he said he had no idea what I was talking about. He told me the same sad story about his childhood. He was so smooth, like always. And when I tried that number again to prove to him that I wasn't lying, it was disconnected.

"But I couldn't let it go. I was obsessed with his lies. And the more questions I asked, the more he started to change. He started throwing my own familial problems back in my face. He became cold and distant and evasive. And then...I guess I started asking one too many questions and he started...punishing me."

Ben's posture stiffened. "What do you mean?"

I pointed to the ice pack on my shoulder. I was pretty sure his nostrils flared. But I couldn't be sure. "His words hurt, but I never expected him to be that way. I stopped asking questions. But he *never* stops."

"He's hurting you?"

I nodded my head.

"Addy, we need to call the police."

"They won't listen," I said with a shrug. "They think I'm crazy."

"That's bullshit. If he's hurting you, we can show them the evidence. I knew you didn't injure your shoulder falling. I knew it and I didn't press it. Come on, we're going down to the police station." He stood up, like our evening had been decided.

"It's a waste of time." I looked out the window. "I'm a clumsy housewife who has a tendency to hurt myself for attention."

"Addy, I can vouch for you. I'm the eyewitness you need. I can help you. Let's go down there right now and get him arrested."

I shook my head. "Ben, there is only one way out."

"The police..."

"No." I didn't want to tell him the real reason why the police wouldn't listen. That I was crazy. He wouldn't understand. And I wasn't ready for him to stop looking at me like he wanted to devour me. Instead of looking at me like I was insane. "I have to kill him."

So much for that. He was already looking at me like I had lost my mind.

CHAPTER 27

"If we don't kill him, he'll kill us," I said. "He'll definitely at least kill you."

Ben laughed. "Wouldn't it be easier to just divorce the guy?"

"It's not that simple, Ben. He's dangerous. He's taken everything from me. And running is useless. He found my dad who was trying to remain hidden. And I don't know the first thing about disappearing."

Ben's expression turned serious. "You're right then. We have to kill him."

"Okay, where do we start?" I asked.

"We'll need the perfect plan. Does he usually come in the front door or the back door?"

"Front door."

"Okay," said Ben. "Do you have any paper? No, scratch that. We need poster board."

"I think so..." I got up and rummaged through the closet. For some reason, we actually had some. I grabbed it and brought it back to Ben.

He smoothed it out on the table and popped the cap off a sharpie with his teeth. I wasn't sure I had ever seen anything sexier.

He started drawing the floor plan to my house.

"How do you know my house so well?" I asked. "You really have been snooping around a lot, huh?"

"What? Oh." He laughed. "My house has the same design. Anyway, what do you like better for the front door? A toolbox booby-trap above the door, or an electrocuted doorknob?"

"Hmm...I think the electrocution would be better. But only dialed up to like, half power. Not enough to incapacitate him. The gawkers might see it if he collapses on the front porch."

"Oh, absolutely. Good call. Electrocuted door knob it is." He drew a lightning bolt on the front door of the floor plan. "What does he usually do next?"

Hurts me. "Walks upstairs."

"Does he take his shoes off?"

"Yes."

"Okay. Why don't we smash some Christmas ornaments right in front of the stairs then."

"Oh, I like that."

Ben drew it on the plan. "For the stairs, there's really only one choice."

"Loaded shotgun with a trip wire?" I asked.

Ben shook his head. "Na, too loud. I say we put a paint can on a rope. If we make the rope just the right length, he'll take it right in the kisser."

"And it'll knock him back onto the broken ornaments."

"Boom. Double whammy. I love it when a plan comes together. What's next?"

The conversation went on like that for at least half an hour. By the time we were done, the poster was covered in all sorts of booby-traps. Light fixtures replaced by blowtorches, kerosene in the toilets, staple guns hidden in door knobs. We had it all. We even had a zip-line from the bedroom window to a tree out back to use as our escape.

"This plan is great," I said. "But I'm worried about all the evidence it will leave. What are we going to tell the police when they come looking for him?"

"We'll just tell them that we caught the sticky bandits. They'll understand."

"Huh?" I asked.

"You know...in Home Alone?"

"Wait, you're going to make me be home alone when I do this? We're going to have to rethink everything then. How am I supposed to lure him into phase 2 if you're not there to release the paint can?"

"What? No. The movie, Home Alone. You do realize that we basically just combined all the traps from Home Alone 1 and 2 into this plan, right?"

I laughed awkwardly. "Of course I do. So scrap all that then." I eyed the detailed poster board. *Damn, such good ideas.* "Maybe we're over-thinking it?"

"Definitely. Let's just go get a couple of unregistered guns with silencers and shoot him." He leaned forward and lowered his voice. "It'll be totally untraceable. Easy peasy."

"Yeah. Or we could ambush him when he comes home tomorrow night. We could each stand on either side of the front door and hit him with shovels when he walks in. He'd probably try to overpower me, but he wouldn't see you coming."

"Sounds perfectly reasonable."

I didn't expect him to be this agreeable so quickly. It was all coming together. "I've always thought burying him alive would be satisfying. But it's better if we know he's dead. So once he has no pulse we can bury him in the backyard. There's a spot back there with a few rocks. I figured we could move them a little, dig the hole for him there then put the rocks back. That way there won't be freshly dug dirt visible. Or maybe the woods would be better..."

"Jesus, Addy, I was joking."

"But you just said..."

"I thought we were playing around. Like a back and forth of things we'd never actually *ever* do. That's why I mentioned Home Alone."

"Oh. Ha. Me too." *Crap, I thought he was on board.* I needed to watch whatever movie that was. It seemed to have good ideas.

"We can't kill your husband." He was staring at me in the way I loathed. Like my mind was slipping.

Technically we can if you stop being so disagreeable. "I know that. Obviously. I was just joking." I laughed awkwardly.

"Were you, though? It sounded pretty well thought out to me."

"So did your plan." God, I sounded like a child.

"But I was actually kidding. You..." he scratched the back of his neck. "You've clearly planned it out."

I laughed. It sounded forced. "Ben, I'm not a crazy person. Of course I'm not going to murder him." *Damn it.* The look he was giving me was the proof I needed. My plan was insane. Which meant all the doctors were right. That my husband was right. Just the thought made my stomach churn.

Ben didn't say anything. He was just staring at me, probably trying to tell whether he was safe sitting next to me. I wasn't sure why he was looking at me like that. I had no intention of hurting him.

I leaned forward and lightly punched his arm. "Geez, learn how to take a joke, Mr. Serious."

He finally laughed. "Addy, you really had me going. I thought you were a psychopath for a second there."

Psychopath. Huh. That stings. "You should have seen your face," I said and laughed again. "Yeah...no...I'm not a murderer." I tried not to sigh. "Let's just pretend I never said anything. Do you want to watch that movie you mentioned? Home Alone?"

He was still staring at me like I was crazy again. "You just told me that your husband beats you. No, we can't watch a movie."

What did he want me to say? He wasn't down with my awesome murderous plan and I wasn't down with his lame plan of calling the cops. Stalemate.

"Can we just rewind for a second," he said and exhaled slowly. "If you don't feel comfortable going to the cops without hard evidence, then let me help you get the evidence."

"How?" I thought about the box. The basement was calling for me. But I refused to go down there with Ben. It was too much. Besides, as far as I knew, the box didn't exist. And pictures wouldn't help anything. Pictures could be explained away.

"As much as it pains me to let him put his hands on you again, we have to videotape him doing it."

My mind starting racing. Him calling me a psychopath was weighing on me. What if I was making everything up? What if the videos showed nothing? "I don't know..."

"What other option is there? You won't go to the cops. You won't run. If you want me to talk to him..."

"No. You can't, Ben. I'll do the tapes." I swallowed hard. "But how do you think we can get him on camera? He'd see them. And if he found the tapes...I don't know what he'd do to me."

"I can have the video-feed sent to my computer instead of yours. I have a few small cameras we can use that he won't see unless he knows to look for them." He stood up. "I'll go grab them and get them set up tonight. Hopefully we'll catch him tomorrow and he'll be behind bars by the weekend." He started to walk out of the family room.

"Why do you have cameras like that?"

He stopped and turned back toward me. "Oh." He laughed. "You know the group of deer I mentioned that roam around in the woods behind my house? They just had a fawn. I thought it would be cool to get video of her."

"That's odd. Aren't fawn usually born in the spring?"

"Yeah. Normally the spring through early summer. Not this one, though. I'll be right back."

For the first time I got the sense that maybe it wasn't so odd for Ben to be falling for me. If he was filming some oddball fawn in his free time, he was clearly pretty lonely.

I heard the back door shut and sighed. I had been so close to getting him to help me commit murder. But maybe this would be better. Getting evidence against my husband was better than getting myself sent to prison. I wouldn't do well behind bars.

But my plan was foolproof. If this deer camera thing didn't work, I'd revert back to my first plan. This time, I'd just leave Ben out of the particulars. I was strong enough to lug my husband's body out of the house and into the backyard. Especially once my ankle and shoulder were healed.

I looked down at my hurt ankle. *Hurry up and heal.* It ached today. A throbbing pain that was almost all-consuming. Much like the feeling in my fingertips. Because they ached to feel my lovely husband's bones snap beneath them.

CHAPTER 28

I lifted up another slice of pizza and took a huge bite. Cheesy goodness from Grotto's was everything I needed to calm myself. It really did seem like Ben was real. If he wasn't, surely he'd be more agreeable. If all of this was in my head, I'd have an actual plan of attack. As it was, the gorgeous specimen installing a camera on the corner of one of my cupboards was real.

Just the thought made me smile. *I'm not insane.* Well, despite the fact that he called me a psychopath. But there was no reason to dwell on that one comment. He was here helping me.

"Aren't you going to eat anything?" I asked before taking another bite.

"Just one more sec." The sound of the drill drowned out our conversation. "Done." He hopped off the ladder with a smile on his face.

"So what else do you have to do to link them to your computer?" I looked around at his toolkit and didn't see his laptop anywhere.

"It's already set up. I had them outside my house feeding to my computer already. Having them a few doors down shouldn't matter any."

"Did you manage to get much video of the fawn? I'd love to see it."

"I didn't realize that you were that interested in deer."

"Who doesn't like baby animals?"

He laughed as he sat down across from me. "Fair point. Can I ask you something?" He lifted up a slice of pizza. He was lucky there was any left. After my little stunt earlier, my stomach was left completely empty. I was ravenous.

"It depends on the question," I said. Now that my lies were diminishing, it was easier to be frank with him.

"Don't be fooled by what you see," he said slowly. "It's the things you don't that really matter."

Him repeating my own words back to me gave me chills down my spine.

"What did you mean by that?" he asked.

I hadn't expected such a serious question. Why did our conversations always do a 180?

"Was that about the fact that you were married?"

He wasn't letting it go. I bit the inside of my lip. "It's about everything you can't see. You say you like me, but you barely know me." I didn't want him to walk away now. I didn't want to be alone anymore. And he knew too much.

He put the slice of pizza down. "I know you, Addy. You're feisty, yet kind. And beautiful." His eyes fell to my lips. "God, you're beautiful."

"Maybe you don't understand because you don't see the worst in me."

"The worst in you?" He flashed me a smile. "There is nothing wrong with you."

Oh, yes there is. "I've done some...bad things." I fiddled with the crust of my pizza slice.

"What kind of bad things?"

I looked up at him. His eyes had narrowed slightly. He wanted to know. He was eager to know. And I desperately wanted to share with him. I wanted to tell him about all the hurt. All the lies. Everything.

But my body didn't care what my head wanted. I stood up and walked over to him.

"I've cheated on my husband." I straddled his lap. I wasn't sure where the sudden surge of confidence came from. Maybe it was because he wanted to know what was behind my pretty face. He wanted to see what lay beneath the surface. I ran my fingers down the back of his neck and tried to keep breathing as I watched his Adam's apple rise and fall.

"You've barely cheated on your husband," he corrected, his hands settling on my waist.

"We could fix that, you know." I wanted him to kiss me. I had already made the first move. It needed to be him. He had to choose whether or not he was okay with this. Suspecting was one thing. Knowing was another.

"What other bad things? Because I don't think you and I can be classified as bad. This is too good."

I sighed, pressing my forehead against his. *So good.* "Remember when I said everything is black or white? That there is no in-between?"

"I remember." His fingers wandered into my hair and he took a deep breath, like he was inhaling my scent.

"I'm one color."

He shook his forehead against mine. "I don't think that's true, Addy."

"It is. I've done things...there's no going back. You asked me if I was good or evil. And I didn't answer. Because I didn't want you to know that I was the latter."

"You, Addy, are anything but evil."

"But you have no idea what crazy thoughts run through my head." I held my breath as I waited for him to respond. No, I hadn't actually told him I was insane. But it was close to a confession.

"You're not crazy to want to get back at him for hurting you." His fingers fell from my hair and he pulled his forehead off mine.

That wasn't what I had meant. But he was looking at me like he understood my pain. Like he wanted to help carry my burden.

"You don't have to stay here and try to get him on film. Come home with me. Let me protect you."

I wanted to say yes. I wanted to play the damsel in distress and have him carry me back to his place. But I was terrible at admitting when I was wrong. Maybe that's why I hadn't asked for help when the abuse first started. Because I was the idiot who married a monster. And I was going to be the one who stopped him too. I needed this.

"I'm tougher than I look," I said.

"I wasn't implying that you weren't. You're one of the strongest people I've ever met." He gently brushed the side of my jaw with the back of his knuckles.

It was a startling contrast when I was used to knuckles on my skin being anything but gentle. I was so sick of being numb. I wanted him to be the one in my bloodstream instead of the remnants of medicine. I wanted him to be what was pulsing through my veins at all times. I wanted him to be the only thing messing with my head. I needed him. I was just about to open my mouth when he broke the silence.

"We can take our time. There's no rush."

He was so gorgeous. It was hard to say anything to him, let alone beg him to take me. But I had the strangest sensation that I was running out of time. "Some things don't need to be drawn out."

"You deserve to be savored. And our first time isn't going to be like this. Not when your mind's moving a mile a minute. Not after what you just told me."

"So much for coming in my back door," I whispered.

He didn't laugh. He looked like he was in pain. "I'm going to help you, Addy. We're going to figure this out together."

"How do you always know the right thing to say?"

"Oh, I've watched a lot of movies."

I laughed. "It shows." I didn't want to climb off his lap. I felt whole when we touched. My hands slid to his shoulders. "So what if he hurts me somewhere besides the kitchen?"

"I have more cameras. Where else should I put them?"

The thought of Ben watching me in the bedroom made me feel nauseous. I didn't want him to see me with my husband. Him seeing me in the kitchen was bad enough. I tended to lose myself in the kitchen. I couldn't even count how many times I threw things out of the pantry or ended up in a ball crying on the tiles. That was bad. Seeing me sleep? Seeing me with my husband? That was significantly worse. "Never mind." I looked down at the buttons on his shirt. I just wanted to undo them and forget about this conversation.

He tilted my face back up to his. "Where, Addy?"

"In my bedroom."

"If this doesn't work, I'll kill him myself."

For the first time, I wondered if he was just one color too. Because there was darkness in his eyes. I knew better than anyone what that looked like. Ben Jones wasn't quite as perfect as I had imagined. And that made him even more perfect for me.

CHAPTER 29

I stared at the dresser in my bedroom. The small camera was visible next to my jewelry box. But only because I knew it was there. No one else would ever know.

I had asked Ben to stay. It had taken every ounce of restraint not to beg him. But he said he wanted to make sure the feed was working. Which meant he was probably watching me right now.

Like he watched the fawn. *Huh.* Ben had never answered my question about that. Had he gotten video footage of the fawn? Was he getting footage of me right now? I wasn't sure how it worked. But it probably recorded everything. He'd have to sift through it and trash unimportant files.

My heart rate accelerated at the thought of him sitting at home watching me. Did he find it more fun than the deer? Animals were innocent creatures. I wasn't. There had to be something enticing about that. Or did he just view me like an animal? Something to watch? Something to study?

I pulled my robe off my shoulders and let it drop to the floor. I was sitting on the bed in nothing but a short, silky nightgown. My eyes were locked on the camera. *Are you watching me, Ben?*

Of course he couldn't hear my thoughts. I sighed. Why'd he have to leave? My throbbing ankle made me turn from the bed. I'd left the Advil on my nightstand. I was just about to unscrew the cap when my phone buzzed.

I lifted up my cell and smiled. Ben had texted me. I clicked on the message, forgetting about the pills.

"Go to bed, Addy."

I turned toward the camera. "Are you watching me, Ben?" I typed out and pressed send. My heart stammered in my ribcage as I waited. But no response came. I sighed and turned the lights off, wondering if he could still see me. His binoculars had night vision. The cameras might too.

I lay down on top of the covers. My whole body felt hot. I had been so close to finally experiencing all of him tonight. He stayed after I'd told him about my husband. He stayed after I'd said I wanted to murder him. And he was watching me now. He didn't have to admit it, I could feel it. That feeling was what was causing me to be so hot.

It may have disturbed most people, knowing that someone was watching. But I had never been most people. It was easy to fall asleep with his eyes on me. Easier than it had been in years.

***

"Always."

I couldn't stop staring at the text. I had woken up to those words. I had asked him if he was watching me, and he'd responded, "Always."

There was a tightness in my chest that I couldn't shake. My father had abandoned me. My mother never wanted me. My husband loathed me.

But Ben? I looked up at the camera mounted on the side of the cupboard. He was watching me. Always.

I felt safe. And content. Which was odd. It was a Friday morning. Normally I'd be in a frenzy cleaning. Making sure there wasn't a thing out of place for when my husband came home.

Friday's were the worst day. But I felt cheery. I felt like singing and dancing.

My mind was clear. Everything was so freaking clear. Tonight my husband would come home and assault me. Ben would take the video footage to the police. And I'd be free.

I bit the inside of my lip. Or would I be? According to the state, I couldn't make decisions for myself. Would they lock me up in a madhouse? Would they take me away even though my husband was so clearly the mad one?

Probably. Ugh. I pushed my bowl of cereal away.

What I needed to do was figure out how to prove I was mentally sound. Ben had come up with the idea to videotape my husband. It was a good plan. If I let him in, would he be able to figure out a plan for the second part of the problem too?

I was twisting my hands into knots on my lap. I didn't want to go from one hell to the next. But I didn't know if I could confide in Ben without him running away. Who wanted to be with a psychopath? That was what he had called me after hearing my murderous scheming. *A psychopath.*

No. I couldn't tell Ben. The only way that the videotapes worked would be if I had an escape planned out. I'd still need to run away. It was probably easier to hide from the state than it was to hide from my husband. Surely they wouldn't look so hard. It wasn't like I knew any of their secrets. I had always been uninterested in history. And I was no Nicolas Cage uncovering national treasures and espionage schemes. The thought made me laugh.

Stop. Only crazy people laugh at their own jokes. *Right?* Or maybe only crazy people talk to themselves. I abruptly stood up. Jokes and thoughts aside, I needed an escape plan and a go-bag. Despite how silly it seemed, the rope from my bedroom window to a tree outside wasn't the worst idea, Home Alone-esque or not.

Besides, it sounded like that little boy from those movies kicked some serious butt.

I walked into the family room and stared down at the sketch Ben had drawn. It wasn't a bad plan. Glass shards in his feet, paint cans to his head, kerosene in the toilet. I was especially fond of the blowtorch. Although the feathers seemed like an unnecessary touch. That was the only thing I could see wrong with the plan. Unnecessary feathers.

I sighed. Murder involved running away. Video footage involved running away. Was there another option that didn't involve running?

I could divorce him like a normal person. Ben made it seem simple. But knowing too many of my husband's secrets wasn't the only issue. He also knew too many of mine.

I turned around and stared at the basement door. All of our secrets were filed away. Clearly labeled and dated. All those files. I swallowed hard. The cops would look at that. Everyone would know our secrets.

But they didn't have to know. I could destroy everything I could get my hands on. And I could destroy his computer. All the evidence of my insanity would be gone. All my wrongdoings wiped away.

I walked over to my laptop and switched it on. A few minutes later I had filled an Amazon cart with a paper shredder, a scanner, and a few other random items that happened to be from the Home Alone master plan. It was good to have a backup plan, just in case.

I'd get the evidence on my husband. And then I'd erase all the evidence he had on me. *This could work.* I was about to press the checkout button when I realized the problem. My husband would look at our joint Amazon Prime account. The stuff I had ordered was strange. Explainable, but suspicious. I signed out of our joint account, made a new G-mail address, and then created a new Amazon account. *Perfect.* Free trial of Prime. It was my lucky day. I added everything back into my cart and was about to check out again, but paused. *Damn it.* My stupid husband looked at the credit card statements too. He'd want to know what I purchased. I stared at the items in the cart. I wouldn't risk it. I'd have to ask to borrow Ben's credit card.

I glanced at the timer counting down how soon I'd have to place my order if I wanted to get it in two business days. I had a few hours. Ben would be here soon, and I'm sure he wouldn't mind if I used his credit card. I'd pay him back in cash. Although, it was best if he didn't see the items in my cart either. I exed out of the screen to hide it and rubbed my hands together. I felt like a diabolical genius.

On Monday I'd be able to start getting rid of all the documents. In the meantime, it would be good to see what I was up against. I walked over to the basement door and undid the latch. I tried to pretend I was going into a normal basement. A dank and scary place with tons of spiders and mold.

I walked down the plush carpeted stairs. The windows along the top of the walls illuminated the space so much that I didn't need to turn on the lights. I looked around at all the file cabinets. All the shelves with different color binders. All the folders lining every inch of shelf space. I crossed my arms in front of my chest, suddenly cold. It was more than I remembered.

I walked over to one of the shelves and lifted up a folder with my name and a date. It was a copy of a psychologist appointment with an updated list of meds. I shoved it back into place. This had gotten so much worse than the last time I'd been down here.

I ran my fingers along the folders. Every appointment. Every checkup. Every single misstep. Every. Single. Fucking. Thing.

I took a step back and stared at the shelves. Thousands of documents all proving that I couldn't take care of myself. That I was crazy. These shelves were what was crazy. He was the one that had lost his damn mind. Who did this? What kind of sick person kept tabs on their wife like this?

What was I thinking? It was all too much. It would be better to just set the whole freaking house on fire. It would take me forever to shred all these documents. And my husband would surely notice before I could even make a dent.

Luckily I had added kerosene to my Amazon cart on a whim. That smart little boy was on to something. It would be better spread around down here than in a toilet bowl though. I was just about to head back upstairs when I noticed a space along the wall that wasn't as colorful. Actually, it was completely black.

A huge safe had been installed against one of the walls. It took up a whole row of shelf space. I walked over to it and studied the keypad. When had this been put in? I typed in my husband's birthday and it buzzed at me. Then my birthday with the same response. Both our names, our last name, a few combinations of out birthdays and initials. Nothing.

I slammed my palm against the keypad, making it buzz again. *You stupid piece of shit!* I wasn't sure if I was referring to my husband or the safe. *What are you hiding?* I grabbed both sides of it and tried to shake it, but it stayed completely still.

"Addy?" Ben's voice drifted down into the basement.

Oh, shit. He couldn't see any of this. *Shit, shit, shit!*

CHAPTER 30

It was hard to run up the stairs on a sprained ankle. Not impossible, just terribly, excruciatingly painful.

Ben made it to the top of the staircase before I was even a few steps up.

I could not let him see all this. "Just a sec!" I called as I forced myself to keep going.

He took a step down toward me.

"I said I'm coming. Hold your horses."

He laughed. "Let me help…"

"I'm fine!" My voice was shrill and not nearly as demanding as I would have hoped. It sounded crazy. *How utterly fitting.*

"Someone's in a good mood today," Ben said with a laugh. He started walking down the stairs toward me, completely ignoring my demands.

The audacity of this man. "I said I was fine. Go back upstairs." It sounded like I was shooing a pesky dog.

He stopped on the step above mine. "Nice to see you too, Addy." He had such a charming smile, I almost forgot about the horrible files behind me. *Almost.*

"I'm sorry. My ankle just hurts." I shifted to try to block his view. "And I actually need help with something upstairs. Something really important. So if we can just…" I let my voice trail off. It was useless. His eyes had already moved past me.

He scanned the walls. Or lack of walls. No wall was visible behind the rows and rows of files. "What is all this?" he asked.

"Nothing. Will you help me back upstairs?" I pressed on his chest. "I have that thing I need help with."

He continued to ignore me as he stepped down to the stair I was on.

I grabbed his arm. "Please, Ben."

It was like he was transfixed by what he shouldn't be seeing. My arm slipped from his as he kept walking. I couldn't let him see it. "Ben, stop."

He didn't.

So I did the only thing I could think of. I jumped on his back. Ben was strong enough to support my weight. His muscles had muscles. I could even feel them beneath my flailing body.

But he hadn't been expecting me to leap onto him at full force.

"Addy, what the heck are you doing?" He tried to peel my arms off of him.

And he definitely hadn't been expecting me to kick him in the backs of his knees when he didn't immediately fall. I had taken one self-defense class the first time my husband had hurt me. This was the only thing I had learned from it. The rest of the class was complete garbage. When would walking with a buddy help when you were being hurt in your own house?

Ben and I tumbled to the ground, a pile of tangled limbs. It was like that first day I'd met him. Except I had landed on a pile of bags that day, not on top of him. Ben groaned.

Oh God, I hurt Ben! I didn't want him to see the files. But I didn't want to hurt him either. What a pair of useless murderers we would be if we were both injured. *Stop it. He didn't agree to be your accomplice.*

The room vanished around me. All I could see was the back of Ben's head. And the fact that he was no longer moving.

"Ben?" I lightly shoved his shoulder. "Ben?" I pushed it a little harder. "Ben!" I tried to roll his body over so that I could see his face. "Ben can you hear me?" *No. No!* "Ben!" A sob erupted from deep in my throat. "Ben wake up. Please!" The tears ran down my cheeks freely. I needed to call an ambulance. I needed to move but I was paralyzed with fear. "You're all that I have," I whispered.

And then suddenly I was on my back, his strong arms pinning me to the ground.

"Got you," he said with that stupidly perfect smile of his.

"What is wrong with you? You scared the shit out of me, Ben!" I tried to squirm out of his grip to no avail. "I thought..." but my words died away as he started tickling my sides.

"Ben!" I screamed through my laughter.

He didn't stop. His hands were all over me, a relentlessly torturous tickling. They felt amazing yet horrible at the same time. The amazing part was winning in my mind though.

"Stop! I can't breathe!" But I didn't really want him to stop. I never wanted him to stop touching me.

I tried to tickle him back but he barely flinched.

The warm breath of his own laughter was hot against my neck.

I stopped trying to fight back. I let my fingers wander into his thick hair.

He continued to tickle me until I started taking awkward gulps of air. His fingers stopped. I wasn't even sure if I was having trouble breathing because of the laughter or because of the excitement coursing through. The hard plains of his body were pressed against mine. It's all I could focus on.

"You win," I conceded. I was panting, my fingers still lost in his hair.

He smiled down at me.

And God was his smile breathtaking.

He leaned down slightly, his lips a fraction of an inch from mine. I was tempted to pull his face down to me, but I kept the pressure even on the back of his neck. I wanted him to come to me. I needed to truly know if this was okay with him.

"Addy." My name was a groan on his lips. It was like a fuse had been lit. I could practically hear the hissing as the fire spread. And the clanging of my heart beating. A steady bang. Bang. Bang.

Take me.

"Someone's knocking on your door," he whispered against my lips.

That was a weird metaphor, but I didn't mind. I was weird too. "And my door is open for business."

He laughed, pulling back slightly. "No, Addy. Someone's knocking upstairs."

"Oh. Ignore it." I tightened my grip on the back of his neck. He was about to lean back down to kiss me when I heard it again. "Wait." I put my hand on his chest. "No. I need to get that. I have no idea who it is."

"So let them walk away."

"No one ever visits me. Ever. I mean, except you. It could be important." I always hoped for bad news. A plane crash. A car explosion. A random bird attack. Death by birds would be a terribly wonderful way to go. I desperately wanted it to be bad news that I would find good. What if my problem had just disappeared?

I slid out from underneath of Ben. "I'll be right back." I was halfway up the stairs when I turned back to him.

He was adjusting his pants.

His pants. And there was a noticeable bulge pressing against his zipper. Jesus, what is wrong with me? Why did I have to break that connection? I swallowed down the moan in my throat.

The knock sounded above again.

"Ben, can you come up? I mean, no stay down here." *Oh frick buckets.* What was I supposed to do with him? "Yeah, come up."

He laughed as he looked around the basement.

Stop doing that! "Ben, please." I couldn't have him looking around.

Another knock.

Damn it. "Can you just close your eyes for a minute?"

He laughed and walked over to the bottom of the stairs. "You want me to just stand down here and close my eyes?"

Bang, bang, bang.

"Yes! Please, I mean."

"Well, since you said please." He placed his hand on the banister and slowly closed his eyes.

Oh, you're a freaking prince, Ben Jones. "I'll be right back." I stumbled up the stairs and down the hall. I was completely out of breath when I threw open the door.

Charlotte was just walking off the front porch. She turned around at the sound of the door opening.

"Adeline. You poor thing." She hurried back up to the door.

Why was she saying that to me? I ran my fingers through my hair. I thought about being pressed against the floor, laughing hysterically. *Oh my God, I have sex hair. I have sex hair and I didn't even have sex!* I could feel the color rising to my cheeks.

"Did I wake you, hon?" she asked.

Oh phew. Not sex hair then. Just crazy sleep hair. "Yes. I've been so exhausted ever since I hurt my ankle. I guess healing takes it out of me." I laughed awkwardly. "Um…what's up, Charlotte?"

She raised her eyebrow. "Nothing is *up* with me." Her tone couldn't have been any snootier.

Geez, she knew what I meant. Why did she have to be such a witch? I could have sworn she gave me an up-down with her prissy gaze.

"I just wanted to check up on you. To see how you were feeling." She smiled sweetly.

"Oh that was really kind of you. But as you can see, I'm good. Thanks for stopping by." I started to close the door, but she put her hand out, stopping me.

"I was worried, Adeline. After you scadoodled out of the meeting the other day."

Who talks like that? "I'm fine. Thanks." My fingers gripped the door harder. *Please just go away.*

"I know you don't have many other friends in the neighborhood to check in on you. You know that you're always welcome at my place. Or maybe the girls and I could come here sometime?"

She looked over my shoulder like she was trying to study my foyer. I wasn't an idiot. There was nothing remotely interesting in my foyer. Such a thing would lead to a discussion. I hated discussions. So my foyer was barren. The thought rolled around in my head. Why had I used such a horrid term. I cringed, trying to focus on the conversation.

"Sure," I said. "Some other time. As you know, I haven't been feeling well."

"Us girls were thinking next week? Maybe Wednesday afternoon before the civic association meeting? It'll be fun."

The way she said it made it seem like it would be anything but. And who invited themselves to someone's house? For such a perfect housewife, she was rather rude. "Um…I guess," I said.

"Oh great." The fake smile returned to her face. "It's a date then. Also, could I speak with Ben?"

I felt faint. *I knew she knew. Oh God.* "Ben? Ben who?"

"Ben Jones. Your gardener."

"Oh." I laughed. "I had forgotten his name. He's not here."

"Of course he is. That's his truck, isn't it?" She pointed over her shoulder.

I leaned out and looked at the driveway. Sure enough, Ben's truck was parked right in the middle of my driveway. Like he freaking lived at my house. *Why the hell is his truck here?* I had told him to come around back. He knew I was married. What was he doing? I had just smoothed everything over with the gawkers. And now this? There was no coming back from *this*.

"Oh, silly me," I said. "He's fixing my…water heater. It's all…broken. I completely forgot he was even here." Why did I pick the one piece of equipment in this house that I knew nothing about?

"That's so nice of him. Could I speak with him for a moment?"

"What about?"

"About Sally Ann of course."

"Who?"

"The girl I'm trying to set him up with. Sally's daughter."

"Her daughter's name is Sally Ann?" Was she joking?

"No, actually it's Sally just like her lovely mother. Her middle name is Ann. She's just always gone by both. I guess it made things easier growing up."

"Mhm." *How stupid.*

"So, can I speak with him?" Charlotte asked.

"He's pretty busy fixing that water heater. It's not much use when it doesn't…heat." I sounded so dense.

"It'll just take a minute." She walked past me into my house.

Maybe I was born to be a gawker. Because I was certainly gawking at her.

"Ben!" she called.

The last thing I needed was her to see my basement too. "I'll go grab him. Wait here one sec." I hobbled down the hall an turned the corner to the basement stairs.

Ben was still standing there, holding the banister. His eyes were closed and there was pure amusement on his face. He had clearly heard our whole conversation. At least someone was finding it humorous.

"Ben. Can you come up here?"

"I'm a little busy," he said.

"Charlotte needs to talk to you.

"I'm preoccupied, Addy." He pointed to his closed eyes. "Can you take a message for me?"

Oh for goodness sakes. "Ben please," I hissed. "You can open your eyes. And you can come up."

He slowly opened his eyes and smiled at me. "Why thank you, doll." He pretended to tip an invisible hat at me as he made his way up the stairs.

"Be cool," I whispered. "And don't call me that in front of company."

He laughed. "I'm always cool." He winked at me and made his way to the foyer.

Please don't make this any worse. I followed him and stood awkwardly to the side as Charlotte gave him a hug. *A hug.* The act of her touching him made me shiver.

"Good to see you again," she said with a giggle. "You haven't returned my calls."

"I've been busy. Picking up odd jobs during the offseason. I'm sorry I missed your calls, Charlotte."

"Please, call me Char."

I swallowed down the laugh in my throat. *Char?* Who was she kidding? There was not one casual bone in that woman's body. It probably hurt her teeth to say such a nickname.

"Char, then" he said. "What can I help you with? I'm just finishing up a job here. I should be done soon."

For some reason his words hurt. He'd be done soon? Was that all this was to him? A job? I thought back to when we first met. He had offered to help me out while I was hurt. I bit the inside of my lip. Was I just imagining the sexual tension? Had I imagined all of it? I put my hand to my forehead. A sharp headache had just hit me.

"It's nothing work-related," Charlotte said.

Her stupid sing-songy voice was driving me insane. I wanted to clock her in the face.

"I just wanted to make sure you'd gotten Sally Ann's number. I heard she's free tonight." Charlotte's eyebrows seemed to disappear under her bangs in anticipation.

"I haven't had time to call her yet," Ben said.

Yet. It was like a knife to my heart. He had been planning on going on a date with Sally's daughter the whole time. What horrible lies had I been telling myself? He was 23 years old. He was young and handsome and *not* a murderer. My mind was growing fuzzy.

"Now's as good a time as any," Charlotte said. "I happen to know she loves that new Italian restaurant on Concord Pike."

"I'm a little busy at the moment," Ben said. "I have that water heater to fix."

"Oh come on, Ben." Charlotte grabbed his arm and gave it a light squeeze. "You should go ahead and give her a call now."

"I probably should finish this first."

Finish with me? Well screw him. I needed to be alone. The foyer was starting to sway in front of me. I swallowed down the lump in my throat. "That's okay, Ben." My voice sounded foreign to my ears. "I actually watched a YouTube tutorial on water heaters. I think I can fix it myself."

"I can stay..."

"I don't need you," I said, cutting Ben off. "Really. I don't. So go have fun on your date. Tell Sally I said hi. Or Ann, or whatever her name is. I'll let you both out." I walked past them and opened the door.

"It was great seeing you," Charlotte said. "Try to stay off your feet, hon. And we'll see you Wednesday!"

"Great." I hated the fake smile on my face. I kept it as I turned toward Ben. "Thanks for all your help." I waved my hand through the door to show him to keep walking. "See you around the neighborhood." Even though I wouldn't. I'd go through with my original plan without him. And then I'd hightail it out of this stupid town.

He stepped through the door, but quickly turned around when Charlotte was out of earshot. "Addy, what are you doing? I..."

"Just go, Ben. I don't need you to finish anything here. I am perfectly capable of taking care of myself." I slammed the door in his face.

The door swayed in front of me. I had lost my mind. I stepped back, tripping on nothing but my own feet.

Ben pitied me. *No.* Ben wanted Sally Ann. *No.* I had imagined everything. The sexual tension. The lust in his eyes. Him wanting to help me out of this hell.

I laughed. The sound echoed around me in the empty foyer.

CHAPTER 31

I stared at the computer screen. I had added even more to my cart than before. This wasn't a backup plan anymore. I was going to kill my husband. And even though the idea of setting booby traps seemed ridiculous, I couldn't think of anything else. The plan that Ben had set up consumed me. I'd show him I could do it without his help.

My order was all ready for checkout, but I didn't know what to do. The countdown timer was clicking down. I was running out of time if I wanted the items in two days. The Christmas ornaments stared back at me, mocking me.

If I ordered with my credit card, my husband would see it. But I needed those items. Stupid Ben with his stupid face had ruined everything.

I pulled out my credit card and quickly typed in the numbers before I could change my mind. I'd tell my husband I didn't order anything and that our credit card must have been stolen. Or that I'd ordered him a gift. Christmas was only three months away. It wasn't that preposterous.

Before I could chicken out, I pressed the place order button. It didn't matter now. It was done. I exed out of the internet browser and stood up. Today was just another Friday. And I needed to clean before my husband came home. If he saw the poster board or leftover pizza he'd have too many questions.

***

The poster board was the last thing to go. Everything else had been thoroughly cleaned and scrubbed. Any trace of Ben had been completely wiped away. Except for his scent. His grassy smell seemed ingrained in my nostrils. I had even blown my nose several times. I wiped it absentmindedly with the back of my hand as I spread the poster board out on the counter to study it once more.

I knew where everything went. My husband wouldn't just end up dead. He'd end up tortured and fairly humiliated. A smile curled onto my lips. It was the perfect plan.

I was just about to throw out the poster board when I spotted the camera out of the corner of my eye. It was silly to even think about it. It's not like Ben was watching me right now. He was probably busy getting ready for his date. Or maybe he was already out.

But I didn't want him to see me go through with the plan. I didn't want him to be able to see me at all. I grabbed a stepstool and wrapped my hand around the camera.

My phone buzzed and I almost slipped off the ladder. I stared daggers at the little device and hobbled back down the ladder. There was a message from Ben. I glanced at the camera for a second and then opened up the text.

"Addy, don't."

I exhaled slowly. He was watching. Well, I had something to say to him too. I flipped over the poster board and wrote on the back in big, bold letters: "FUCK YOU, BEN." I held it up to the camera.

Another text came through. "What about the plan?"

I lifted up the poster board again and tapped it with my index finger before ripping it in half and throwing it in the recycling bin.

My phone buzzed but I ignored it. I walked back up the ladder and tried to yank the camera out of place. But Ben had freaking screwed it into the cabinet. How had I not realized that he was ruining my kitchen? I looked down at my watch. I only had 20 minutes until my husband would be home. I didn't have time to figure out how to dismantle it.

I gave the camera the middle finger and then went to get some duct tape. I wasn't sure when my tears had started to fall. But I felt them. Big, fat tears rolled down my cheeks as I placed the duct tape over the camera lens.

My phone started ringing now, but I ignored it.

I did the same thing to the camera upstairs before changing into a dress and matching sweater. I slid on my engagement and wedding rings and went back downstairs.

I counted out the number of pills I should have taken from each container and then dumped them in the trash. After the trash and recycling were taken out, I smoothed my dress, buttoned my sweater and plastered my fake smile on my face. I was close to escaping. Just one more week of hell. But this weekend had to be completely normal. I'd be on my best behavior. I'd do everything my husband wanted.

And then next Friday when he came home at 5:45 pm, I'd murder him.

My phone started ringing again. Damn it, Ben couldn't keep calling me. He'd ruin everything.

I slid my finger across the screen to accept his call. "Don't you have better things to do than spy on an old lady, Ben?"

"What the hell are you doing, Addy? We had a plan."

"Plans change."

"This was going to work. Take the tape off the cameras before he gets home. We'll capture it on film. We'll get him sent away."

I'd had all afternoon to think about the plan. And I didn't want to send him away. I wanted him to stop breathing. There would be no prison bars for my dear husband. I still planned on burying him in the backyard. "I don't want you watching me."

He groaned, as if I was the most frustrating human being he had ever met. When in reality, he was the frustrating one.

"Addy, listen to me..."

"I've done enough listening. Go have fun on your date and forget you ever met me."

"Forget I ever met you? What are you talking about? I can't just sit here knowing what you're planning to do. You can't kill your husband, Addy!"

Oh yes I can.

"Adeline, I'm home!" my husband said from the hallway.

I hadn't even heard him walk in. How long had he been here? Ben was already ruining my weekend before it had even begun. "Would you please be so kind as to place me on your do not call list?" I said, waiting for my husband to emerge into the kitchen.

"Is he there?" asked Ben. "Jesus, Addy, don't do anything stupid."

"Thanks. You have a good day too. Bye."

Right before I hung up, I heard Ben say: "How can you even ask me to forget about you? You know how I feel about you, Addy."

I pressed the end call button. My heart was beating so fast it felt like it was slamming into my ribcage. I thought I knew how he felt. But all of that was a lie. I wasn't sure why I was stuck on that part of the conversation. I should have been worried that Ben would try to stop me. He said he wouldn't sit around while I killed my husband. And he didn't know that I was waiting on a very important Amazon order. He might think I was going to try to kill him tonight. Or sometime this weekend. I bit the inside of my lip. What if he showed up here trying to stop me?

"Who was on the phone?" my husband asked as he walked into the kitchen.

"Just a telemarketer. How was the rest of your week?"

"Good." He cupped my face in his hand. "But I was worried about you."

"I've been doing a lot better. I've been taken my pills again. And you're right. I needed them. I'm so sorry that I worried you. But everything's fine now." It was easy to smile. Because soon everything would be fine. As long as Ben stayed out of my way.

"Let's go out and celebrate tonight," I said. I couldn't stay here, waiting for Ben to barge in and ruin all my plans. At dinner I'd sneak away to the bathroom and send Ben a text. I'd let him know that I wasn't planning on going through with it this weekend.

"That's a wonderful idea, Adeline. There's a lot to celebrate tonight. I have some exciting news as well. Call and make a reservation while I go freshen up." He placed a kiss against my lips. "We have a lot to talk about tonight."

Somehow I was able to manage a calm, "That's lovely," before he exited the kitchen. *What the hell else are we celebrating?*

CHAPTER 32

My husband reached for my hand in the middle of the table. I was trying to grab a roll. Couldn't he see that? My stomach growled as he kept my hand in his. I stared at the rolls longingly.

"Adeline?"

I looked up at him. There was a tiny spot of salad dressing on the side of his mouth. A good wife would tell him about it. But that certainly wasn't me. Instead, I smiled, enjoying the fact that he was making a fool of himself.

"It's good to see you so happy," he said. "It's been awhile since I've seen your smile so carefree."

It was true. I couldn't contain my excitement for next weekend. Hopefully he wasn't growing suspicious. "I really do feel great. I'm sorry I worried you earlier this week."

"It's alright. I know that sometimes the autumn is hard for you."

The smile twitched on my face. It was like he wanted my good mood to crumble.

He sighed and leaned forward. The elbows of his crisp suit looked out of place on the linen tablecloth. "I'm sorry, I shouldn't have mentioned that." He squeezed my hand.

"It's okay." But it wasn't. It was as if he wanted me to be miserable. But that shouldn't have been a surprise. The man loved seeing me cry. I needed to change the subject. "What was your good news?" I bit the inside of my lip. Why had I asked him that? I didn't want to know.

"I got that promotion. I'll be working from home now."

"Congratulations." Could he hear the anguish in my voice? When was this happening? I needed more time.

"And I thought maybe a change of scenery would be nice. Since I'll be around more and we can really focus on your health. Maybe somewhere down south? Florida perhaps?"

"I don't want to move."

"Adeline." He squeezed my hand again. "I spoke to Dr. Nash on the phone this afternoon after I got the news. And she thought a move would be very beneficial. New scenery. A fresh start for both of us. Maybe we can try to have another baby."

I pulled my hand out of his. Way too fast. Too brash.

His eyebrows lowered.

"You talked about your promotion with Dr. Nash before you told me?" It was irrational for me to be upset, but why would he tell good news to that woman before he told me? I shook away the thought. I never told him anything.

"I was excited to tell you about the move. I wanted to make sure it was in your best interest first, though. I didn't want to see you get your hopes up only to squash them later."

Didn't he, though? "Is Dr. Nash so eager to be rid of me?"

He laughed. "No, I don't think that's it. We both think this move would be best for your health."

My health? Yeah right. He was running from something. I didn't believe this promotion shenanigan for a second. People in his line of work didn't get promotions. Unless there had been a lot of death and destruction.

"What do you say, Adeline? We can start looking for houses this weekend. I already have a flight for us that leaves tomorrow morning."

This weekend? I thought about Ben. I didn't want to move. Yes, I was mad at him, but that didn't mean I didn't still like him. I couldn't move away from him. Just the thought made me feel like I was being strangled. But what did it matter? Ben didn't even like me. I tried to swallow down the lump in my throat, but I couldn't. My whole body was starting to feel sweaty. "Can't we look at houses online?"

"You need to feel the air down there. See how much of a difference this will make for us. We can fly down there, pick a house and stay. We'll have movers send our things. We can be out of Delaware by the end of the weekend."

What?! "That's not how these things work. We need to pack. And we need to find a buyer for this house."

"We don't need to sell before we can afford to buy a new home. We'll put it up for sale once we're out."

"But buying a new house takes time. There are inspections and..."

"We can stay in a hotel until closing."

My fingers fumbled with my purse. I needed to text Ben. Not to tell him that everything was fine. But to tell him that I had moved up my plans. That my husband needed to die tonight.

"Adeline."

"No!" My eyes got round as soon as the word fell from my lips. A few people at nearby tables turned their heads toward us. I leaned forward and dropped my voice. "I'm not moving."

"You haven't even seen..."

"You can't make me."

"Darling." He reached out and grabbed my arm because I refused to give him my hand. "We both know perfectly well that you have to do as I say." His fingers dug into my forearm.

"You're hurting me."

He didn't let go.

"I don't want to leave. I've finally made friends. Charlotte and the other girls are coming over on Wednesday."

Nothing I said was helping.

"And I..." God, what could I say to make him change his mind? That I was in love with someone else? Just the thought was jarring. *In love?* I wasn't in love with Ben Jones. I barely knew him. And he didn't even like me back. "I'll...kill myself if you make me leave."

He let go of my arm, like my skin burned him. "Why would you even say that?"

"Because it's true. I love it here, and I won't be happy anywhere else you take me. For once in your life, would it hurt you to ask what I want?"

"I've already made up my mind. We'll look online for houses if that's what you want. But we're moving, Adeline. I have a few meetings this week that I can't reschedule. I'll leave Monday morning and be back Wednesday night. Take the time to pack and say goodbye to your friends. I'll pick you up after my flight on Wednesday night and we'll leave together."

For the first time in years, I saw the tick. He hid it well. He always had. But I could see it now. He was clenching his jaw, grinding his teeth back and forth. He was nervous. Something wasn't right. The promotion. The move. "What did you do?" I whispered. Because whatever it was, it had most likely put me in danger too.

"If you don't have anything productive to add to this conversation, then it would be best if you said nothing at all."

"What are you running from?"

"Enough, Adeline." His tone was harsh but his voice was quiet.

I nodded and looked down at the salad I hadn't touched. "I need to use the restroom."

He grabbed my hand before I slid out of my seat. "I love you, Adeline."

"I love you too." The words were hollow. And I breathed easier the farther I walked away from him.

CHAPTER 33

Wednesday night. It moved up my timeline, but it was still doable. Definitely still doable. I started pacing back and forth in the restroom. The stuff from Amazon would come Monday night at the latest. I could get it all set up on Tuesday. And I'd have Wednesday morning and afternoon to perfect everything.

No. Charlotte and the gawkers were coming on Wednesday. That would ruin everything. I'd need to call her and tell her not to come. I sighed and looked up at the ceiling. I didn't have the witch's number. I had none of their numbers because I wasn't actually friends with them.

My eyes stayed glued to the ceiling as someone else walked into the restroom. I didn't care if I looked like a crazy person. I was a woman with a deadline and I didn't give a shit about anything but the end result. I'd figure out the Charlotte issue. Even if I had to walk down the street and tell her to stay away from me. Was her number in the phone book? Did I even have a phone book?

The click of the lock made me tear my gaze from the tiles on the ceiling. Ben was standing there with his arms folded across his chest in the sexiest way possible. His face was stern and his eyes were staring daggers at me. But he was wearing a ridiculous fake mustache and a baseball cap. We were at a fancy restaurant. What was he thinking?

"What the hell, Addy?" he said.

It took me a second to realize he was really there. That the man with the weird mustache was actually Ben in the flesh. "What are you doing here?" For a moment I wanted to run into his arms. Like he was here to protect me from that monster sitting across from me in the restaurant. But I knew that wasn't why he was here. He was probably going to report me to the police. Was planning a murder a crime if I hadn't done it yet? I'd feign innocence. I'd tell them that Ben made the sketches.

"Are you serious right now? You tape up the cameras so I can't see you and then you leave the house. I wanted to make sure you were okay."

"You followed me here?"

"Yes. I was worried about you."

"Well as you can see, I'm perfectly fine. And he's still alive too. So stop worrying about everything so much."

"Addy…"

"And stop stalking me."

He took off his baseball cap and fisted it in his hand. "I'm not stalking you. I'm trying to protect you."

"By dressing up like a homeless man?"

He exhaled slowly. "It's a disguise. I didn't want anyone to recognize me."

"Why? So that you can't be brought down as an accomplice?"

He took a step toward me. "You are planning on doing it, then?"

"I didn't say that." I kind of had. His stupid disguise was distracting me. "I'm definitely not doing it this weekend, so you don't need to worry."

"We're leaving right now. Before he gets here. Walk out of the back of the restaurant and get in my truck. We're going to the police station."

For a stalker, he was pretty bad at stalking. "He's already here. And I am not going to the police station." I turned away from him and washed my hands, hoping he'd leave me alone.

Instead he walked over to me, sandwiching me between him and the sink. I could barely turn around to face him.

"We're leaving right now."

"You can't tell me what to do!" I was breathing too fast. The anger coursed through me. I could make my own damned decisions. Why did everyone always try to make up my mind for me? I tried to shove him away from me.

He didn't move, but his gaze softened. "I'm asking you to come with me, Addy. Please."

"To turn myself in? I don't think so." I shoved him again but he grabbed my hands. I struggled against his grip until suddenly I wasn't struggling at all. I was pulling him closer. My anger had completed transformed to lust. And God, I wanted him.

His mouth paused a fraction of an inch in front of mine. "Please, just walk out that door with me. I'll protect you."

I laughed. This time when I moved back, he let me slide from his grip. "What are you really doing here, Ben? Just say it. You think I'm crazy and you're worried I'm going to murder my husband." He should be worried. But I hated that he thought of me that way. I thought he liked me. I wanted to scream, but I didn't want anyone to hear us.

"I don't think you're crazy for wanting to do that. He hurts you. It's normal to want to hurt him back. But that's not why I'm here."

"Then why? Don't you have a date with Sally Ann, the doctor that's apparently perfect for you? I have to get back to my husband before he comes wandering back here."

He grabbed my shoulder. "Yes, okay? I'm worried that you'll do something that will get you sent to prison rather than him. Take the tape off the cameras. Let me help you."

"I don't need anyone's help. Especially not some 23 year old boy who doesn't actually give a shit about…"

His mouth was on mine. He pushed my back against the dirty bathroom wall. How could I not kiss him back? I was falling for him. All I wanted was to spend the rest of my days kissing this man. Even if his fake mustache tickled my upper lip in the most annoying way.

I could taste his anger on my tongue. I could feel it in the way he was holding me. In the way that his fingers tugged at my hair. Anger wasn't love. But it was an emotion I understood. And I was getting drunk on his anger.

He pulled away far too soon. "Tell me I don't like you, Addy. Tell me you can't feel this."

"That's the problem, Ben. I do feel it." I was seconds away from crying. "And I don't deserve it. And we both know you could do better." I unlocked the door but he grabbed my hand to stop me from leaving.

"Addy, I know how I feel. And you're lying to yourself if you think this isn't real."

I've told myself so many lies that I don't even know what's true anymore. I tilted my head slightly to the side as I studied him. Did he realize that? That I didn't even know if this conversation was real or if it was in my head?

"I know he has something on you," he said. "It's why you won't leave. But it doesn't mean the police won't believe your story."

I shook my head. He really didn't understand. "It's not just one thing, Ben."

"Yeah, I kind of gathered that. Your basement looks like a freaking serial killer's lair." He smiled, but I didn't find his joke funny at all.

"I'm glad you find my issues hilarious."

His smile vanished. "That's not what I meant. But if the police saw all those records…"

"You were supposed to keep your eyes closed."

"It was a little hard not to see any files when there were thousands."

"Just stop, okay?" No one needed to tell me how many problems I had. I was well aware of my own shortcomings. And I knew what was in each of those damn files. "It's not your problem. *I'm* not your problem."

"You are my problem, Addy! Why won't you believe me when I tell you that I like you?"

"I don't know, Ben. Maybe it's because Charlotte has your phone number. Or you said you just needed to finish up at my house."

"You asked me to play along…"

"Or that you agreed to call Sally Ann?"

"And what about me, Addy? How do you think it made me feel that you pretended you didn't even remember your gardener's name?" His chest rose and fall when each word. He raked his fingers through his hair. "Are you coming with me or not?"

I wanted to tell Ben how I really felt about him. And I wanted to tell him that if I came with him, his life would be in danger. As far as I knew, it already was. I needed to focus on my plan. And Ben was nothing more than a complication. A complication that happened to have the thing I currently needed most. "Can you text me Charlotte's number?"

"What?" He was staring at me like I had just said the most incredulous thing ever. "Did you just hear anything I said? I want to talk about this."

"I need her number."

"You're infuriating, Adeline."

Maybe that's why my husband beats me. It was a numbing thought. A thought a crazy person would think. Between that and the way Ben was looking at me, I suddenly believed Dr. Nash. I probably was insane. Because there certainly was no box of evidence. And I was most definitely going to attempt murder.

"Would you please just take off the tape?" It was a final plea. He knew I wasn't going with him. He was finally giving up on me.

"You should probably take off that mustache before your date." I opened the door and left him alone in the women's restroom. But his scent was on me again. On my tongue. On my lips. In my hair.

I went back to my table but it was empty. The paid check was sitting there. I walked out of the restaurant and found my husband sitting in the car, which was already running. He honked the horn. So much for not angering him this weekend.

CHAPTER 34

I hated being wrong. I had made a sequence of terrible choices in my early twenties. One bad decision after the next that had all led me here. And I hated that I was still unable to make good ones.

The footage of him beating me would have been perfect. A flawless angle. Apparently I wasn't grateful. Apparently I had made a scene at the restaurant. Apparently I was worthless.

My hands shook as I removed the tape from the camera lens. And apparently I was an idiot that couldn't learn from her past mistakes. I blinked at the camera.

Was Ben watching? I wanted him to be. Could he see the bruise on the side of my jaw? I hoped he could. We could have captured my husband's abuse on film. But I had been too stubborn. Too caught up in a love story that would never see fruition. *Save me from myself, Ben.* I stared at the camera, willing him to help me.

But my phone didn't ring or buzz. All I could hear was the water from the shower upstairs. Ben wasn't watching. And why would he be? I told him not to. I had covered up the cameras. I had ruined everything. Ben was right. This would have been a better way. How much more guilt could I carry before I broke? If I hadn't already broken.

God, I shouldn't have fought with Ben last night. Maybe he had just come to the restaurant to make sure I was okay. He had kissed me like he cared. I ran my index finger along my bottom lip, remembering his lips against mine. But he wouldn't listen to me. I couldn't go to the police. He had seen the files downstairs. It wasn't hard to put two and two together. If he had picked up any of them, he already knew I was insane. It was the words in the files against my own. And it felt like Ben wanted me to go to the police to confess what *I* was planning. I pinched the bridge of my nose. Or had I misread that whole conversation?

I wanted to throw something. What did it matter? Ben had never denied calling Sally Ann. Or setting up a date with her. It was done. *We* were done. I stared back at the camera. Obviously we were done.

The shower was still running upstairs. Over-thinking everything wasn't helping. I had more to do than wallow. This was the first time I had been alone since my husband came home. If I was lucky, I'd slip up again and he'd punish me. And we'd get it on camera. And if I wasn't? I still had another plan.

In the meantime, I needed to try to get into that safe. My ankle still ached as I made my way down the stairs, but it was getting better. If I was lucky, it would be completely healed in another week or so. Not soon enough for my master plan. But that was why it was such a good plan. I just got to watch it unfold from a safe distance. The boy from Home Alone was a genius.

I ignored the files, my eyes honing in on the keypad of the safe. I tried our birthdays, names, and other important dates again, this time writing down each thing I tried in a notebook. *Nothing.* I bit the inside of my lip. I tried the dates backward. What was his favorite holiday? Christmas? I tried that. *Nothing.*

I slapped the side of the safe. *Work, damn it.* I thought of his parents' names from the marriage certificate and tried them. The stupid machine just beeped innocently back at me. And I knew it wasn't innocent. I knew there was something terrible in there.

Something worse than all these files and the memories in my head.

The water stopped. I looked up at the ceiling and then back at the safe. "I'll be back, you son of a bitch." I pinched the bridge of my nose again as I made my way upstairs. My head was pounding. I needed an Advil. Or maybe I just needed to stop talking to inanimate objects.

I stepped into our bedroom just as my husband was coming out the bathroom. A towel was slung around his waist. Water dripped down his chest and abs. Any woman who didn't know him would drool. But the façade didn't fool me. I knew the darkness that lurked beneath his physique. And he was hideous to me.

I turned away from him and grabbed the bottle of Advil from my nightstand. *Huh.* It was regular Advil. Not extra strength. I rotated the bottle in my hand to look at the back. I knew it had been extra strength. Because I didn't like it. And it didn't seem to work. Where had this come from?

"Did you put this here?" I asked as I turned to my husband.

"It was there since I've been home. Even though it doesn't belong there."

The snide remark wasn't lost on me. But I wasn't talking about it not being in the medicine cabinet. I meant the actual existence of the bottle. "Did you pick it up for me? I thought we had extra strength."

He grabbed it out of my hand and placed it back on the nightstand. His fingers gently traced the bruise on my jaw. "Are you in pain, Adeline?"

I tried not to recoil from his touch. "I'm fine." That wasn't why I was asking about the Advil. I was asking because a bottle that hadn't been in our house a few days ago had miraculously appeared on my nightstand.

"I can make you feel better." His mouth fell to my neck and I cringed.

"I'm not really in the mood."

He ignored me and leaned forward, pushing me against the bed.

No. My eyes gravitated to the camera on the dresser. I had taken off the tape from it earlier. But I didn't do it so that Ben could see this happen. I never wanted Ben to see this.

He's not watching. The voice in the back of my head made me close my eyes. *He doesn't care about you.* If he did, he would have tried to call. He would have seen the bruise. He would have seen your tears. *You're all alone.*

The thought of Ben not watching made me even nervous than if he had been watching.

"Really, I'm not in the mood." I tried to push on his shoulders.

"I know it hurts. I'll make it better. I always make it better."

I felt nauseous. "Please."

He didn't hear me begging him not to. He never could read me. Instead he took it as an invitation. He actually thought I wanted him. It would have been funny if I was miles away from him. But here in his arms? Nothing was humorous.

His lips crashed against mine. He forced my lips to part with his tongue.

I missed Ben's touch. Ben's taste. But for some reason, it was harder to remember now. Our parting last night felt final. The memories were slipping. Just like everything seemed to slip from my mind.

The thought was terrifying. And the harder he kissed me, the harder it was to remember. His soft hands wiped away the feeling of Ben's rough ones. His groans made Ben's groans vanish. He was taking everything from me. I tried to push against him again, but he just clutched me harder. And his painful grip erased the memory of Ben's loving touch.

I was in hell. He pushed the hem of my skirt up. I was in hell and there was no escape. Killing him wouldn't take away my pain. Nothing would. I didn't resist his advances any further. There was no point. It's not like I had anything left to save.

But the sharp knock on the door was a welcome reprieve to his burning kisses on my flesh. I pushed away from him.

"Ignore it," he said.

"It might be important." Even though I knew it wasn't. It was probably just some door-to-door salesman.

The knock sounded even louder.

He groaned. "Fine. I need to get dressed. Answer the door."

I took the escape. My head cleared as soon as I was out of our bedroom and away from him. But that thought lingered. Killing him wouldn't erase the memories. The only thing that seemed to make me not think about my husband's touch, sight, smell, taste, and sound was Ben. He made me feel whole again. Alive again. He filled up every one of my senses so I couldn't feel anything but him.

I opened up the door and it was like my guardian angel had appeared. Ben was standing on my front porch and he was every bit the heaven to my husband's hell.

CHAPTER 35

"What happened?" Ben asked.

I stepped out onto the porch and closed the door behind me.

He reached out and touched the side of my jaw. The way he touched me was soothing. It was affectionate. Protective.

"I'm sorry." My lower lip quivered. "I should have listened to you. If I had taken the tape off the cameras we would have caught him."

"It's okay, Addy." He kept his hand on the side of my face, not caring at all that my husband could open the door any minute. Or that the neighbors could probably see.

And for just one moment, I didn't care either. I wrapped my arms around him, pressing the side of my face against his strong chest. I just wanted to feel safe. "Why are you still wearing that ridiculous mustache?" I mumbled into his chest.

He laughed. "You said your husband was dangerous. I wanted to be untraceable."

I reluctantly stepped away from the safety of his arms. "The mustache won't help. Or the baseball cap." He actually did look good in the baseball cap, though. For just a moment I could see our future. Cheering at a Phillies game, embracing after a home run.

But first I had to take care of my past. "You need to go before he comes down."

"Actually, I was hoping to distract him for a while. Talk shop."

I stared at him.

"You know...what hedges he wants trimmed. That kinda thing."

"So your plan was to wear a fake mustache and tell him that you're Ben Jones the landscaper? That's a terrible, awful idea. You need to go. Now."

"He'll know my name, but he won't know what I look like. It's fine."

"Please trust me on this. If he sees your face, you're as good as dead. That mustache isn't fooling anyone. Please go, Ben." I looked over my shoulder at the door. We were running out of time.

"And I always thought doctors were bad with faces." He laughed when I didn't say anything. "You know...the bad bedside manner and everything. Have you seriously never heard that stereotype?"

"No, I have. But my husband isn't a doctor." What was he talking about?

"I thought you said he was a doctor."

"I never said that. He's an insurance collector." *Of sorts.* "Ben, you really need to go. He's gonna open that door any second."

"Are you sure you don't want me to..."

"Absolutely not."

His eyes searched mine. I could tell he didn't want to abandon me. And I appreciated that more than I could say. But this was my battle, not his.

He sighed, finally conceding. "Call me if you need me, okay?"

I turned back to the door without responding to him.

"Promise me that you'll call, Addy."

I grabbed the doorknob. "I will. And thank you for saving me. You came over just in time to prevent..."

"He was going to hit you again?" There was a vein in the side of his neck that seemed to bulge. I had never seen it before. He was a little young to show signs of stress.

"No, that's not…wait, you didn't see?"

"I saw your face. I came as soon as I could."

"You have perfect timing." Just like a knight in shining armor would. "This will all be over soon." In one way or another. "He'll be gone again Monday morning."

"I'll see you Monday morning then." He looked sad and a little dejected, just standing there on my porch in his silly disguise. I didn't have the heart to tell him that if we didn't get my husband's actions on film, or if my other plan didn't work, that I was going to be leaving. That Monday may be one of our last days. I couldn't tell him, because he was already hurting. I could see it in his face, his eyes, his posture. I was feeling that same hurt. But we couldn't afford to comfort each other.

I stepped back into the house just as my husband was coming down the stairs. I quickly closed the door so he wouldn't see Ben.

"Who was it?" he asked as he clasped his watch. He didn't even look at me when he stepped off the stairs.

I sighed with relief. He definitely hadn't seen Ben. "It was just one of those door-to-door people like you thought. They wanted to give us a quote for new siding."

"New siding? This house isn't even five years old."

I laughed. "That's what I said."

He shook his head. "Don't they look at the signs posted at the front of the neighborhood? We should report them."

"It's fine. It wasn't a bother. And if we needed new siding then it would have been nice that they stopped by."

"Still. Who tries to sell siding in such a new neighborhood? You'd think they'd do more research before breaking the law. If we weren't moving soon, I'd report them."

I pressed my lips together. Since when did he care about breaking the law? I didn't know whether it was better to provoke him or not. Yes, getting him on camera would be good. But killing him would be better.

"Speaking of which," he said before I could decide what to say. "Browse some houses today. I'm leaning toward something in the 33109 zip code. Let me know if you find something you like."

"What are you going to do?" I asked as I followed him through the hall. "I thought you might want to look together." I could set my computer up in the kitchen and try to get him to hit me. Even though the thought made my stomach turn over.

"I have some work to do." He unlocked the basement door and opened it.

I had done something to earn another file. But I didn't know what. Was it because of our fight last night? My "scene" at dinner? I hadn't done anything wrong. "What are you working on?"

"Just writing down a few things before I forget. And I need to box up some of my files for the move."

Of course he did.

"There's some boxes in the garage if you want to start packing too. But look at the houses first. I know you're going to find something you like."

I strongly doubted that. "What's in the safe down there?" I was feeling bold. And I was also only a few steps away from the kitchen. If he hurt me, I'd have a record of it. A real one that I hadn't misplaced.

A smile curled onto his lips.

Not a regular, "you're stupid, Adeline," smile. This one was sinister. And bone-chilling.

"We both know what's in there," he said.

I didn't. I'd remember if he had told me. I didn't even know it had been installed. He was keeping me I the dark, but trying to make me feel like I was crazy. He was a manipulative asshole. "What's the password?"

"Stop being silly. You're the one that made it, Adeline."

I wasn't being silly. For some reason I found that word extremely condescending. "That's not funny. You know I didn't make the password. I didn't even know the safe was there until yesterday when I…happened upon it." Crap, now he'd know I was snooping. I took a step back toward the kitchen. Come get me, you sick bastard. "And I want to know what's inside."

"Give your medicine a few more days to kick in and I'm sure you'll remember, babe." He switched on the light and was about to step down when he paused. "Are you feeling okay? You look a little pale."

He was taunting me. I just didn't know why. What was his end game here? "I'm fine."

"Great. Have fun looking at houses." He disappeared down into the basement.

CHAPTER 36

He'd been down there for hours. *Hours.* I stared at the computer screen, clicking through the images of the house I'd pulled up. It was beautiful. With breathtaking views of the ocean. It was someone's dream house.

But I wasn't living a dream. I was living a nightmare. I eyed the basement door. Really. What the hell was he doing down there? It didn't take this long to toss a bunch of files into some boxes.

I stood up and stretched, almost tripping over the box on the floor that I had been packing. It was odd playing along. Looking at houses, packing up plates. Everything in this house would be ash by Wednesday night.

Except for the stuff in that safe. It looked industrial. It was probably fireproof. What had he meant that I set the password? I pinched the bridge of my nose, trying to ease the headache that was coming. Maybe he was down there trying to crack the code that I had set. Was it possible that I had actually set it?

I looked up at the camera. *Sorry Ben. I tried.* My husband would still be home for one more day. Maybe I'd wake up with more courage to antagonize him. It's not like it took much. I walked to the top of the basement stairs and looked down. There were boxes on the floor and files strewn everywhere.

It didn't seem like he was packing. It seemed like he was looking for something. He wasn't in my line of vision. Every nerve in my body wanted to go down there and look at the open files. But what was the point? Stirring up memories wasn't going to help me now. "I'm going to bed!" I called down the stairs.

"Night!" he responded.

"You're not coming?" How was I supposed to catch him in the act if he refused to even be in the same room as me?

"I'm a little busy, Adeline. There's a lot to do before Wednesday."

At least that much was true. He was being uncooperative. So he had just made my week a lot harder. If he kept this up, I'd have no choice but to kill him.

I smiled as I wandered upstairs. Sunday. Monday. Tuesday. Death Day. My week wasn't looking so bad. I just needed to survive one more day of him.

It took me a long time to get ready for bed. For some reason, I couldn't stop thinking about the safe. Even though I knew my husband was just messing with my head. I sat down on the bed and stared at the camera.

Maybe I was imagining it, but it was like I could feel Ben watching. I lifted up my phone and sent him a text wishing him a goodnight before sliding under my covers.

My phone buzzed on my nightstand. I lifted it up to see a text from Ben.

"Goodnight, Addy. Everything's going to be okay, I promise."

He promises. He was young and naïve and so freaking wonderful. I turned off the light and rolled over onto my side.

My eyelids felt heavy but my mind was still racing. I had been trying passwords I thought my husband might use. I hadn't tried any that I thought I might use. *He's lying, Addy.* I squeezed my eyes shut. Why would I believe the word of my husband over my own memory?

***

A knock on the door made me yawn. "You get it," I mumbled and reached over for my husband. But the sheets were empty.

Another knock made me sit up. The bed was perfectly made on my husband's side. He had never come to sleep. I rubbed my eyes and climbed out of bed.

When my feet reached the bottom stair I froze. The mailman smiled at me as he handed my husband a huge package. A package with Amazon tape wrapped around it. What the hell was my package doing here? It was supposed to be two business days. And it was Sunday. When had packages started coming on Sundays?

It was almost like the mailman could feel my distress. Like he enjoyed torturing me. His smile grew.

I narrowed my eyes at him. *What happened to our understanding?* We had a routine. He always just left packages on the front porch.

But it didn't really matter. It wasn't his fault that Amazon had lost their damn minds. Sunday packages. Completely preposterous.

"Have a good day," the mailman said to my husband and walked away. He probably had no idea that he had just ruined my whole day.

I wished that Ben and I had thought to put cameras in the foyer. The tiles were cold on my feet as I quickly walked toward the kitchen.

"What is this?"

I turned back to my husband. "What is what?" Playing dumb was the worst idea ever. What was I doing?

"This." He kicked the package with his foot.

I thought of all the murderous valuables. "Don't!"

He folded his arms across his chest. "So clearly you know what it is. Open it up."

"I didn't realize it was coming today. When did they start delivering packages on Sundays? Mailmen need a day off."

"Adeline, what's in the package?"

For the first time I realized how tired he looked. His hair was matted on the side like he had fallen asleep on something hard. There were dark circles under his eyes. Something was definitely bothering him. He was hiding something. The reason why we were moving. *He's running.*

"Adeline!"

"A present. It's a Christmas present for you, honey."

He eyed me coolly. "It's a little early for Christmas, isn't it?"

"It's almost October. I like getting my shopping done early. I always have." It was true. But I wasn't sure if he knew that or not.

He leaned down and ripped off the tape.

"Stop it." I ran over to him. "You'll ruin the surprise." I grabbed his arm to stop him from opening it. He hit me across the face with the back of his other handing, knocking me to the floor.

"A paper shredder. Paint cans. A blowtorch." He laughed. "A scanner?"

I clutched the side of my face. He had hit me in the same place that I already had a bruise. And he was laughing. I clenched my jaw.

"Rope. A staple gun. Kerosene. And...Christmas ornaments."

"I told you it was a Christmas related purchase."

He tossed the ornaments back into the box and I heard them shatter.

Jokes on you. I needed to shatter them anyway.

"Why do you need Kerosene and a blowtorch?"

"I'm making you something. You'll have to wait until Christmas to find out." *Too bad your body will be rotting in the ground long before then.*

"I'm going to ask you one more time. What are you making?" He walked over to me.

"I just told you it's a Christmas present. I'm not going to ruin the surprise."

He grabbed my hair in his fist and yanked my head back so that I'd look at him. I swallowed down the cry in my throat.

"Tell. Me."

"I'm going to use them to murder you."

He laughed and released his hold on my hair.

I touched the back of my head. Sometimes the smallest actions hurt the most. My whole scalp burned. I walked backward until my calf hit the step. It would have been easier to run to the kitchen. But now I'd have to go up the stairs. *Frick.* He'd easily catch me and pull me back down. I needed to calm him down somehow.

"You think I'm joking? Just watch me do it." Why? Why would I say that of all things? *God, he's going to kill me before I even get a chance to kill him.*

"Adeline." He made a tsking noise that caused my stomach to flip. "Oh, poor, sweet Adeline." He reached forward and gently ran his fingers through my hair. The action was even worse than when he pulled my hair. Fake. Everything he did was fake.

"We both know that I'm not sweet."

"That's true. Your mind is sick and twisted. You've done unthinkable things. But killing me? No. No, that's never going to happen."

"After everything you've done to me? What makes you think I won't?"

"I'm not saying you won't try. I'm saying you can't succeed."

"Yes I can." I was clenching my jaw so hard that I was getting a headache. I wanted to bite my teeth into the side of his neck, but I stayed where I was. I clenched my jaw so that I wouldn't try.

"Besides, Adeline." He touched the side of my forehead. "You really think I'd just go away? Nothing ever leaves this." He tapped the spot he'd been touching. "Your brilliant, broken mind. I'm unforgettable. You've made me unforgettable."

"No." I shook my head.

His fingers slid underneath my chin. "Oh, babe, I'm already there. You're already doubting yourself. I can see your mind working. You're wondering if I'm right. And deep down you know I am. You will never escape me."

"No." My voice was sad and quiet.

He made the tsking noise again. "Take your meds. We have lots of work to do today." His fingers fell from my skin.

"What work?"

"The packing." He gestured around the house. "Box it all up. I'll be downstairs."

"Doing what?"

He smiled. "Making sure you can't possibly forget me."

Oh, I was definitely going to kill him. And he had no one to blame but himself. But as he walked past me down the hall, I did start to wonder if he was right. If killing him would ever be able to erase the years of pain. The memories.

I was hopeful that it would. Besides, my memory wasn't very good. And I could thank him for that. He was the one that made me take my medicine.

CHAPTER 37

I placed the last pan into a box and taped it shut. There was something satisfying knowing that when the house burned down everything would be organized. I wiped my hands off on my jeans and stood up.

We had a lot of useless kitchen appliances. I had never been much of a cook. It would have been better to donate the boxes to Goodwill than to let them all burn. But how suspicious would that be? *Well. Maybe not that suspicious.* If we were moving, we would have a reason to donate stuff. I just couldn't donate everything. Now *that* would be a red flag in any investigation afterward. And I couldn't afford any kinks.

I sighed. *Kinks.* I still had one major one. I lifted up my phone and typed out a text to Ben.

"Can you please send me Charlotte's number?"

His response came almost immediately. "Where is your husband? I haven't even been able to get him in the frame. Let alone any evidence. Her number is 555-2583."

"He's working on something in the basement. Thanks for her number." I was about to type her number into my phone when another text came through.

"Organizing his serial killer files? Seriously, Addy. What does an insurance collector even do? I've been doing some research and that's not a real job title."

I swallowed hard. No, it wasn't. But it described what he did perfectly. "Ben, stop doing research. You're going to get us both killed."

"He does something illegal, doesn't he?"

"I'm serious, Ben! Stop researching it." I looked up at the camera and made a swiping motion across my throat. I was not going to get this close to freedom only to wind up dead.

"We have a lot to talk about tomorrow."

I stared down at his last text. Yes, we did. There was no reason to respond. Instead, I typed in Charlotte's number and put my cell phone up to my ear. She answered after two rings.

"Hi! Charlotte Hallady speaking."

"Hey Charlotte, it's Adeline...Bell."

"You're the only Adeline I know," she said with a laugh. "How are you feeling, hon?"

"A lot better, thanks."

"Me and the girls are so excited to spend time with you on Wednesday. I've already picked out the perfect bottles of wine."

Bottles. Maybe Charlotte was a drunk. It would be nice if there were flaws behind that perfect facade. "Actually, I have some bad news, I..."

"Oh, don't you dare cancel on us, Adeline. We're so looking forward to it."

"Well, that's the thing. I'm moving..."

"No! When?"

"Wednesday night."

"So it'll be a farewell get-together then."

"No..."

"We're going to hate to see you go, but you'll have to let us send you off in style."

"Can't we do it earlier in the week?" *Or not at all?*

"It'll be fine. We'll bring everything. No need to fuss. I can't believe we're losing you."

"I really think it would be best if we did it maybe tomorrow night?"

"Nonsense. It's already set in stone. We'll see you Wednesday afternoon. Bye now."

"But…" the line was already dead. *What a bitch.* She couldn't come on Wednesday. I needed all day to booby-trap the house. I'd call her again tomorrow and be more firm about my demands. Sometimes I thought I hated Charlotte more than I hated my husband.

I eyed the basement door. What on earth was he up to? He'd been hard at work all day down there. He hadn't even stopped for lunch. Despite my conversations with Ben and Charlotte, I felt relatively calm. Packing tended to do that for me. I liked that everything had a place. And that everything ended up in said place once packing was complete.

I opened up the fridge and pulled out some lunch meat and lettuce. The least I could do for my dear husband on one of his last days was make him a sandwich.

Besides, I had always loved making him sandwiches. I hated mayonnaise. Just the thought of it made me want to gag. He happened to like it. But I always felt satisfied smearing it onto his bread. This gross, gloppy stuff. I liked to pretend that I was ruining his sandwich. That he'd choke on the greasy mess.

I smiled as I placed the slice of bread on top. *Perfectly disgusting. I might actually miss this.* I laughed out loud in the empty kitchen. Who was I kidding? I wouldn't miss a thing about him. I walked down the basement steps to find my husband pulling a folder out of a filing cabinet.

"I brought you a sandwich. You could probably use a break, huh?"

"Thanks, babe." He took the plate from me and set it and the file down on a folding table.

"Have you found what you're looking for?" I couldn't help my curiosity. He was so intent on finding something. And I had no earthly idea what he was looking for.

"No, not yet." He took a bite of the sandwich.

I smiled at the thought of the gross mayonnaise. *Take that.*

"Thanks, this is delicious."

He had the palette of a child. "Mhm." I rested my back against the banister. "What is it exactly that you're looking for?"

He looked up from the file. "You'll see soon."

How irritatingly vague. "I was thinking. If we move...I'll need to find a new doctor. Maybe I could choose my own this time?"

He sighed and closed the file, tossing it into a nearby box. "That won't be necessary." He walked over to the filing cabinet and pulled out another file.

"You think I'm well enough to stop going to therapy?"

"No, I didn't say that, Adeline. Dr. Nash will be joining us in Florida." He opened up the file and started reading it. As if he hadn't just said the most absurd thing in the world.

"She can't come with us. She has a practice here. I'm not her only patient."

"You've made a lot of progress with her guidance. I don't want our move to have negative consequences for your health. The whole idea is that this will be best for you."

"She won't agree to it. She hates me."

He looked up at me. "Dr. Nash doesn't hate you. And she's already agreed to come."

"What do you have on her?"

"Excuse me?" He put his hand down on the file.

"Are you blackmailing her?"

He laughed. "What are you talking about? No, I'm not blackmailing your psychologist. But I am paying her handsomely for the inconvenience of moving. That's probably motivation enough."

"That's crazy. I can just find a new doctor."

"It's already done." He lifted up the file and tossed it in the box.

"But..."

"Go get some rest, babe. You look tired."

I wanted to argue with him. But it was like a wave of exhaustion hit me. All the packing had worn me out. I watched the back of his head as he pulled out another file. I truly was exhausted. Of him. Of us.

"If you could do things differently...would you?" I asked.

He turned toward me. "What do you mean?"

"If you could go back and marry someone else. Someone less..."

"Never. I love you, Adeline."

I nodded.

"I think a nap would do you some good."

Why did he keep trying to make me go to sleep? My eyelids felt heavy, even though I didn't want them to. "Maybe a nap would do me some good."

"Yes. It most definitely would. I really do need to get back to these files. We're running out of time."

We most certainly were. Somehow this was the nicest exchange we'd had in years. And it made me incredibly suspicious of him. "If you were in trouble, you could tell me, you know," I said.

"I know."

There was no reason to press it. He'd tell me if he wanted. But it was disconcerting. Depending on what mess he was in, it could haunt me after he was dead. And I was so tired of running. I was so tired in general. I started to climb the stairs.

My ankle barely hurt anymore. In a few days, I'd probably be able to run again. Right around the same time when I'd never need to run again. I smiled as I made my way upstairs. Three more days.

CHAPTER 38

I pulled back the curtain and watched my husband's sedan pull out of the driveway. It was go time.

I threw open the flaps of the Amazon box. The blowtorch looked especially fun. But if I was being honest, I didn't know what to do with it. I didn't really know what to do with any of the items unless I was at close range. Which wasn't an option. I knew from experience that I couldn't overpower him.

Even though Ben didn't approve of my plan, he was the one that had come up with it. He'd be able to help. I shot him a text letting him know that my husband was gone.

There was one other person that could help me. The little boy from Home Alone. And it would be nice to see how everything worked out for him. Because I was pretty sure I'd need a little luck on my side.

I dragged my box of equipment into the family room, put everything on the coffee table, and pulled up the movie On Demand. A light study session was just what I needed. It had been years since I was I college, but I was pretty sure I still knew how to take notes.

***

"Why are you watching Home Alone?"

My notebook fell out of my hands at the sound of Ben's voice. "What the hell, Ben? How did you get into my house?"

"You gave me a key, remember?" He sat down on the couch beside me.

"No, I don't remember giving you a key." I didn't really care that he had one though. I was just upset that he had nearly given me a heart attack.

"Well, maybe I just picked the lock."

My breath caught in my throat. *Crap. He knew.* I had been so consumed by my scheming that I'd forgotten about what I'd done. "Ben, I'm so sorry. But your basement door was the only thing that was locked. Obviously that's not an excuse. At all. But I couldn't *not* try to get in. I..."

"Addy, it's fine. You told me your secret. It's only fair that you know mine."

"Right." I didn't know his secret, though. I hadn't successfully broken into his basement. But he didn't know that I didn't know his secret. And I was dying to know what it was.

He had a strange expression on his face. Curiosity maybe. It's like he was waiting for something.

A chill ran down my back. What if me "knowing" was a bad thing? What if he was here to kill me? I was about to tell him the truth, when he started to speak.

"We definitely need to talk about all this," he said and gestured to the stuff on the coffee table. "And about how there's tons of boxes packed up in the kitchen. But I think we should address the elephant in the room first. Addy, I'm so, so sorry."

"Well...you should be sorry." *Possibly?* "Thank you for apologizing."

He lowered his eyebrows. "Addy, you overreact to everything. How are you not upset with me right now? And how have you played it so cool for the last few days? I didn't even know that you knew until this morning." He pulled out the broken bobby pin from his pocket and tossed it next to the staple gun on the coffee table.

I was supposed to be upset? What the hell was his secret? "Of course I was upset…at first. I mean, you lied to me about…" What? Or had he lied at all? What was I even saying? "About everything," I said. *Maybe?*

"Not everything." He grabbed my hand in his. "I never lied about us. My feelings for you are real."

My heart was racing uncontrollably. He was lying about something, but not his feelings. Who cared about the rest? I had been lying to him the whole time too. Sometimes there was bliss in lies. We could still be happy. We could still have a future.

"I wasn't supposed to get involved with you, obviously."

Obviously. No sane person would. But I still had no idea what he was getting at here. And I wasn't sure I even wanted to know. "Ben, it's fine. I forgive you." I patted his knee. "Let's watch the rest of the movie. Actually, let me rewind it." I grabbed the remote off the coffee table. "I don't want to miss anything important." I leaned my head against his shoulder.

"It's fine? None of this is fine." He shifted away from me. "I should have figured it out by now. Before he was able to do this to you." He touched the side of my face.

"What does this have to do with him?"

He just stared at me. "Everything."

It was as vague as my answer about what he lied about. "Ben, I asked you not to look into him. That it was dangerous. What are you doing? You're going to get us both killed."

"I'm doing my job. I'm trying to crack this case before he strikes again."

His words settled around me. Maybe he was the insane one. "You're a landscaper, Ben."

He laughed. But his laugh quickly died away when he saw my face. "Did you not see my basement?"

"Not exactly. The bobby pin snapped. My phone was missing so I couldn't look up how to pick a lock. So I was kinda just guessing how to do it. And I couldn't figure it out. I never got down there."

"You just..." He ran his hand down his face. "You just flipped me."

"Sure?"

"You flipped me without even realizing it." He leaned back. "Jesus, Addy. You should be freaking CIA."

I laughed. "Or maybe you're just terrible at your job. Whatever that is. Look, Ben, I don't know exactly what's going on, but it's probably best if I don't know. Right? And I have a really busy day. So let's just watch this movie and then get the house set up..."

"Addy we're not Home Alone-ing your husband. I have a few days left to get the evidence I need. He's planning on a move right? I saw the boxes."

"But, Ben, I have it handled." I pointed to the movie. "I was hoping you could help me set up a few things, but I have the general idea. He's not going anywhere. He'll be dead by Wednesday night."

"Addy, you don't understand. Your husband is a very dangerous man."

"You think I don't *know* that?" My eyes had welled up with tears. I quickly blinked them away. "Ben, I know that better than anyone."

"This is bigger than you. I'm not trying to diminish what he's put you through. I want to kill him myself. But, Addy, it's bigger."

"It's not. He's an insurance collector. He..."

"Do you really think that's true? That's not even a real job title." He pulled out his phone and typed something on it. "*This* is your husband." He handed me his phone.

He had pulled up an article. About a serial killer that they had dubbed "The Doctor." I didn't need to read it. I got the gist from the headline.

"Don't you have anything to say?" Ben asked.

"You think this doctor fellow is my husband?"

"Yes. I'm 99 percent sure it's him."

"What a ridiculous name," I said with a laugh. "My husband is too stupid to be a doctor. He barely got his bachelor's degree."

"That's all you have to say? Addy, this is serious." He tapped his phone. "He's killed over 20 people and left zero evidence. The man's a freaking ghost. He's untraceable. A tiny breadcrumb led me here, but I have *nothing*. And we're running out of time. He's about to disappear. *Again*."

"And who are you, Ben Jones?"

"I'll tell you everything if you promise to help me." He put his hand out for me to shake.

I knew my husband was a killer. I had seen it with my own eyes. And I knew exactly what he did as an insurance collector. I wasn't sure I could help Ben become 100 percent positive though. There wasn't any evidence in our house or on his computer. I had looked. Of course I had looked.

But the safe. I didn't know what was in the safe. Maybe Ben could break into it. It could have what he was missing.

"If I help you, he'll go to prison?" I asked.

"Yes. And not just for a few years for domestic violence. For life. And depending on the laws of the places where he did the murders, he could get the chair, Addy."

I looked at the items on the coffee table. That plan seemed complicated. This new plan seemed easy. I could just sit back and relax while Ben broke into the safe. I liked uncomplicated things.

"You'll answer any questions I have?"

"Yes." He lifted his hand again.

This time I didn't hesitate to shake it. I had just freed up my next two days to finish packing.

CHAPTER 39

I looked down at our intertwined hands. It seemed too good to be true. I slid my hand to his wrist and pinched him.

He jerked away from me. "What was that for?"

He is real. I had been putting off doing that for awhile because I was scared I was imagining him. Or am I supposed to pinch myself? I pinched myself too just in case. It hurt. It didn't wake me up from a coma or anything, though. "I just wanted to make sure this was really happening."

He stared at me incredulously as he rubbed the inside of his wrist. "My feelings for you are real. I didn't lie about any of that."

I was glad he had misunderstood me. I was testing to see if *he* was actually real. As a person. Not his feelings. But I was glad to hear him say his feelings were real. Because mine were too. There was so much else to ask him, though. I could finally get answers to all the questions I had. I knew exactly what I wanted to ask first. It's all I had wanted to know for days. "Did you go on a date with Sally Ann?"

"That's your question?"

"My *first* question. You said you'd tell me everything I wanted to know."

He ran his fingers through his hair. "No, I didn't go on a date with someone else. I've told you that I liked you. I spoke with her once over the phone to let her know I was seeing someone."

Seeing someone? I smiled to myself. *We might actually work.* By Wednesday, the man who had ruined my life would be gone.

Maybe sooner. And I could actually have a real chance at happiness. I didn't even care that I didn't deserve it. "That's all I really care about," I said.

He shook his head, like he didn't believe me. "Look, I'm just going to put it all out there from the beginning. I need to get it off my chest."

"If it makes you feel better."

He gave me that same dubious look. "A little over three years ago I got this case about The Doctor. We had nothing to go on. We were chasing a ghost. But then about six months back we got a lead. Some internet blip unscrambled whatever firewalls were on the killer's computer. We were able to get a general location. A block of houses in this neighborhood. I've been here undercover ever since. I'd like to add that it was my job to talk to everyone. Charlotte is one of the most annoying people I've ever met in my life."

"I know!" I was aware that I was focusing on the unimportant revelations. But they were the parts that mattered to me. Everyone had secrets. Nothing Ben said would make me change my opinion of him. "She's the absolute worst."

He smiled. "I'm still kicking myself that I didn't know about those stupid civic association meetings. It would have been easier to meet everyone."

"Let's actually rewind for one second," I said. I had finally heard something important to fixate on. "You mentioned that the killer lives in one of the houses near here. Why do you think it's this one?"

"Something you said tipped me off initially. You were talking about your marriage certificate. How your husband's last name didn't match his parents' last name. Whenever we're close to catching him, he disappears. He must be changing his name. Do you have a copy of the marriage certificate? It could really help. I looked through some of the files downstairs…"

"You did?" I thought he had kept his eyes closed. My heart rate accelerated.

"I wasn't joking when I said it looked like a serial killer's basement. I was trying to get a read on your reaction when I said that."

It felt like all the wind had been knocked out of me. "Were you using me to get to him?" I wanted to believe that he liked me. But the circumstances had just changed. Of course he was using me. He was freaking using me right now. I bit the inside of my lip.

"No. Never. I did need to talk to you just like I needed to talk to everyone on this street. It was lucky that you came to me. But I didn't use you to get to your husband. He's the only person left I haven't spoken with. And when we met, I wasn't even sure if the killer was a man or a woman." He pressed his lips together. He looked so guilty.

"You thought *I* might be the killer?"

"It was a possibility…"

"When did you change your mind about me? Before or after we kissed?"

"Honestly?" he said with a sigh. "Not until after. And I'm sorry that…"

"You've been manipulating me this whole time, Ben! If that's even your real name."

"It is. But my last name is Harlow, not Jones."

Benjamin Harlow. I knew he had a cool name. Ben Jones had never fit him right. Ben Harlow. Adeline Harlow. I liked it. *Damn it.* Again, I was focusing on the wrong things. "So what? You thought if you could get in my pants I'd tell you I was a crazy murderer?"

"That wasn't..."

God, I was such an idiot. This whole thing was a game. He was playing me right now.

"I know you're not a murderer. It's my job to be suspicious. Addy, look at me."

I hadn't even realized that I was staring out the window. I turned back to face him. He looked genuinely sorry.

"I know you wouldn't hurt anyone."

But my husband would. Neither one of us had to say it out loud.

I cleared my throat. I hated the awkward tension in the room. "Does this have anything to do with the fact that you stole my shoe?"

He laughed. "I didn't steal it. I confiscated it for evidence."

"I knew it!"

"But before you get upset, everyone on the block is missing a shoe. I even swiped one of your husband's. The killer's been slipping up recently. Ever since we've pinned his location down. A shoe print was found at the scene of the crime of one of the last murders."

"Was there a match?"

"No. Unfortunately not."

I guess he wouldn't have needed my help if there had been. "Is there anything else I should know about? You know...that you did to investigate me?"

"A few things, yeah. Just try to put yourself in my shoes for a second. I think you'll see that I deserve the benefit of the doubt."

"Okay." I could tell it was going to be bad.

"Nothing major. I went through your trash to see what pills you were on. I took images of your fingerprints when you were sleeping because there were none in the database. I went through your purse and I've run a DNA test. I did a thorough analysis of your phone and called all of your contacts to make sure they were legit. Before we set up the cameras, I was spying on you with those binoculars you saw at my house. And I did have a key made to your house. This wasn't the first time I've been here without you knowing."

I stared at him. "Is that all?"

"Oh. And the Advil I gave you were actually pretty strong sleeping pills so that I could snoop around your house."

"What the hell, Ben? I've been taking those non-stop." *No wonder I keep feeling so tired.*

"When I realized that, I switched them out. I'm sorry. I didn't realize you were still taking the ones I gave you until I saw them on the surveillance cameras. I assumed you'd swap them out for the ones you liked."

I thought about the bottle on my nightstand. How it had changed. "Did you find anything interesting when you were snooping around?"

"Nothing but the files. And that safe. What's in it?"

"I have no idea. But I think it might contain the evidence that you need. I asked my husband about it and he was really evasive. And he was down there all weekend."

Ben shook his head. "I can't believe I didn't get any footage of him. I think he was on the screen when you taped the lenses, but you can't really make it out."

"Sorry about that."

"Not as sorry as me." His eyes traveled to the bruise on my jaw. "I didn't see any photo albums or anything around. If you could give me a picture we could run it in our system. Maybe stop him before he strikes again."

"I don't have any photos."

"None?"

I shook my head. "He's weird about having his picture taken. And I don't...I didn't..." I let my eyes meet his. "Why would I ever want to look at his face when he was away?"

"This will all be over soon, Addy. We're close. I can feel it."

"What is it exactly that you do? I mean, who do you work for?"

"The FBI." He sighed. "You weren't supposed to learn my real identity. My cover's been blown. Technically I should call this in. I should pack everything up and let someone else finish this."

I bit the inside of my lip. "Please don't leave me, Ben."

"I'm not going to. We're going to bring this son of a bitch down together."

I glanced toward the coffee table strewn with murderous tools.

"Not that way, Addy." He grabbed my hand. "The right way. You never answered me. Do you have a copy of your marriage certificate?"

"No. The last house we lived in burned down. We lost everything." *Maybe that's what happened to my box.* I couldn't actually picture it in this house. Was it really that long ago that I had given up hope of him going to jail? The thought was numbing.

Ben lowered his eyebrows slightly. "The files downstairs are dated as far back as five and a half years ago..."

"They're copies. I don't know if he has a storage unit somewhere or what. But they aren't the originals."

He nodded. "Do you remember his parents' last name? That would be a good place to start."

"I'm sorry. It was so long ago." It was on the tip of my tongue. God, why couldn't I remember? "He's had me on a lot of pills. They've messed with my memory."

"Your plan to kill him is awfully tempting." He didn't laugh.

And I was happy for the moment. Because I knew he wanted to protect me. In that one line, I knew how much he cared.

Ben shook his head and sighed.

Maybe having so many secrets wasn't the best policy. If he liked me, he needed to accept me. He needed to fight for me. It was possible he could even help me get out of the mess I was in. "I'm not insane."

"I never said you were." He put his hand on my knee.

"No, I know. But…everyone else does. My husband had me declared legally insane after an incident several years ago." I ran my thumb along the lines on my wrist. "The state took away all my rights. That's why he keeps all the files. To prove I'm incapable of making my own decisions. To keep me doped up on meds. To keep anyone from believing me."

"It's okay. I believe you. And a court is going to believe your word over a serial killer's."

"Maybe. Maybe not. But it's more complicated than that." *Just rip off the Band-Aid, Adeline.* "We have an unspoken arrangement. I keep his secrets and he keeps mine."

"What secrets?"

I wanted to tell him. I really did. But something prevented the words from coming out. Fear. Shame. I swallowed down the lump in my throat. *Do it.* Tears pooled in the corners of my eyes. "I don't even know where to start. I've done something terrible Ben. I've tried so hard to forget."

He squeezed my hand. "It's okay, Addy. Whatever it is, I can help. We're going to fix this mess that your husband made for you. We'll figure all this out together. You have my word."

I so badly wanted to believe him. But I knew my next words would change everything. "It wasn't just because of all the files that I didn't go to the cops. I was worried what my husband would tell them if I did." I took a deep breath and let the words come out in my exhale. "Because four years ago, I killed my father. And my husband watched me do it."

CHAPTER 40

Ben's hand felt like lead in mine. Someone else might not have noticed the shift, but I did. He was losing faith in me. And he had every right to. He was chasing a murderer. But I was one too.

"What happened?" he asked. "You said your husband was going to help you find him. I thought you wanted a relationship with your dad."

"I did. I mean…I thought I did. But he was nothing like what I expected. Or maybe he was everything I expected." I shook my head. "That not true. Those were my husband's thoughts. His words. He said them over and over again. He told me my father thought I was worthless. That he didn't regret abandoning me." *Stop.*

"So you *killed* him?"

"My husband knew my weaknesses. He played to them. He got in my head. He gave me the gun and convinced me to pull the trigger." I ignored the tears running down my cheeks. "I was already broken." My voice cracked. "This was six years after we'd gotten married. He had been hurting me for so long. He was already forcing me to take pills. He knew how to control me. He knew I'd do anything he said in order for the pain to stop. A few years before this happened I had tried to take my own life." I ran my thumb along the scars on my wrist. "Because I'd just had a miscarriage." I shook my head. "People always refer to that as losing a baby. But I didn't lose my baby. He killed it. He hurt me." I tried to blink away the tears. "And I couldn't take the pain. I was drowning. I just wanted it all to end."

"Addy." The name held so much agony on his tongue.

"And my father didn't deny any of what my husband said, Ben. He just stood there." I shook my head. "He had my eyes. And his weren't filled with dread like mine. He had lived a great life without me. A better life without me. Everything my husband said was true. Every. Single. Thing. He turned me into a monster."

"Addy. You're saying that your husband forced you to hold a gun. That he convinced you to pull the trigger."

"What does that matter? I was the one that pulled it! I killed him." It felt like I was back there. Like my memories had swallowed me whole.

"You were on prescriptions you didn't need. You wouldn't have done it without his encouragement. Addy, look at me."

I forced myself to look into his eyes. His face was blurry through my tears. I could have had happiness. I could have continued my lies. I could have finally been free. But there was something freeing about telling him my secret.

"A serial killer forced you to kill. After years of abuse. I think we'll be able to sway the court's mind."

"Ben, I killed someone. Nothing will take that away. I've tried to rationalize it in my mind for years. The pills. The depression. Him egging me on." I was gasping for air. "My life was over anyway. He killed my soul. And I was so angry." I covered my mouth with my hand.

Ben did the last thing I expected him to do. He shifted forward and wrapped his arms around me.

I cried into his shoulder until no more tears would come. I got out all the hurt. The years of pain and secrecy. And he rubbed my back the whole time.

"Let's take that son of a bitch down," he said as my tears slowed.

I pulled away, wiping the rest of my tears away. "This is where you're supposed to arrest me."

He shook his head. "My whole job is about secrecy. You don't think I'm capable of keeping your secrets?"

"I'm not asking you to, Ben. You're only 23 years old. You have your whole career ahead of you. Your whole life. The last thing I want to do is jeopardize that."

"Addy, I'm not a 23 year old lawn care specialist. I'm a 32 year old FBI agent, and I'm perfectly capable of making my own decisions. I've already broken the rules by getting involved with you. What's one more?"

"You're 32? I knew you looked older." The more we talked, the more I thought we could work. He wasn't some young man. He was two years older than me. He wasn't missing out on a lifetime of happiness by choosing me. I could be his happiness.

He shrugged. "My boss thought that saying I was younger would make people more likely to confess to me. A boy-next-door vibe or something like that. In a way, I guess it kind of worked. I got you to confess." He gave me a small smile.

I exhaled slowly. "You were never supposed to see the good in me."

"It's a little too late for that, Addy. You're beautiful and smart. You're the strongest person I've ever met. And one mistake doesn't define you."

"It wasn't *some* mistake. I just confessed to murder. I'm guilty."

"And no one else was listening. You've been to hell and back already. You've suffered enough, Addy."

I let his words settle around me. He was the only other person that knew the truth besides for my husband. And he was saying he'd keep my secret.

"Unlike what you think, the world isn't black and white. There are blurred lines. Most everything is gray."

I didn't agree with him. But I was relieved that he had such a naïve view of the world. And he was right about one thing. I had suffered enough.

I just needed to get through the next few days. And then maybe I'd finally wake up from the nightmare I'd been living. "I regret it," I said. "I know it doesn't make any difference, but I do. And you're right. I've paid for sins I haven't committed. I've already suffered enough."

"I'm not going to tell anyone."

I nodded. I never thought I'd tell another living soul about what I had done. But I also never thought I'd feel like I could trust someone. And I knew I could trust him. And I could trust him to do the exact opposite with my husband's secrets. Because he seemed to hate him as much as I did. It was time to end this. "What else do you need to know about my husband?"

CHAPTER 41

I was expecting him to fire questions at me. I didn't expect him to grab my hand and lead me out of the family room. Out the back door and into the woods.

The fear of being back here usually paralyzed me, each step becoming harder than the last. But with my hand in his, it was easy to breathe. He had taken a weight off my shoulders. And it didn't feel like anything could put it back.

My feet crunched through the fall leaves. I actually enjoyed it. I was almost sad to leave the cover of the trees when we reached his backyard. And I had the strangest realization that I would follow this man to the end of the earth.

I followed him into this house and held my breath as he pulled out a key and opened up his basement door. "After you," he said and gestured for me to enter.

I felt like a child in a candy shop. I practically ran down the stairs. His basement wasn't that dissimilar from mine. But instead of files lining the walls, there were zigzags of yarn between newspaper clippings and pictures.

"This is everything I have," Ben said.

I stared at the image of myself. My eyes were closed. It was taken from far enough away that my shoulder was showing. My sweater had been pushed down, revealing the bruising on my shoulder. I yanked the picture off the board and turned to Ben.

"When did you take this?" I asked as I stared at the image. It was strange, seeing myself so peaceful. I never felt calm when I was awake. Did I really dream at night? I could only remember nightmares.

"When you slept over."

Maybe I was peaceful now because of Ben. I stood on my tiptoes and placed a kiss against his lips. "Thank you, Ben. For reminding me what it feels like to live again."

His hand was soft on my lower back as he pulled me closer. "The feeling is mutual. And in a few days, when all of this is over, we can finally be together."

"I already belong to you, Ben."

He frowned as he pushed a strand of hair out of my face. "You don't belong to me. You don't belong to anyone. You're your own person with your own dreams."

But I did belong to him. He had what was left of my heart. My soul. My everything.

"So you haven't been looking at deer in the woods this whole time?"

"No, I've been a little preoccupied watching you."

A lot of people would have felt uneasy by his words. But I loved that he was watching. And I'm pretty sure I was falling in love with him.

***

"I wish I knew more. But he barely talks to me." I watched Ben as he tried another lock combination. We had been down here for hours with no luck.

"Anything you can think of?" He tried another code. "Anything that he might use as a code?"

"I already tried everything."

"Then just tell me about him. About your relationship. Anything."

"Please don't make me do that, Ben."

Ben looked up at me. "It might help us get in. We're running out of time."

I sat down next to him. "Can I ask you another question instead?"

He didn't say anything. He just tried another code.

"Why do people call him The Doctor?" It had been driving me crazy.

"The rumors are that he's a psychologist." He cursed under his breath as he tried another wrong code.

"Ben, he's been manipulating me ever since we got married. He's been piling evidence of my insanity so that no one would ever believe my word." I gestured to the boxes of files. "He paints me as a lunatic really well. But he's no psychologist."

"They're just rumors. We think that he targets people in online forums. Individuals who search the internet as a last resort for drugs. Most of the victims have been in and out of therapy."

Like me.

"He prescribes them drugs to get their address. It's pretty easy for him from there."

"Who would accept drugs from some fake doctor online?"

"People who are desperate for a cure. People who would do anything for help. Not everyone has access to the care they need. You'd be surprised at how many black markets there are for prescription drugs."

Hearing that made my chest hurt. Here I was, throwing pills down my garbage disposal, when there were people out there that desperately needed them. "But you didn't say that the victims are sick or dying. So they wouldn't necessarily have high life insurance policies. Your theory doesn't make any sense."

He stopped fiddling with the safe. "Perhaps."

"I was always suspicious of what he did for work. Every now and then he comes home with a scratch on his neck or a speck of blood on his collar. All easily explained away. But he didn't hesitate to tell me the truth when I asked. He was proud of himself. I'm very aware that my husband is a monster. But he doesn't do *that*."

"So what do you think he does?"

"I don't think it. I *know* it. He works for some thug. He's sent to collect debts. He kills people who owe his boss money and collects their life insurance as a last resort to settle the debt. My husband is the muscle, not the brain."

"And I'm hoping you're wrong. Because that means it's bigger than him. I just want this to all be over. If he has a boss, another insurance collector will be hired. The murders won't stop."

"You'll still have caught a serial killer."

"It's not a serial killer if he's being paid to kill. That's just a hit man." Ben focused on the safe again.

"I'd still call that a win."

"I didn't say it wouldn't be. No matter what, your husband deserves to go to prison. He deserves it just for putting his hands on you." He sighed. "Maybe we should take a break." He put his hand on top of one of the moving boxes as he stood up. "You're sure we shouldn't look at the files? Maybe..."

"Ben, they're all lies. They're transcripts of my therapy sessions. Summaries of my apparent insanity. They have nothing to do with this." I pointed to the safe. "Can't we just melt it with the blow torch I got?"

Ben shook his head. "No, this is top of the line. It's virtually indestructible."

It was built to contain the darkness. I stared at it longingly. How badly I wanted to get inside. How badly I wanted my husband to pay for every crime he had ever committed. *The Doctor.* What a load of crap. He was nothing more than a weak man who pushed me around to feel better about himself. The name glorified him. Didn't the media see that? He probably got off on it. He probably loved it.

But he certainly liked pushing drugs on me. It was the only thing that aligned with Ben's theory. At the same time, though, he needed Dr. Nash to force me to take the drugs. He couldn't prescribe them.

"He's not a doctor," I said. "So how can he even prescribe medication?" *Got you, Ben.*

"The black market I mentioned. It would be easy for someone like him to get drugs." He was eyeing the moving boxes longingly.

Someone with money. Again, the thought made my chest hurt. "So why did he make me go to a legitimate psychologist? Why wouldn't he just give me some of his illegal drugs?"

"You're right." He grabbed both sides of my face. "You brilliant woman. Maybe they're working together. What did you say your psychologist's name was?" He let go of my face and pulled out his phone. He was already typing something into it.

"Dr. Nash."

"I'm going to go pay her a visit. I'll be back later."

"Can't I come with you?"

"Keep trying combinations. It's better if I question her alone." He was already making his way up the basement stairs.

"Ben, you can't believe a word she says. She's a liar. She just listens to everything my husband says and never…" I stopped mid-sentence. "Oh my God. What if she's been in bed with him this whole time?"

"Addy, I think you may have just cracked this case wide open."

The smile on his face was contagious. I turned back to the safe. Now if I could just figure out the code. Everything was falling perfectly into place. I typed in the first thing that crossed my head. NASH.

The safe clicked open.

CHAPTER 42

That bitch is sleeping with my husband. I didn't even understand my reaction. Why did I care what he did with his free time? I'd rather her be under him than me. It was just this sickening gut feeling. I immediately dismissed the thought. It didn't matter if she was sleeping with him. All that mattered was they were clearly working together. He had made the code her freaking name.

All those years of appointments. It was right in front of me the whole time. She never listened to me. It was just some sick game my husband was playing. Controlling my mind. *Not anymore.*

I stared at the safe. Now that it was opened, I was almost scared to look at it. What if there was a dead body? Or tons of evidence and I accidentally touched everything? I could ruin the whole case. *Maybe I should wait for Ben.*

But my hand had a mind of its own. My fingers wrapped around the metal door. I held my breath as it squeaked open.

The whole thing was blindingly white, like it had recently been scrubbed with bleach. It almost sparkled. Blindingly white. And alarmingly empty. *No.* Of course he had scrubbed it clean when he was down here for hours the other night. He had hidden the evidence. *No!* I slammed the side of the safe and something slid out of it onto my feet.

A white envelope. I hadn't seen it against the whiteness of the safe. My hands shook as I lifted it. There was nothing on the envelope. No address or name. I turned it over in my hands. It felt heavy even though it was thin. Like it held every piece of evidence imaginable. I had waited my whole life for this moment. I tore it open and pulled out a letter.

Adeline,

If you're reading this, there isn't much time left. You stopped taking your medication. Why? Why do you constantly insist on torturing yourself? Why do you never listen to me?

I'd advise you to go back on your meds, but we both know you won't. Your mind is already made up. You're feeling better, I know. I wish it was permanent. I wish you could find peace. But Adeline, that is never going to happen. I'm sorry, but it's not. And honestly, you don't deserve it.

If you figured out who I am, it's only a matter of days now until you know the truth. It comes back in a wave. An intoxicating rush. Don't fight it. There's no point. It's easier if you embrace it. Not all problems are meant to be solved. Not all issues can be fixed.

All I can do now is delay the inevitable. I hid what you're looking for. I promise it'll all make sense soon. Enjoy your last few days of sanity. It goes away in the blink of an eye. And the worst is yet to come.

XOXO,

-Dr. Nash

Well, the joke was on her, because I literally had no idea what any of that meant. All I knew was that Dr. Nash was trying to ruin my life. Just like my husband was. I wanted to scream.

The safe was supposed to have the answers. Instead I was left with riddles from a psychopath. And I was never going back on my medicine. If this letter was here to convince me I was crazy, she had done a terrible job. It just made me think she was crazy.

I started pacing back and forth in the room as I reread the letter. *Running out of time.* She was the one that was out of time. And the joke was on her. I was finally finding peace. In Ben. She could keep my husband. I had found someone so much better. Someone who treated me right. Someone that was going to help me escape all of this.

I slammed the safe closed. The next time I saw Dr. Nash she'd be behind bars. Maybe I'd visit her and tell her she was the insane one. Maybe I'd visit her every day and reinforce that fact. I'd ruin her life like she tried to ruin mine.

The words echoed around in my head. *I hid what you're looking for.* That was the only thing in the letter that mattered. She had hidden the evidence that my husband was a killer. And I was going to find it. I went up the stairs. I just needed to think about where she'd put it. If her and my husband were working together, maybe they hid it together.

I pinched the bridge of my nose. Where would the two of them hide something? I was always here. They wouldn't have hidden it in the house. I looked out the back window at the woods. But my husband didn't know I was scared of the woods. I turned back to the kitchen. *Where?* I looked back down at the letter. *Where, you crazy bitch?*

No. I looked up from the letter and back out the window. My husband didn't know I was scared of the woods. But Dr. Nash did. I told her about the time I went running. How I had gotten lost and screamed for help.

No one had been able to hear my cries. I had wandered around for hours until I found my way back. *She buried the evidence in the woods.*

It was rational to wait for Ben. But I was so close. I was so close that I could taste victory. I opened up the back door and walked down the steps. It would be easy. They wouldn't have wandered far.

This time the crunch of the leaves made me cringe. Without Ben's hand, I wasn't calm. If anything, I was frantic. I turned around in a circle. There'd be a freshly dug patch of dirt if they had hidden it recently.

I walked a little farther into the woods and turned in another circle. I'd find it. I had to.

CHAPTER 43

I had just walked past that tree. Hadn't I? I wasn't sure how long I had been looking, but I didn't know where I was. The sun was starting to set and the trees seemed to be closing in on me. Each time I turned around, the woods felt smaller.

Focus. There wasn't much light left. I needed to find it. A mound of dirt caught my attention. I dropped to my knees and started digging. I was about to give up when I was elbow deep in soil, but then my fingers brushed against something hard.

I pushed the dirt away to reveal a box. Just a regular shoe box. But I instantly recognized it. *My box.* The box full of pictures of my abuse. Enough evidence to put my husband in jail even if we couldn't put him in for life. I opened up the lid, expecting to see the stack of photos. I wasn't expecting an unaddressed envelope on top of it.

I remembered what Dr. Nash had said. That she had been to my house. That she had looked for the box. I didn't remember her coming. What if it was because she *did* come and *did* find the box and then made me forget? What if she gave me the perfect cocktail of prescription drugs to mess with my mind? Because that bitch had clearly found my box. And decided to hide it from me. And made me feel insane for not remembering.

I took a deep breath. I had a feeling this would be filled with more riddles. But maybe it held the truth. She had said she'd hid what I was looking for. And I was looking for answers. I tore open the envelope to find another letter.

Adeline,

You didn't deserve it. No one deserves it. But that doesn't excuse what you did. We both know that. What you don't realize is that this isn't what you're truly looking for. Not even close.

The only thing these photos do is prove that you're guilty. Yes. You. I know you don't believe me. You're probably tempted to show the photos to the police. But it is my professional recommendation that you wait a couple of days to make that decision. Because if you found this box, you have less than 48 hours until you know the truth.

You've held onto your secrets this long. What's one more day? And if you don't believe me, the proof is in the images.
XOXO,
-Dr. Nash

Professional recommendation my ass. I looked down at the first picture. It was an image of myself staring back at me. With a black eye. The proof was in the images. The proof that my husband was monster. I turned it over. My handwriting was scrawled on the bottom, dating the image. It was from nine and a half years ago. The very first picture I had taken of the abuse. When I still thought there was hope of escaping him.

My phone buzzed in my pocket. I pulled it out and answered Ben's call. "Ben! I just…"

"There's nothing here," he said.

My exciting news died in my throat. "What do you mean nothing's there?"

"I mean the office is vacant. There isn't any record of her ever being here. Her office isn't even listed on the directory in the entrance."

"I was just there last week. Office 215. It's on the second floor. Right next to a podiatrist. God, what's his name?"

"William Antony?" Ben asked.

"Yes, that's it! Dr. Antony. He's this small balding man."

"Yeah, I talked to him. And the owners of several other neighboring offices as well. They all said that office 215 has been vacant for years."

"Talk to Dr. Antony again. He'll be able to tell you where it is. You must just be walking past it."

"It's not an issuing of finding 215! I'm literally standing outside of it."

I swallowed down the lump in my throat. The box had started shaking in my hands. I didn't like when people yelled at me. Angry tears welled in my eyes. "Don't talk to me like that." I was surprised by the venom in my voice.

"I'm sorry, Addy." His voice was soft. "I didn't mean to yell. I'm just frustrated. And I am standing outside of office 215. There's a vacancy sign hanging in the window. I can see in. There's nothing there. I don't know what to tell you, Addy. It's just not here."

"And I'm telling you that's not possible." *He's losing faith in me.* I was holding a letter from Dr. Nash in my hands. It's not like I made her up. I had been forced to see her for years. *Dreaded* it for years. And now the psychopath was following me and my husband to Florida. *Florida!*

"Ben, my husband convinced her to move with us. She probably already packed everything up. Maybe she's already in Florida. That would explain everything."

"The neighbors would have remembered her being here then."

"Not if they were paid to stay quiet. They *must* have paid them. They're covering their tracks."

"Addy, it didn't seem like they were lying."

"Of course they were lying! Don't you believe me?" My voice cracked. Maybe there was some other clue in the box. Another letter or something. I sorted through the images. *Anything. Please.*

"I do believe you, Addy. But I...I believed them too. We're missing something. I don't know what's going on, but we're going to figure it out. I'm on my way home now. We can talk about it when I get there."

"I'm not at home. I'm in the woods."

"What the hell are you doing in the woods?"

Dr. Nash warned me not to tell. What if she was right? What if her advice was finally worth taking? Ben clearly didn't believe me. Would he believe these notes? Believe the evidence? My fingers stopped and I lifted up one of the images.

It was growing dark, but I could still clearly see that it wasn't a picture of me. It was an image of a young woman, probably in her early 20's. She had bruising around her neck like someone had tried to strangle her.

"Addy, where are you?"

Darkness had surrounded me. "I don't know, Ben." I stared at the image. She looked so familiar.

"Stay right where you are. I'll come find you. Did you go straight into the woods from your backyard?"

I was transfixed by the picture. "I don't know." Maybe it was her eyes. They held the same pain as mine.

"Addy, it's a simple question."

No, it was more than just her eyes. I *knew* her. But I had no idea how.

"Addy?"

"Ben, I don't know." My vision was starting to blur. I closed the lid of the box and stared at the darkness around me. I had told Ben about my past. I had told him everything. So why was I scared to tell him about this? Why was Dr. Nash's warning stuck in my head?

The proof is in the images.

I felt like I was going to be sick. What proof? That my husband abused other women? A serial killer with a side hobby of assault? *Vile. Disgusting. Horrible man.* He was already abusing me. I didn't need other proof. So why did I have these images? Why were they in my box? And why did she look so damn familiar?

"I'm coming, Addy." Ben sounded out of breath like he had been running for a while already. "Stay where you are. I'll find you."

He was running toward me. I could hear the crunching of leaves. So I did the first thing I could think of. I put the box back in the hole and shoved the dirt back on top. And then I started running in the opposite direction of the crunching leaves.

CHAPTER 44

I peeled off my muddy clothes and put them in the waste bin. My ankle throbbed. I wasn't sure how I had evaded Ben.

I stepped into the hot shower. My mind was always clearest when I ran and when I showered. And I kept coming back to one conclusion. My husband and Dr. Nash were framing me. My fingerprints were on the box. On the safe. And they were both conveniently not here. The only two questions were what were they framing me for exactly. And why.

My husband didn't need to frame me for anything. He had convinced me to kill my father. And he made the state think I was insane. It was his word against mine. Any competent jury would convict me. So what else were they planning?

I closed my eyes and let the water hit my face. The water burned the cuts and scrapes on my face from rushing through the trees. And all I could hear were the autumn leaves beneath my feet. I was going in circles. I wiped the water from my eyes and opened them.

It was like I was stuck in the woods. Why couldn't I focus? *Think, Adeline. Think!*

I started to scrub off the mud that was caked onto my skin. The FBI was closing in on my husband. He needed a scapegoat to get them off his trail. And who better than his loony wife? He was going to make me pay for his crimes.

I realized my skin was growing red from all the scrubbing. I stepped back under the water to rinse off and heard the crunching of leaves again. *Stop.* I switched off the shower and wrapped a towel around my body.

My husband was trying to frame me. I nodded to myself. But I wasn't going to let that happen. I just needed to figure out if Ben would believe me. If I could trust him, then I could show him the letter from the safe. I could show him the box in the woods.

I eyed my jeans in the trash. The letter from Dr. Nash was nestled in the back pocket. Instead of lifting it out, I opened the bathroom door.

My ankle hurt. And I was exhausted. I changed into a pair of pajamas as I looked down at my phone. I had silenced it when I was running home. There were several missed calls from Ben.

He was worried, but I couldn't see him right now. My mind was a jumbled mess. He'd want to know why I was in the woods. And I didn't know what to tell him. He had doubts. I could hear it in his voice over the phone. He was doubting my story.

I pinched the bridge of my nose as I sat down on my bed. I was doubting my story too. *Stop.* Dr. Nash was in my head. A woman that had vanished without a trace was trying to ruin my life.

I needed sleep. I needed time to process the notes. And that girl's face. I could still see the fear in her eyes. I popped some of the Advil off my nightstand and pulled the comforter up to my chin.

All I could see were the woods when I closed my eyes. And I wished that the Advil were still sleeping pills.

***

I woke up to the smell of bacon. *Bacon?* I sat up and rubbed my eyes. Someone was cooking downstairs. *My husband's home early.* He wasn't supposed to be back until tomorrow night! *Shit!* I quickly got up and dressed. He'd see the Home Alone items on the coffee table. And the movie was under recently watched on the TV. He'd know what I was planning.

Had he seen my clothes in the bathroom trash? Did he know I had gotten into the safe? My heart was racing as I went into the bathroom. The note was still in the back pocket, but it didn't mean he hadn't seen it. I folded it in half, tucked it in my jeans' pocket, and made my way down the stairs. *Please be in a good mood.*

I turned the corner to see Ben at the stove flipping pancakes. The sight of him instantly made my heartbeat return to normal. I sighed with relief. But then he turned to me. His face had cuts and scrapes, just like mine. I had run away from him in the woods. I had run away and all he had been trying to do was help.

And all I wanted to do was inspect every inch of him to make sure he was okay. I cared about the man in front of me. And I knew in that moment that I could trust him.

"I'm sorry, Ben. I'm so sorry."

"You ran from me. Why did you run from me?" He turned off the burner.

"I panicked."

He carried two plates over to the table.

"You didn't believe me on the phone," I continued when he didn't say anything. "You yelled at me."

He abandoned the plates and walked over to me in the doorway. "I'm sorry that I raised my voice. But, Addy...your stories aren't lining up. I'm frustrated because I can't solve this case if you're lying to me."

"I'm not lying, Ben. She's real. She *is*. I was just there the other day." I fished the note out of my pocket and handed it to him. "She wrote this. It was what was in the safe. She's real." I never thought I'd need to convince him of this. But the note proved she was real. "The code to the safe was Nash. It all revolves around her."

He stared at me and then lifted the note out of my hands.

I wished I had gotten the box and the other note. It would be hard to find again. But I could try to retrace my steps from last night. Ben would know what to do. I watched him reading the letter. Figuring stuff out like this was his job. He'd clear all this up in a flash.

Ben shook his head and looked back up to me. "This is a bunch of nonsense. There's nothing coherent in this note. It's just riddles."

"I know. She's trying to mess with my head. Don't you see? And I know she just moved. My husband told me she did. She's in Florida. We can find her."

"Addy, I didn't just talk to the owners of the neighboring practices. I talked to receptionists and even patients. There's no way they were all paid off. So I started digging..."

"Of course they were paid off. It's the only thing that makes sense!"

"Addy, I need you to sit down for a moment, alright?"

"Why?" I could feel a headache coming on. "She's real, Ben." I couldn't make myself sit down. "She's real."

"I'm not saying that Dr. Nash wasn't real."

I heard the past tense and my body felt like it was shutting down. I somehow managed to sit down before I fell to the ground.

"I'm saying that she hasn't been alive for over 4 years. And she was never located here. She was from New York City. Whoever you've been going to see was posing as her. Your husband must have hired someone to play a role."

"There are probably a lot of Dr. Nash's. Maybe you just found the wrong one."

"No. She had the same letterhead as the Dr. Nash in your files." He opened up a box on the floor. It was one of the ones from the basement.

"I asked you not to look through those, Ben." It felt like my throat was constricting. How was I supposed to trust him when he did the opposite of what I asked him to?

"These files are dated from when she started her practice, up until today," he said, ignoring me. "The files before her death have an address in New York City." He opened one up and showed it to me. "The files after her death have an address here." He showed me one of those too. "You don't appear in any of the files when she was actually alive. Only once she passed away. Addy, your basement is filled with files from a dead psychologist. Which is odd, because her offices burned down. She died in that fire too. So why do you think you have files that had apparently burned in the fire that killed her?"

"I have no idea." I lifted one up. Betty Ann Tompkins was written at the top. "They're not all about me?" I looked up at him.

"No." He sat down across from me. "And the ones about you aren't real."

I had an unsettling feeling in my stomach. "Ben, I don't know. I was definitely seeing someone. They prescribed me drugs..."

"I believe you. But you weren't seeing Dr. Nash. And there's a link here. Clearly your husband killed Dr. Nash. And what if some of his targets are people in these files? There's too many for me to sort through, but I'm having some people pick them up to analyze. This could be the missing link."

"Ben, I don't think that's a good idea. If my husband sees that they're missing..."

"This could be what puts him away. He won't even get a chance to see that they're gone. We'll arrest him before he even steps foot back in this house."

"You really think there's a link?"

"Why kill Dr. Nash and steal the files if there isn't? He's called The Doctor because we thought he was posing as a psychologist. He's been using *her* name. And he could have been finding his targets with those files. They're all mentally ill just like the victims and they..."

"You're not necessarily mentally ill for going to a psychologist, Ben. Some people just need someone to talk to. Others are abused." I could feel tears welling in my eyes.

He sat down next to me and grabbed my face in his hand. "I know, Addy. I'm sorry." He wiped away my tears with his thumbs.

"For years I wished I had someone to talk to. Someone that was on my side."

"I know." He placed a soft kiss on my forehead. "Now you have me."

God it felt good to have his hands on me. I felt calmer as soon as his skin touched mine. "But you're right. Some of them probably are mentally ill."

He nodded. "I think we've got him, Addy."

A knock on the door made me jump.

"It's alright. It's just forensics for the boxes."

I watched silently as men took box after box out of my home. As each box was removed, the unsettling feeling in my stomach got stronger. When the door finally closed, I had eaten far too many pancakes. Since when have I eaten my feelings? I pushed the plate away. The meds must have messed with my appetite. Maybe I was just making up for years of missed meals.

"What about those?" I asked. There were a few more boxes from the basement that they hadn't taken.

"Those are the ones about you. They aren't real so they don't need them."

"What about fingerprints or something? They could find out who the imposter Dr. Nash is that I've been seeing."

"I have a feeling her fingerprints will be on the old files as well. I can run a few tests of my own, but it's better that those files stay here. We don't want to give anyone more of a reason to believe your false insanity title."

And I thought I couldn't trust him? He was helping me bury evidence against myself. "Maybe we should burn it."

He gave me a weird look.

"I have a bunch of kerosene and a blow torch."

"Addy, you need a permit to set a fire outdoors."

"Oh. I have a shredder too." I had been planning on destroying all the files. Thank God I hadn't.

"Let's wait to see what forensics comes back with first. Then I'll know if I need to look for fingerprints."

"So that's it? We just…wait?"

"I'm sure they'll find a pattern. We just have to give it some time."

Time. I felt like a clock was ticking down in my head. I still felt like I was running out of time.

CHAPTER 45

It was easy to forget when I was with Ben. Curled up into his side, I felt so calm and happy. I took another sip of wine. "It's not your turn. It's mine."

"You're taking too long to ask a question."

"Fine." I looked up at him. "Where do you want to be five years from now?"

He laughed. "You're going to steal my question without even answering it first?"

"It wasn't your turn and it's a good question." Besides, I wanted to know. I could picture us together five years from now. Could he?

"I want to be married with a few kids."

"Hmm." That's what I wanted too.

"Hmm? All you have to say is hmm?" His thumb traced circles on my hipbone.

"Well now that I know that you're actually 32, it's not very alarming that you want to settle down soon."

"No, it's not."

"So do you see someone in particular filling the role of wife in your mind?"

"It's not your turn anymore."

"But your answer was hardly groundbreaking. Everyone says they want to be married with kids eventually."

"Well, what about you, Addy? I sat in that appointment with you when you said you were positive you didn't want children for at least three more years. Is that really the case?" His thumb never stopped tracing circles on my hip.

"I don't want kids with *him*. I couldn't handle losing another child. I barely kept going the first time. And actually having one with him would be worse. What if he hurt our baby too? What kind of mother would I be if I couldn't protect my own child?"

"I don't mean with him. He'll be in prison soon and you'll be divorced."

"Is that so?"

Ben nodded. "It's as good as done."

"So who would I be having children with in this very plausible but still hypothetical situation?"

"Someone who cares for you. Someone who would never hurt you or your child." He tucked a loose strand of hair behind my ear.

"And who might that be?"

"It's not your turn for a question."

"I hate 21 questions. It was like this game was designed to torture me."

He laughed. "Would you be open to the idea of having children with someone else?" He had reworded his question from earlier so that I'd give him the answer he wanted.

"Yes, I still want children. Are you implying that you want to knock me up?"

"I'm breaking the law for you, woman. My intentions are certainly clear."

I started to laugh, but it died away when I looked at his face. He looked genuinely serious. I wanted to tell him how I felt. I needed him to know that I was falling for him. That I could see the same future he could. *He broke your trust by going through those files.* I grabbed my glass of wine and took another sip. The files didn't matter. It was good that he went through them. They were going to help.

I pulled away from him, his hand falling from my hip. I needed space for a moment. It was hard to think straight around him. I took another sip of wine. Or maybe the alcohol was making my brain fuzzy.

He looked concerned. I knew he cared about me. If he didn't, he wouldn't be sitting here right now. He opened his mouth, but I started talking before he had a chance to say anything.

"Ben, I have a hard time trusting people. Every time I open myself up, I'm crushed. My mother was very honest about not wanting me. My husband..." my voice trailed off and I looked down at my lap. "How am I supposed to believe you really care about me when I don't know what it feels like to be cared about?"

"I believe you do know. It feels like this, Addy." He placed his hand on my shin. His touch instantly soothed me.

I looked back up at him. "You mean that warm fuzzy feeling I get when I'm around you? Like nothing in the world seems bad anymore?"

"Oh, no. Not that."

"No?"

"No, Addy. I believe that warm fuzzy feeling is more than caring. I believe that's love."

Love? My husband always said he loved me. And I mindlessly said it back. I wasn't sure I had ever loved anyone. Even when I married my husband, it was to take care of my ill mother. And I certainly didn't love my mother. I took care of her out of obligation, nothing more.

"You think I love you?" I asked. "I barely know you, Ben."

"I think that maybe you have a hard time trusting, and caring, and loving. You've been through a lot. But I don't think it means you're incapable of those things. I understand if it takes you longer to feel the same way that I feel about you. You're lucky that I'm a patient man."

"You love me?"

"I've already let you ask a few questions in a row. Do you see yourself staying here? I primarily work in D.C. so it is a bit of a commute. But it's not impossible."

I just stared at him. It was like he knew exactly what he wanted. All I had wanted for the past decade was to get away from my husband. It's the only thing I dreamed of. Well, that wasn't entirely true. Ever since I had first seen Ben mowing lawns, I had dreamed of him. It seemed like all my wildest dreams were about to come true. "I wouldn't mind a change of scenery."

"Good to know. And in answer to your earlier question…I love my job. I wouldn't risk it for a simple crush. I think you're amazing. And beautiful. And intoxicating. And yes, I could see myself five years from now with you by my side. With little kids with blonde hair."

I smiled. He knew my darkest secrets. He knew every part of the evilness that had seeped into my soul.

"I'm falling in love with you, Addy." He didn't ask me the question back.

But he didn't need to. "I'm terrified that I've already fallen," I said.

He leaned forward and cupped the side of my face in his hand, drawing my lips closer to his. "I will never hurt you. Never."

I believed him. I did. But an unsettling thought crossed my mind. For some reason, I was more concerned that I might hurt him.

His lips brushed against mine.

I pushed aside the thought and let myself get lost in his kiss. Lost in him. And for the first time in my life, I did feel loved. Whole. Safe. And happy.

CHAPTER 46

I re-taped the box from Amazon and pushed it into the corner of the family room with the rest of the moving boxes. That was the last of it. I had organized everything into two groups. Things that were my husband's that I didn't want, and the items that were mine that I did want.

I stared at the boxes filled with files. Ben hadn't heard back from the forensic team yet. The files could still be important. I shoved them into the "keep" pile. It wasn't much. I had really only wanted my clothes and a few other knickknacks. I would be starting a new life tomorrow. I didn't want to be weighed down by anything from my past. Besides, my husband was extremely wealthy. And I was about to get half of everything in the divorce. *Or will I get everything in the divorce since my husband's a serial killer?*

The doorbell rang. For the first time, I was excited to answer it. This would be the last time I ever had to see the gawkers. And there were only a few more hours before cops would swarm my house and arrest my husband. I couldn't wipe the grin off my face.

"Hey, girls," I said as I opened up the door.

Charlotte's eyes wandered over me. She had a look of utter disapproval on her face. "Were you not expecting us, hon? I thought I said 3."

"What? I was expecting you." I stepped to the side, welcoming them in.

"Oh." She laughed awkwardly. "Pretend I didn't say anything. We brought wine and snacks." She, Rosie, and Phoenix each walked in carrying a bottle of wine and covered dishes.

"You look fine," Rosie said. "Ignore her. The last time I packed, it was 90 degrees out and our air conditioner was broken. I was a complete mess. You, on the other hand, look super cute."

I looked down at my outfit. I was dressed in a pair of yoga pants and a tank top. Was that why Charlotte had said that? She thought I was inappropriately dressed? *Give me a break.* I pulled my hair out of its messy bun as they stared at me. *Screw you, gawkers.* I walked towards the kitchen and ran my fingers through my hair. "I left a few glasses out. They're pretty much the only things I haven't packed."

"I can't believe we've never been here," Phoenix said as she eyed the boxes in the kitchen. "You're moving and we never really even got to know you."

And whose fault is that? She didn't blame Phoenix and Rosie, though. If anything, they had been the nicest to her in the whole neighborhood. It was Charlotte who was the ringleader of evil looks and snarky comments. She had probably told them not to hang out with me. "It's okay, I know you were all probably super busy." I eyed the bottles they placed on the table. "Crap, I packed up the corkscrew. One second, I know it's in one of these boxes." I turned toward one of my husband's piles.

"It's okay, I came prepared." Phoenix reached into her designer purse and pulled out a bottle opener.

Charlotte shot her a disapproving glance and grabbed it from her. "Ladies, I say we make a toast." She opened up the bottle and started pouring the wine. "To new beginnings." She raised her glass.

"Hear, hear!" *Far away from you.* I clinked my glass to hers, downed the whole thing, and put it back on the table a little harder than I meant to. I was lucky it didn't crack. They all stared at me. It had only taken me 5 seconds with Charlotte to realize that I needed to be more than tipsy to get through the next couple of hours with her. They'd have to deal. I poured myself some more.

Charlotte cleared her throat and sat down at the table. "I still can't believe we never even met your husband."

Of course they wouldn't remember seeing him at the neighborhood picnics. He always promised that he'd come. But then he'd only stay for a few minutes before leaving for an important business call. It was always the same lame excuse. "He travels a lot for work. He's incredibly busy." I sat down across from her. It felt like I was about to partake in the ultimate showdown. Snooty gawker versus tortured housewife. This was a game I could win.

"What does he do for work?" she asked.

He's a serial killer. "He's an insurance collector of sorts."

"That sounds interesting," Rosie said. "What exactly does that entail?"

Murder. "Honestly, I'm not really sure," I said with a laugh. "What do your husbands do?"

"I'm actually very involved in my husband's business," Charlotte said. "We're in real estate together. I handle staging the houses before showings. He always says I drive all the sales. God, I can't imagine just sitting around all day doing nothing. How boring would that be?"

For just a second I wished I had booby-trapped the house. For *her.* She knew I didn't work. I took another huge gulp of wine and pulled the aluminum foil off the closest dish. It was covered in chocolate chip cookies. "Oh, yum. These look great." I stuffed one in my mouth.

"I made them from scratch," Charlotte said.

I grabbed a napkin and spit it out. "I'm so sorry." I wiped the corners of my mouth. "There was a hair in it," I lied.

She gasped. "What?" She snatched the plate and stared down at the cookies. "I'm going to have to have a word with the bakery about that." As soon as the words slipped out of her mouth she laughed awkwardly. "I mean I..." her voice trailed off. She sighed. "I ran out of time today. There was a showing this morning that took longer than expected."

"That's okay," Phoenix said. "I just dumped a pile of Chex mix in a bowl."

"I was too busy to cook anything too. Pretending to be a perfect housewife is exhausting." Rosie laughed and revealed her dish. "I added some sour cream on top to make it look homemade. But I bought the dip from the grocery store."

"You know, I have some mint chocolate chip ice cream in the fridge," I said. "Does anyone want some?"

"That sounds amazing," Rosie and Phoenix said at the same time.

"Is it dairy free?" Charlotte asked. "I don't eat dairy products. I can't believe how they treat the poor cows."

"No. It's the good stuff." I rummaged through a few boxes and pulled out spoons and bowls. Charlotte glared at us as we stuffed ice cream in our faces. I honestly liked these girls, Charlotte excluded. We could have been friends. If my life had been different, maybe we would have been.

I felt so normal. For an hour, my problems evaporated. I laughed more than I had in years.

My phone ringing pulled me away from the conversation. It was Ben. We had only been apart for a few hours, but I missed him. I quickly answered his call.

“Hi!” I said. “What’s up, I’m a little busy hanging out with my girls.”

Rosie raised her glass to me and took another sip.

“Are you drunk?” he asked.

“No.” I laughed. “Maybe a little.”

"Do you want the good news or the bad news first?"

"Good news."

"Okay. So you know how the serial killer had been targeting men? And then the wives were going missing?"

"Yeah. My husband was probably selling the women into prostitution." *As if he could be any more of a monster.*

All three women looked up at me with shocked expressions.

I held my hand over the receiver as I shrugged and mouthed, "Telemarketer." That just made them even more shocked. I walked out of the kitchen to continue the conversation in private.

"Maybe," said Ben. "But that's not the important part. What's important is that we finally found a concrete link between all the murders. Up until now, we'd been looking at what the men had in common, since they were the primary victims. But when we went through your husband’s files, we realized that all the men's wives, the ones disappearing, were all patients of Dr. Nash."

For some reason I felt a tightening in my chest. I was Dr. Nash's patient too. I felt camaraderie with those women. No, I hadn’t disappeared. But it felt like a piece of my soul had disappeared the first time my husband ever put his hands on me.

“Yeah. It’s bigger than we originally thought. We think he might have killed the women too. But now that you bring up the prostitution thing, I guess that's a possibility. We haven't been able to find the women's bodies. That might be why. I'll run it by some of our human trafficking guys. Either way, this link combined with all your statements should be enough to prevent your husband from getting bail while we piece the rest together."

"What about the prints on the files?" I asked. "Isn't that the final bit of evidence that we need?"

Ben cleared his throat. "That's the bad news. His prints weren't on the files. Not a single one."

"Of course they were. He made the files. Have forensics look again."

"We already double checked," said Ben. "Honestly, the lack of prints make your husband look even more guilty. It's super weird. I mean, the files were in his house. He would have had to have been extremely careful to never get his prints on them."

"Right. I hadn't thought about that. What about Dr. Nash? Were her fingerprints on them?"

"No, but I didn't expect them to be. You said you thought you lost the original files when your last home burnt down two years ago. These were just copies. Dr. Nash has been dead for four years, so her fingerprints wouldn't have been on them. But, there is some good news here. There *was* one other set of prints besides yours. They belong to a Maria Gonzalez. We're still trying to locate her. She's originally from the Bronx, but her last known address is abandoned. Regardless, we think she must have been the woman impersonating Dr. Nash. The one that's been prescribing you medicine you don't need and helping your husband commit these murders."

"No, she's my..." The word got stuck in my throat. A word that made no sense at all. I immediately coughed. *No.* The side of my face twitched. *No.*

"Addy, do you know her?"

I thought about the box in the woods. The box that I had completely forgotten to tell Ben about. The picture of the other woman seemed to focus in my mind.

"Do you know her?" Ben repeated.

Maria Gonzales. I did know her. She was the woman in the picture. She was… I shook away the thought. My memory was playing tricks on me. "She's an old friend," I said. Lies had always come easier to me than the truth.

"You showed the files to her?"

"No…I…" my voice trailed off. "Yeah, that sounds right. I showed them to her."

"Do you know where she is now?"

"No, I haven't seen her ages."

"How long has it been? Has she been to your current house?"

I pinched the bridge of my nose. "Um…yes, I think she's been here. It must have been a year ago or so."

"Okay. Then she's not the one impersonating Dr. Nash. I'm going to stop by and pick up a few of the other files to run for fingerprints. Maybe we can still figure out who the imposter is. Or find somewhere your husband slipped up and left his prints."

I eyed the boxes of files in the corner. "Ben, I'll bring them to you, okay? Give me a few minutes to finish up here."

"I'll see you soon…"

I hung up the phone while he was still trying to talk to me. My whole body felt numb. My vision was turning red. The gawkers had gathered in the doorway and were gawking at me in true gawker fashion. *Stupid gawky gawkers.* "I have to get going," I said without even looking at them. "If you ladies don't mind letting yourselves out."

"Was that Ben Jones?" Charlotte asked. "You've been spending a lot of time with him."

"Well, that's because we're having an affair." Maybe that would make her leave.

Charlotte gasped.

"Now can you please leave?" My voice was calm, but my mind was zooming. I felt like I was going to faint. I needed to find the picture of Maria Gonzalez. I needed to make sure.

"What was that about fingerprints?" Rosie asked. "What's going on? If you and your husband are having issues, Phoenix and I know a great couples' therapist."

"You have to leave." My voice came out in a whisper this time. They blurred in front of me. I walked past them back into the kitchen and grabbed my glass of wine.

Phoenix cleared her throat. "If you want to talk about it..."

"Please just go." My memories were wrong. But the image was as clear as day. That picture was of Maria Gonzalez. I remembered something that didn't make any sense. I downed the rest of the wine and grabbed one of the other glasses off the table.

"You need to go!" I screamed when they didn't move. "Get out of my house." I threw the wine glass against the wall.

Charlotte dove to the floor and covered her head. "I knew you were crazy!" she yelled as she scrambled towards the hall.

"Me? I'm the crazy one?" I threw another glass. It shattered right behind Charlotte's feet. "You don't even know me! You never bothered to try!" I threw another glass.

All the women ran for the front door. They didn't know me. I placed my hand on the wall as I chased them out. The whole house was spinning. I didn't even know me. "You don't know what I've been through." I was choking on sobs. I heard the slam of the front door and my knees buckled beneath me.

The image of Maria Gonzalez was all I could see. But the memories were wrong. They had to be. The years of pills had messed with my head. I dug my fingers into my scalp. The pain in my skull was unbearable. I screamed at the top of my lungs. "You're messing with my head!" I yelled into the empty house. It was directed at my husband, but I knew he wasn't there.

I was all alone with the thoughts tumbling around in my head. Mashing together in illogical ways. I wasn't allowed to work. I wasn't even supposed to leave the house. So how could Maria Gonzalez have worked for me?

CHAPTER 47

The crunching of the leaves was driving me insane. Almost as much as the clock ticking down in my head.

Something had gone terribly wrong with my brain. Incomprehensible flashes of memories screeched through my mind. Nonsense. Complete and utter nonsense. Everything was garbled together and flipped upside-down, careening off the edge of reason.

I felt a raindrop land on my forehead. I looked up past the trees to the darkening sky. It felt like the storm clouds were fusing with my brain.

The proof is in the images.

Dr. Nash's words turned over and over in my head. What proof? They were just pictures. Pictures proved nothing. I knew that better than anyone else.

I didn't know where the box was. I had turned in so many circles the other day that I couldn't possibly find it. But my feet seemed to remember. Like they had walked this path hundreds of times.

I stared at the ground. No, my feet didn't remember. There was an actual worn path in the dirt. The leaves were matted down, and not just from the rain. Someone had definitely walked this same path through the woods over and over again. And recently. I turned around. If I squinted, I thought I could see my house in the distance. The path led directly to my backyard. How had I missed that the other day?

My husband must have been coming out here. That explained it. My vision blurred as I turned back to the path. *It's him.* It all went back to *him.*

But you knew Maria Gonzalez. I pinched the bridge of my nose, trying to erase the pain searing through my forehead.

I saw the mound of dirt to the side of the path up ahead. I ran as fast as I could and started digging.

I lifted off the lid and sifted through the pictures. Tons of them. Mostly of my injuries, but there were pictures of other women too. Gashes, bruises, pain in their eyes. They had all been terribly hurt. Their stories swirled around in my brain, colliding with everything else that made no sense. Had my husband killed these women? Had he told me about them?

No. He hadn't hurt them. I shook the thought away. How could I know that? He had hurt me. What would have stopped him from killing these women?

I found the image of Maria Gonzalez. I could hear her laughter. I could hear her sobs. It didn't feel like I had heard stories of her. It felt like I had known her. That maybe we'd been friends. But that wasn't possible.

The proof is in the images.

"What proof?!" My words echoed around me. I thought I heard a crunch of leaves and lifted my head. But there was nothing. Nothing except for the path that continued farther into the forest. It hadn't been leading to the box.

These pictures meant nothing to me. They were proof that my husband abused me. But the other women? I had no idea what he'd done to them. The fact that their names came easily to my lips was disconcerting. My husband had clearly told me what he had done to them. Told me their names. So why couldn't I remember? I could help save them if they were still alive. *Remember, Adeline.*

Berating myself wasn't helping. I slammed the lid of the box back on and tucked it under my arm. My husband had walked this path countless times. *Finding where it leads might give me answers.*

The box felt heavy in my arms, weighed down by secrets I didn't understand. My ankle throbbed with each step I took. I was exhausted and soaked when my feet reached the end of the path.

But it wasn't really an end. It just...stopped. Right in the middle of the woods. I turned around. I could no longer see my house or any houses from my neighborhood. There was nothing anywhere. Just a dead end.

I wanted to scream. I had been so scared of these stupid woods. If I had ventured out here sooner, maybe I would have found what I needed. Maybe my brain wouldn't hurt.

I kicked some leaves and heard the snapping of twigs. The ground was covered in leaves and sticks. But there was a pattern of sticks. Every few inches one stuck up out of the fall foliage. I dropped to my knees and pushed some of the leaves aside. A tiny cross made of twigs stuck out of the ground.

I pushed more leaves aside to reveal another cross. It felt like my heart was beating out of my chest. There were so many of them. It was a mini graveyard. The thought churned my stomach.

20 murders. Wasn't that what Ben had said? That the serial killer had murdered 20 people? I scanned the crosses. So why were there 27 crosses?

I thought about the women in the pictures. *Please don't have hurt them.* I dug into the dirt in front of one of the crosses, but there was nothing there. I tried another. And another. *Damn it!*

I knocked some of the crosses over into the dirt. I lifted up and threw a few of them as far as I could. I was about to scream when my phone started buzzing in my pocket.

I pulled it out, smearing mud across the screen. It was Ben. How long had I been out here? He wanted the files. But I needed more time. I needed answers. Talking to him would buy me that time.

"Hey, Ben," I said as calmly as I could muster.

"Addy, your husband will be home soon. Let me come grab the files real quick."

I looked down at my watch. I still had an hour until my husband arrived home. My eyes darted around the woods. I had to be missing something. I began to dig where the first cross had been.

"The girls and I are just finishing up. I'll be there in 30 minutes. "

"We don't have 30 minutes. We agreed that you wouldn't be home when he got there. We need to get you to a safe location."

I ran over to the last cross and started digging. My fingers hit something hard. *Jackpot.*

"It's the last time I've ever going to see them," I said. "I just need a few more minutes."

"You really must be drunk. You hate these women."

"Hate is such a strong word." I pulled out a box that was similar to the first and lifted off the lid.

"Come over now. I've already contacted the local authorities. They're bringing him in for questioning as soon as his car pulls in. You don't need to be there for this. It's over, Addy."

I picked up one of the many passports that were in the box. I opened it up and there was a sticky note with my name on it. What the hell? I lifted the sticky note. An image of me stared back at me. But it wasn't me. The woman's name was Jennifer Clarke. How was that possible? It looked just like me. Had someone doctored my passport?

"Addy?"

I grabbed another passport. The name on the sticky note didn't match the name inside the passport again. But the picture in this passport didn't resemble me. It looked like one of the women from my box of pictures. Again, it felt like I knew her. Like we'd used to be friends.

"Addy?"

I grabbed another passport. This sticky note said Juanita Howe. I lifted it off and stared at the passport image of Maria Gonzalez. "Does the name Juanita Howe mean anything to you?"

"No. Should it?"

"Ben, I think that my husband was giving the victims' wives and girlfriends new identities. I found this box..." I let my voice trail off.

The letters from Dr. Nash had warned me not to tell anyone. I suddenly felt dizzy. And the women had been hurt. I had pictures of them in pain. Why would my husband help them when all he had ever done was hurt me?

"A box of what?" Ben asked.

I knew I could trust him. I had already determined that. So why was I hesitating? The stories rolled around in my head. But they were just stories. Planted there by my husband. I never left the house. I didn't have any friends.

"A box of passports," I said. "And there's a sticky note with each one that doesn't match the name on the passport. Maria Gonzalez's passport is one of them. The name on the corresponding sticky note is Juanita Howe." I could hear him typing something on a computer.

"You think that Juanita Howe is her new identity?" he asked.

I looked around at the few remaining crosses. It was like a graveyard. Like old identities came to rest here. I thought back to the passport of Jennifer Clarke. *I think I'd remember being someone else.* But this wasn't about me. This was about helping these women. "Yes, I think it's definitely possible. You said all the women were missing. Maybe you can't find them because they changed their names." I opened and closed more passports, looking for any other names that seemed familiar. There was another letter at the bottom of the box, but I had no desire to open it. Dr. Nash was insane. Her words meant nothing to me. I was never the crazy one. She was.

"I found a hit on Juanita Howe's location," Ben said. "She's actually still in the Bronx. I'm going to make a call to bring her in for questioning. She can probably identify your husband. Maybe the Dr. Nash impersonator too."

"That's great." I continued sifting through the passports until my hand froze. There was a sticky note that read Jennifer Clarke. Which meant Jennifer Clarke had a different identity before she became Jennifer Clarke. My hands started shaking as I lifted up the sticky note. Even though I knew all of it was nonsense. Whatever it said was a lie. Because I was me. I was Adeline Bell.

The pain in my head returned.

"Ben, I'll be over soon, okay?" I hung up before he had a chance to answer.

The woman staring back at me was me. But the name beside it was Katrina Nash. Dr. Katrina Nash.

CHAPTER 48

I'm being set up. It was the only logical conclusion. *My husband is framing me for murder.* I threw Dr. Nash's passport back into the mud and picked up another. And another. And another. All the names swirled around in my head.

I stopped when I opened a passport without a sticky note attached. Tears started running down my cheeks. It was my father. I remembered his face. His voice. His eyes. I had *his* eyes. He had no new identity. Because I had killed him.

I could barely breathe. The memories flying through my mind screeched to a halt. My stomach churned. I leaned over and threw up into the hole I'd just dug. *God.* I wiped my mouth with the back of my hand.

I could still hear my husband's words. I could still feel the weight of the gun in my hand.

But there was no time to be swallowed by grief. I knew what I had done. And I knew perfectly well that any sane person wouldn't have been pressured into pulling the trigger. I was about to close the passport when I noticed the last name. Bell. His name was Richard Bell. What?

The side of my face twitched. Bell? My maiden name was Evans like my mother's. I was Adeline Evans before I married my husband. And my husband's last name was Bell. Adeline Bell. I threw the passport down and rummaged through the remaining ones until I found the one I was looking for. One with a sticky note for Katrina Nash. I lifted it up. Adeline Thompson?

I shook my head. *No.* I was never Adeline Thompson. *No, no, no.* It was nonsense. All the passports were nonsense. I threw it on the ground. I'd have to tell Ben to call off his search for Juanita Howe. There was no way that person was really her. Just like Jennifer Clarke wasn't me. And Dr. Nash wasn't me. And Adeline Thompson wasn't me. But I couldn't stop lifting up the passports. Scanning the sticky notes and names. Tossing the ones I had searched into the mud.

Until I found my husband's. Montgomery Thompson. What a pretentious name. It was the stupidest name in the history of names.

No. That wasn't his name. He was... I pinched the bridge of my nose. *His name is...* My mind was coming up blank. *My husband's name is...* I pinched the bridge of my nose harder. *What the hell is my husband's name?* My hand started shaking, slipping off my nose. Well his last name was Bell, that much I was sure of. Because my last name was Bell. I had married him and taken his last name. These passports were lies. All of them lies. But the cruelty in his eyes was captured in the image perfectly. And his handsome features and flawless smile that had tricked me all those years ago.

Montgomery Thompson. The name flipped around in my mind until suddenly it settled. It was coming back to me now. I had been Adeline Thompson. *Had been.* I had been all these people. I had been running for so long. It hit me like a wave, just like Dr. Nash had warned. Like *I* had warned.

And I wasn't at all surprised that there was no sticky note for him. My dear husband was dead. I had killed him four years ago. I smiled. His blood had felt like the rain falling down on me now. Except it was hot and sticky when it splattered on my face. But still cleansing. Still freeing. I laughed into the emptiness, a laugh I didn't recognize.

No. I dropped the passport onto the ground. No, he was alive. He'd be home soon. He was going to jail for killing all those people. He was a monster. He deserved to die. But I hadn't killed him! *And his name is...damnit what the hell is his name?!*

I felt the trigger beneath my finger. I could see my father in front of me. My husband's words running through my head. And I pulled it. *Twice.*

No. Once. I had pulled it once. *No, you turned and you...*

Stop it. I was losing my mind. I lifted up the second to last passport. It was mine before I got married. When I was Adeline Evans. When I thought I needed a man to save me. I threw it in the mud.

There was one last one. I lifted it up. Adeline Bell. There was no sticky note. 27 crosses. 27 passports.

Adeline Evans. Adeline Thompson. Katrina Nash. Jennifer Clarke. My father, Richard Bell. And my lovely husband, Montgomery Thompson.

26 murders. And then there was Adeline Bell. *But I'm still alive!* It felt like my mind was zigzagging in every direction. *I'm still breathing.* My husband was still breathing. And he was trying to make me think I was insane.

I lifted up the letter at the bottom of the box. *No.* I would not fall for my husband's tricks. I wasn't crazy. I didn't have these past lives. And I certainly hadn't killed the twenty women in that box. I would have remembered killing them. Because I was haunted every day by my father's death. I remembered it like it happened yesterday. *I'd remember taking another life.* And I certainly would have remembered killing my husband because I so desperately wanted to.

I felt his blood splatter against my face again. And the leaves crunch beneath me. And the weight of his body.

No. I didn't remember that. It didn't even align with my first memory of killing him. I was imagining it. I was imagining everything. And even if I had shot him, it didn't mean I killed him. Obviously I hadn't killed him. I'd been trying to get away from him for years. He had been hurting me for years. I'd remember if he was dead.

I needed to get all of this to Ben. He'd help me. He was the only one that would believe me. I threw all the passports back into the box and placed the letter on top before closing the lid. I picked up the box of passports and the box of pictures and stood up.

I was about to run back to the house, but turned back. Something made me stomp on the little crosses that remained, burying them beneath the leaves. I wasn't sure what made me do it. I was tampering with evidence. I smashed the last one. *Stop it.* I took a step back. What was wrong with me? The ache in my head returned.

All I knew was that I needed to run. I followed the path, trying to ignore the searing pain in my ankle. There were two things I was sure of. I was good at dealing with pain after years of torture, and I was damn good at running. Those two things were true. Everything else? I wasn't sure of any of it. But I was pretty sure I knew how to find out. The proof was in my husband's files. If the handwriting on them matched the ones on the passports, I'd know he planted evidence. That he was setting me up to take the blame for his crimes.

I threw open the back door and trudged inside. I was completely soaked. My feet left muddy prints on the sparkling clean tiles. A few weeks ago I would have stopped everything to clean up the mess. But I wasn't sick. The medicine made me sick. It gave me OCD. It gave me nightmares. It numbed me.

It changed me.

I looked down at my watch. My husband would be home in 15 minutes. *Shit.* I was so tired. The boxes fell out of my hands. Again, my body seemed to move without my brain's permission. I lifted up the closest box of files and picked one up, smearing mud across the folder.

My name was Adeline Bell. And before I had gotten married, I had been Adeline Evans. I was not Dr. Nash. I had never been anyone else. The date on the file was clearly my husband's handwriting. I had seen him make these files. I had him now. That stupid bastard. I caught him red-handed. I opened up the file and stared down at the words that the Dr. Nash imposter had written about me. *Wait.* They were in the same handwriting.

What? That couldn't be. I grabbed the box of passports. The sticky notes had the same handwriting. I tore open the box of pictures. The backs of them with the names and dates had the same handwriting. *No.*

I picked up the open file. It was a session from five months ago. Listing my problems. All my problems that didn't exist. Problems that had never been real.

But I did have one problem. One *huge* problem. The handwriting was mine. The file shook in my hands. Not my husband's. Not some mysterious imposter. It was mine. All of it was in my handwriting.

Mine.

How was that possible? My phone started ringing. I pulled it out of my pocket. It was Ben. I ignored it. *God, oh God.* Had I done this? How could I have done this?

I dumped the box of passports out on the floor. I knew it was what my husband wanted. To lead me to this point where I'd be grasping for anything to make sense. To make the false memories go away. I grabbed the envelope and tore it open.

Adeline,

Do you remember now? Do you know what you've done? Or are you fighting it?

You need to embrace it, Adeline. You're not who you think you are.

We've talked about this so many times. Argued about good and evil. Right and wrong. Doing something good doesn't make up for the wrongs. It doesn't change the past. I'm sorry, Adeline. I truly am. You've done so much good. But you've done so much more evil.

Now that you know, you only have one choice.

Unless you're ready to be caught. Ready to face the consequences of your actions. Ready to pay for all the lives you took.

If not, stop pretending you're the one in pain and take your damn medicine. It controls you. It numbs you. It makes the memories fade. I get why you resist that. But in your case, that's a good thing. Trust me. You need to be controlled. You need to be numb. You need for your memories to slip away. Trust me. I'm the doctor. Remember?

And if you're still having trouble remembering, look in the mirror. Those bruises on your face? Those aren't from your husband. He's dead, remember? He was the second life you took. Don't you remember that night in the woods?

XOXO,

-Dr. Nash

I touched the side of my jaw where I knew a bruise was. It was like a switch went off in my mind. Everything came flooding back. The memories of my husband were true. He promised to take care of my mother if I dropped out of college. But he hurt me. I was so scared of him. I was terrified of the man I had married. I wanted an out. He traveled during the week, so I kept going to school. I finished my degree. I kept going until I got a doctorate in psychology. I kept going until I knew I could take care of myself and my mother. And I covered my trail the whole time. Expensive fake personal trainers, cleaning services, anything I could think of that would equal the cost of tuition. And my husband bought it. He thought I had become an entitled housewife, just like he wanted me to be. Everything was going according to plan.

But I never expected to get pregnant. It sped up my plans. I didn't have time to do it right. All I could do was flee. By the time I reached my mother's nursing home, she was already dead. And he was waiting for me. In my haste to get away, I hadn't been checking the mail. I hadn't seen my diploma come. He knew my secret. He had been making plans of his own the whole time. Which included stopping the payments for my mom's medical bills.

My perfect escape plan faded to dust. I kept screaming that I was pregnant, but he didn't listen. He had never hurt me like that. He left me broken. He killed our baby. *My* baby.

I tried to kill myself after that. I had lost everything. Every. Single Fucking. Thing. There was no point in living. But he found me before I died and he sent me away. To a terrible place. Some horrible psych ward. It was like I was still living with him. Every day was worse than the day before. But I escaped. I got out of that wretched place.

I was finally free. I became Dr. Katrina Nash. I started over. But I never forgot my past. I thought becoming a psychologist would be meaningful. That helping others would soothe my own demons. Those women from the passports weren't my friends. They were some of my patients. The ones with problems like mine. It felt like I knew them because they bared their souls to me. But not enough. I tried to help. But I knew what it was like to be abused. I knew how hard it was to trust. I knew what was going on in those women's lives, but I couldn't reach them. I couldn't help them. Not the way I wanted. I even hired an abused woman as my secretary. Maria Gonzalez. That's why her fingerprints and mine were the only ones on the files. Because I was Dr. Nash and Maria worked for me. She was just one of the many women who I couldn't get through to. That I couldn't help with words. I kept trying. And failing. They'd show up with bruises, bandages, casts. I wasn't good enough at my job to save them.

And then my husband found me. I had nothing left to give him. My job wasn't fulfilling. It already felt like my soul was dead. He said he was close to finding my father. My dad was the only family I had left. And technically my husband was too. He promised me he'd changed. He promised he'd be better. He held me as I cried over the loss of our child. The loss of my mother. And he apologized. He said he'd never send me away again. He said he'd never hurt me again.

I knew better. But I let my husband back into my life. He could be so charming when he wanted to be. But the abuse started again. My weakness started again. I couldn't help my patients if I couldn't even help myself.

When my husband finally did find my father, I was a shell of who I once was. And my husband wanted me to kill him. He wanted to trap me back in our marriage. He needed something else to hang over my head so that I'd never run away again. He convinced me to pull the trigger. So I did. I played into my husband's hand perfectly. But what he didn't realize was that I had nothing left to live for. So then I shot my husband too.

I remembered missing. And running. The sound of crunching leaves as I fled into the woods. He tackled me to the ground, but I still had the gun. I shot him and his blood rained down on me. His body collapsed on mine. I couldn't breathe.

No. I tried to make the memories stop. *No.* I dug my fingers into my scalp. *No!*

I remembered killing my new identity of Dr. Nash too. Setting fire to my office. But I took my files with me. I changed my name to Jennifer Clarke. I was so sick of not being able to help. I started striking up conversations with my ex-patients online. Telling them I knew what they were hiding and that I could help. That I had a way out. That I had gotten out. Talking never helped anyone. But action? That fucking helped.

Every Friday, I thoroughly cleaned my house. Not because my husband would be upset if it was dirty. But to wipe away any fingerprints in case the Feds came busting down my door when I was away. Because I traveled almost every weekend. I told myself my husband was abusing me. The past merging with the present was the only way I could justify my actions. But my bruises weren't from him. They were from the struggles with the men I killed. The husbands of the 20 women whose passports I had. I ended those women's struggles. Gave them new identities and a fresh start.

The fee for my help? Half their husband's life insurance policy. A policy which I had made them increase before I came to fix their problems.

Only once had I almost gotten caught. But I hadn't been done my work. I still had a few ex-patients that needed my help. I burned down my house and moved with my files again. But I was close to being done. So close that I changed my name back to Adeline. So close that I used my father's last name. So close that I made myself easy to catch. I left a trail of breadcrumbs right to my doorstep. And it worked. Ben showed up.

But the detective investigating me wasn't supposed to be so freaking handsome. He wasn't supposed to make me feel the way that no one ever had before.

I touched the side of my jaw again. They were bruises from my last victim. Mr. Gonzalez. I was done. I had helped everyone I needed to. I was supposed to surrender now. It was the last thing I had left to do.

Even if I didn't, the cops could put it together. The evidence was in the pictures, just like I had told myself. Pictures of myself with bruises and cuts. I pushed them around, staring at the dates. Some were old, from when I had been trying to prove my husband's abuse. But most of them were taken after his death. I had taken one on each day that I killed someone. To remind myself what the monsters I was killing were capable of. The proof was in the pictures all along. But not of my husband's actions. Of mine.

The cops would see the new names of my patients. They could find them and ask them who killed their husbands. It was only a matter of time before one of them caved. All the evidence was right here. I looked around at all the boxes. Right here in cardboard boxes. Highly flammable cardboard boxes. I bit the inside of my lip.

I *could* turn myself in and face the consequences. Face death. That had been the plan. To help my patients. And then die. There were 27 crosses in the woods. I had already made my own grave marker. I had wanted to die for so long. Until I met Ben. It felt like my heart had started beating when I met him. He had ruined everything.

Turning myself in wasn't the only option, though. I could find new people to help online. In support chats. Or in actual meetings. There were so many people that still needed my help. I knew it in my gut. There was still more work to be done. I should have felt bad about the murders, but I didn't. I felt proud. Doing this was so much better than being a psychologist. I had saved these women's lives. And by doing so, I had given my pathetic excuse of a life meaning. There was no real reason to stop. All I had to do was destroy the evidence. It would be so easy.

But I had already told Ben about the passports. About Maria's new name. I had told him too much. If I wanted to keep going, I'd have to do more than destroy the evidence. Ben was the only one that had ever seen me. He was the only one that knew any of my secrets. He'd be able to find me if I ran.

So I had to kill him.

CHAPTER 49

I poured the remaining kerosene over the boxes of evidence. No, I had never seen the whole Home Alone movie. But I didn't need all the gimmicks. The kerosene would be plenty.

I looked up at the camera mounted in the corner of one of the kitchen cabinets. He was probably watching me right now. Why wasn't he stopping me? He had to know what I'd done by now. Didn't he know I was coming for him next? I walked over to the stove and turned the gas on.

But I didn't light it. I let the gas spread into the room. This wasn't the first time I had done this. I breathed it in. It reminded me of being Dr. Nash. Of being Jennifer Clarke. It reminded me of freedom. This would all be over soon. And I could add a few pills to my cocktail to make myself forget.

"Freeze," Ben said.

I felt the barrel of his gun press into the back of my head. Yes, I had done this before, but never after someone was so close to catching me. This wasn't how Ben and my last moment together was supposed to go. I had forgotten that he had a key to my house. And if I was being honest, there were no pills that would make me forget him. I closed my eyes, wishing I was back in his arms. Just hearing his voice and feeling his presence reminded me of how I felt. I loved him. I could never hurt him. But it certainly seemed like he was about to hurt me.

"I didn't know if you were watching," I said.

"I told you I was always watching."

Something constricted in my chest. Maybe there was another way out. Would he believe me if I told him I was innocent? Would he run away with me? "Ben, whatever you think you know…"

"Save it, Addy. Maria didn't hesitate to tell us everything. That The Doctor was a woman. That The Doctor claimed she understood what it was like to be a victim. That she understood what it was like for everything to be taken from her. Her mother. Her father. Her unborn child."

I swallowed hard.

"Maria said that The Doctor had gotten revenge on her husband. And that she had helped others get revenge too. Maria didn't hold anything back."

That ungrateful bitch. I had saved her from hell and this was how she repaid me? I knew she wasn't my friend. Employees were very different than friends. "It wasn't me, Ben."

The barrel shifted slightly. "Do you even know how to tell the truth?"

"Yes. And the cops are going to be here any second. I need a minute to explain. Can we go for a walk?" I needed to get out of the house. Far away from the imminent fire.

"There's nothing to explain. You murdered your father. Your husband. And 20 other innocent people."

"Innocent? Ben, they were abusing my patients!"

"And they should have gone to jail. Just like your husband should have gone to jail, Addy. The punishment for abuse is not death. I understand that you were hurting…"

"You don't understand! How could you possibly understand what it's like to have your soul ripped out?"

"I understand better than you think." The gun fell from the back of my head.

I turned around to face him. I had never seen such agony in someone's face. Ben wasn't anything like my husband, or my father, or the other men I had killed. He was good. So good.

"How do you think it feels to fall in love with the suspect you're supposed to be hunting down?" he asked. "A person you thought you knew but don't even recognize anymore?"

"Not good." Probably similar to how it felt knowing that I needed to kill him but couldn't. Knowing that I loved him but that I'd never get to be with him.

He laughed, but it wasn't his normal infectious laugh. It was forced. And sad. "Yeah, not great."

"We really should step outside," I said. I heard his words. I did. And maybe I could convince him to let me go. Or even to come with me. But we couldn't do it right here. We were running out of time.

"I can forgive one murder. I can understand that you were hurting. That you were manipulated. That you were drugged. But 22 deaths? Addy, you're the definition of a serial killer."

I'm a monster. He didn't have to say it. I knew what he was thinking. And I didn't disagree with him. "I was still on drugs."

"Drugs that you prescribed yourself! That's not the same."

No, it wasn't. "Ben, when the cops open the front door, this whole place is going to blow up."

He lifted his gun higher. "You expect me to believe that? You're not getting away from me this time. I have everything I need to bring you in."

"Which we can discuss *outside*. I rigged the front door. When it opens the blowtorch will ignite, lighting the trail of kerosene that leads in here." I gestured to the boxes. "Everything's going to explode."

He eyed the stove. I knew he smelled the gas. He knew I wasn't lying.

But he didn't move. He just turned back to me. "Was anything you said to me true? Or was this whole thing just a game to you?" It seemed like he was giving up. That the pain I had caused him really was as bad as he claimed. And it was the first time I had ever regretted hurting someone.

He saw the worst of me. Everything. All the horrible things I had done. Did he still love me? I felt like I could see it in his eyes. But I needed to know. I needed to know if it was possible to convince him to forgive me. I needed to remind him of what he had said to me. "Remember when I told you there was nothing in-between good and evil? That there was no gray? You didn't believe me. You said that was a pessimistic outlook. And that people can commit crimes with good intentions. That's what I did, Ben. I had good reasons. I can't take back what I did. But I'll stop. For you, I'll..."

The sound of the front door opening made all my thoughts disappear. I lunged for the window. I tried to grab his hand but he ducked out of the way. I broke through the glass just as the kerosene ignited behind me.

I fell onto the wet grass and turned around. The whole house was engulfed in flames. *No.* I wanted to destroy the evidence. Not Ben. *No!* I struggled to my feet and ran to the back door. I opened it and a blast of heat almost knocked me backward. I took a huge gulp of air and crawled into the house.

The fire lapped at the walls, burning the cabinets off their hinges. The boxes had already been incinerated. I heard shouting but it was far away.

"Ben!" I coughed.

Smoke curled around me, choking me, getting denser by the second.

"Ben!"

I couldn't see him. I got lower, slinking along the floor. "God, Ben!" He was lying on the far side of the kitchen. His body must have been thrown in the explosion. I crawled over to him.

"Ben, please." I tried to shake him awake, but his head flopped back and forth. I needed to get him out of the fire. I choked on the air as I grabbed his hands and pulled.

It was getting harder and harder to breathe. When I finally reached the back door, I shoved him out of the house. He rolled into the grass and didn't move.

"Ben." I tapped the side of his face. "Ben, wake up." There was blood dripping down from his hairline. I wiped it away. "Ben, I'm sorry. There was truth in my lies. At least one truth. I love you. I didn't lie about that. I fell in love with you, Ben. Wake up."

Sirens sounded in the distance. People were screaming in the front yard. If there had been more time, I could have convinced him to come with me. If he had left the house, we could still be talking. He'd know that I loved him. I'd promise to stop. I'd give it up for him.

"Ben, please."

The shouts were getting louder. People were coming this way.

I didn't know if he was alive or dead. But I knew I'd be caught if I didn't go now. I had to go.

I took one last look at the man I loved. The man I had deceived. The man who didn't shoot me when he had the chance.

And then I ran. I ran like I always did. But this time, I knew why I was so tired of running. Because I could never run away from what I had become.

Despite everything I had done, I only had one regret, though. That Ben would never know the truth in my lies.

WHAT'S NEXT?

Adeline isn't the only crazy housewife in the neighborhood! Meet Violet (and hear a tiny bit more about Adeline and Ben) in Book 2 of the Secrets of Suburbia Series, *Sweet Like a Psycho*!

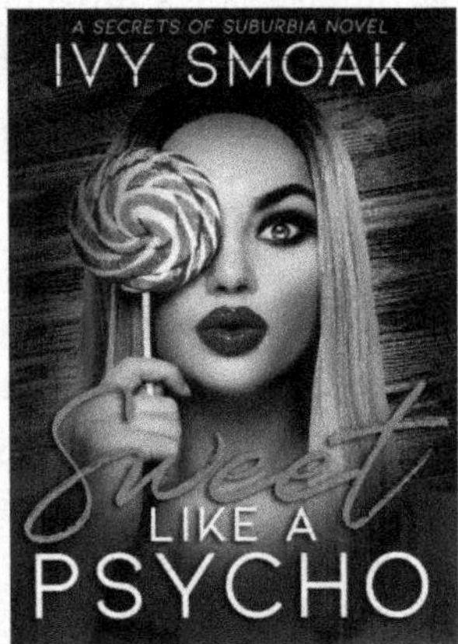

To most people, suburbia is synonymous with good school districts, manicured lawns, and friendly neighbors. But you can never really tell what's hiding behind those white picket fences and smiling faces.

I mean, we all have secrets. The kid down the street steals lawn gnomes. The woman on the corner is having an affair. And me? I'm a murderer. At least...that's what everyone thinks.

Because that's the other thing about the suburbs. Rumors spread like wildfire. Handsome detectives start poking around. Houses explode. You know...the usual.

Yes, I have secrets. But so does everyone else. Welcome to suburbia. I'm one of the smiling faces waving from my front porch. Don't you trust me?

A NOTE FROM IVY

First I'd just like to say that the characters led me here. That unsettled feeling in the pit of your stomach? It wasn't my intention to do that to you. I usually write romance. I'm in love with love. But I always let the characters guide the story.

And Adeline had a story of her own to tell - About the gray area between black and white, good and evil. She was doing the wrong thing for the right reasons. I think we can all relate to that. The pain she suffered through wasn't her fault. The loss she experienced wasn't her fault. But everything else? Those were her choices.

Ivy Smoak

Ivy Smoak
Wilmington, DE
www.ivysmoak.com

ABOUT THE AUTHOR

Ivy Smoak is the international bestselling author of *The Hunted Series*. Her books have sold over 1 million copies worldwide, and her latest release, *Empire High Betrayal*, hit #4 in the entire Kindle store.

When she's not writing, you can find Ivy binge watching too many TV shows, taking long walks, playing outside, and generally refusing to act like an adult. She lives with her husband in Delaware.

Facebook: IvySmoakAuthor
Instagram: @IvySmoakAuthor
Goodreads: IvySmoak

Recommend *The Truth in My Lies* for your next book club!

Book club questions available at:
www.ivysmoak.com/bookclub

Printed in the USA
CPSIA information can be obtained
at www.ICGtesting.com
LVHW041440201123
764224LV00034B/1236/J

9 781942 381174